Cameron's Chase

Whistle and I'll Come · The Kid · Storm South
Hopkinson and the Devil of Hate · Leave the Dead Behind Us · Marley's
Empire
Bowering's Breakwater · Sladd's Evil · A Time for Survival · Poulter's
Passage · The Day of the Coastwatch · Man, Let's Go On
Half a Bag of Stringer · The German Helmet · The Oil Bastards
Pull My String · Coach North

Featuring Commander Shaw:

Gibraltar Road · Redcap · Bluebolt One · The Man From Moscow
Warmaster · Moscow Coach · The Dead Line
Skyprobe · The Screaming Dead Balloons · The Bright Red Businessmen
The All-Purpose Bodies · Hartinger's Mouse · This Drakotny
Sunstrike · Corpse · Werewolf · Rollerball

Featuring Simon Shard:

Call for Simon Shard · A Very Big Bang · Blood Run East · The Eros
Affair · Blackmail North · Shard Calls the Tune · The Hoof
Shard At Bay · The Executioners

Featuring Lieutenant St Vincent Halfhyde, RN:

Beware, Beware the Bight of Benin · Halfhyde's Island · The Guns of Arrest
Halfhyde to the Narrows · Halfhyde for the Queen · Halfhyde Ordered South
Halfhyde and the Flag Captain · Halfhyde on the Yangtze · Halfhyde on
Zanatu · Halfhyde Outward Bound · The Halfhyde Line · Halfhyde
and the Chain Gangs

Featuring Donald Cameron:

Cameron, Ordinary Seaman · Cameron Comes Through · Cameron of the
Castle Bay · Lieutenant Cameron RNVR · Cameron's Convoy
Cameron in the Gap · Orders for Cameron · Cameron in Command
Cameron and the Kaiserhof · Cameron's Raid

Non fiction:

Tall Ships – The Golden Age of Sail · Great Yachts

Cameron's Chase

Philip McCutchan

Weidenfeld and Nicolson · London

Published in Great Britain in 1986 by
George Weidenfeld & Nicolson Limited
91 Clapham High Street
London SW4 7TA

ISBN 0 297 78681 4

Typeset at The Spartan Press Ltd,
Lymington, Hants
Printed in Great Britain by
Butler & Tanner Ltd,
Frome and London

1

IN Norway, far beyond Scottish waters and the ships of the Home Fleet swinging round their anchors in Scapa Flow, the whole area, both land and sea, was covered in swirling fog that had brought the visibility down to a matter of yards. This fog was extending its blindfold grip, reaching its fingers down to touch the winter snow and ice of Scotland. Soon the Scapa base was enclosed in the fog's clutches and the murk was moving down over Caithness and Sutherland, over Argyll and the Tobermory base, over the Perthshire highlands, over the islands to the west, down across Aberdeenshire in the east. By nightfall it had enclosed the Firth of Forth and the battleships and cruisers lying inward of the great bridge that spanned the Firth, while across to the west the chilling embrace rolled down upon the Clyde to enfold the warships at anchor or at buoys off the Tail o' the Bank opposite Greenock.

In the fog-bound waters of the far north a lone Norwegian cyclist – a delivery man, taking in his meat basket some special provisions to delight the stomach of the German Admiral now commanding the port of Bergen – had noted some movement along the Buddefjord that separated the Bergen peninsula from the mainland. Great dark shapes – ships, of course. The delivery man shrugged: only fools would go to sea when they were unable to see the ends of their noses, but the Nazi thugs had never been renowned for their brains – and of course they would find their way by use of the radar. Thoughtfully, the delivery man rubbed his own nose as he pedalled back from the Bergen dockyard, going slow because of the fog and because of the ice that covered the road. Perhaps the Nazis were not such fools after all: the fog was covering their movements, which perhaps they wished kept secret.

The delivery man cautiously put on a little more speed. Some distance from the dockyard he turned down a narrow street of small houses and then, dismounting, pushed his bicycle along a cluttered alleyway that ran between two of the houses. At the end of this alleyway was a wooden shed; from within came the sound of hammering. The delivery man pushed the door open. He said, 'Ivar, a moment.'

The hammering stopped; Ivar Haaland, a grey-haired man wearing steel-rimmed spectacles and a carpenter's apron, looked up. 'What is it, my friend?'

Olav Gjerde went in, closing the door carefully behind him. There was no one else around but he spoke in a low voice. 'In the port,' he said. 'There is, I believe, movement of German warships, Ivar . . .'

ii
As the fog swept down to the Firth of Clyde that evening Mr Bream, warrant engineer of HMS *Glenshiel* of the Clyde Escort Force, was sitting in the lounge bar of the Bay Hotel at Gourock gloomily drinking a half of bitter, which was about all you could get in wartime unless you were one of the nobs, by which Mr Bream meant the wardroom officers – at any rate in an exclusive establishment like the Bay Hotel. Mr Bream would have preferred whisky, but never mind that he was in Scotland, you might as well ask for nectar and be done with it.

Mr Bream belched and said, to no one in particular, 'Pardon me.' Beer had that effect on him, always had, which was one reason he didn't like it. Mr Bream thought about Pompey, where he lived, thought about Queen Street outside the barracks, full of matloes drunk as lords on Brickwood's beer, either that or looking for tarts, or both. Probably both, Mr Bream decided. That was if bloody Goering permitted – all those bombs, HE and incendiaries that had dropped on

2

poor old Pompey and made it largely unrecognizable to its inhabitants . . . and he hoped his missus was all right. He glanced at his wrist-watch: she was all right up to half an hour ago – he'd telephoned from the hotel, a shilling's-worth of reassurance or three minutes of moans whichever way you looked at it; but anything could happen in a wartime half-hour and if the fog lifted the *Glenshiel* was under orders to weigh at tomorrow's dawn, off on another bloody slog across the North Atlantic with a convoy and he virtually watch on, stop on in the engine-room. No more chance to ring the missus then, not for ten days or so.

Bugger the war, Mr Bream said to himself. And then his thoughts shifted from Pompey and the war and he stared open-mouthed, not able to believe his eyes. There was a glass-panelled door leading from the lounge into the hotel dining-room, and one of the panels – as he had already noticed, having an eagle eye for a lack of care and mainten-ance – was missing. Currently there was a Naval officer jumping through it. As Mr Bream watched, the Naval officer crawled across the dining-room floor barking like a dog, rose to his haunches at a table and seized a chrysanthemum in his teeth. Coming back through the glassless panel, he was eating the chrysanthemum with every appearance of enjoy-ment and never mind the scandalized Naval and civilian faces glaring through from the dining-room.

Mr Bream recognized him with a shudder: Sub-Lieuten-ant Poole, from his own ship, talk about disgrace, bloody RNVR! Pissed again. Mr Bream clicked his tongue. Daft young buggers, thought they owned every place they went to ashore. He hid his face behind the evening paper. No point in being seen to scowl; they all thought he was an old fuddy-duddy, a dug-out from peacetime, and in a sense he was, having swallowed the anchor back in 1935 and then been called back by courtesy of bloody Adolf. Looking again at his watch a little later, Mr Bream got to his feet and went to the cloakroom for his cap and greatcoat, the latter bearing on its shoulders the single thin gold stripe and purple cloth of his rank; and then moved out into the fog hoping to find a bus that would penetrate the thickness and take him to Albert Harbour in Greenock for the duty drifter back aboard the destroyer, cold in the pit of his gut on account of the beer.

iii

POLICE were on the move; patrol cars, beat men and bobbies on bicycles, all shouting through megaphones along with the gaitered seamen of the Naval patrol: 'All Naval officers and ratings to report back aboard their ships immediately. Extra drifters are being laid on from Albert Harbour, ships' boats will be using Prince's Pier.' Mr Bream was one of many who heard them, since he'd been forced to walk after all.

He asked a constable, 'What's the panic, eh?'

'I wouldn't know, sir.'

Bream wiped the back of a woollen glove across his nose, catching a drip. 'Careless talk costs lives?' He walked on, making for Prince's Pier instead of Albert Harbour – not so far to go, and the *Glenshiel*'s Officer of the Day would be sending a boat if there was a flap on, as apparently there was.

God, it was cold! Mr Bream hunched himself into his upturned collar, beneath which a thick blue scarf was wound around his neck. Scotland in winter, stone the crows! As if they didn't get enough of it out at sea, though personally he was warm enough down below, but you couldn't be on the starting platform all the time. He moved on towards the embarkation points, one of a large crowd of officers and ratings: the ships always disgorged their companies, or the non-duty watches anyway, *en masse* when they came in after a gruelling convoy run and the skipper rang down Finished With Engines. Booze and popsies . . . Mr Bream was glad to be past all that. Plenty of the men surging along the snow-piled streets of the town had had a skinful and more. Come the next day and they'd be sorry, going on watch with sore heads.

As, half an hour later, Mr Bream came alongside the *Glenshiel* and climbed the quarterdeck ladder from the motor-boat, he was met by the First Lieutenant.

'What's up, sir?'

4

Hastings shrugged. 'No idea, Chief. Father's still ashore, but we got a general signal.' (The Captain was father to the wardroom, the skipper to the lower deck.) 'All ships to raise steam for immediate notice.'

'Thanks very much,' Bream said drily. He swept a hand round. 'In this?'

'In this indeed, and I don't fancy moving in it any more than you do, Chief. They may hold us till the weather clears, I suppose. I wouldn't bank on it, though.'

'Something big?'

'Must be.' Hastings turned away: there was much for a First Lieutenant to see to. Mr Bream went below to his cabin, where he shifted into white overalls. The filth outside seemed to have penetrated everywhere, bringing a nasty cold fug. He went down to his engines, to his kingdom, the part of the ship where he was God. Chief Engine-Room Artificer Downs was already there, on the starting platform. Bream's eagle eye swept around, noted that everything was shipshape: Downs, his right-hand man, was dependable . . . like himself, Downs had been called back to service in 1939. The engine-room was under the charge of old-timers and in Bream's view was the better for it. Too many hostilities-only men in the wartime Navy. . . .

'All set, Jack?' Bream asked.

The Chief ERA nodded. 'All on top line. What's the buzz, eh?'

'No idea.'

'Don't like the weather, sir.'

'No more do I.' Bream reckoned there was a degree of daftness around, sending ships to sea in pea-soup. But maybe, as Jimmy the One had hinted, they were just being brought to immediate readiness to move out the moment the fog lifted a little. In any event they'd have to go out dead slow, just feeling their way like zombies, blind except for the radar which was just another of those new-fangled gadgets that always packed up when you needed them most. Mr Bream's mind roved from his engine-room and floated towards the places of power where decisions were made that affected the lives of seamen: what the bloody hell was in the air? It wasn't often that all ships in an anchorage were ordered out at a

5

pierhead jump . . . maybe there had been a big battle in the North Atlantic, another convoy decimated and most of the escorts gone – a troop convoy from the States that stood in urgent need of warship reinforcement, though by this stage of the war the Nazis weren't having it all their own way. Well – no doubt they would know soon enough. The skipper was never slow to keep his ship's company informed. For an RNVR, Lieutenant-Commander Cameron was pretty good.

iv

CAMERON had been summoned along with all other commanding officers in the anchorage, summoned by general signal before the fog had settled in so thickly, to attend upon the Flag Officer in Charge. It took a while for all the officers to assemble; when all were present, the Rear-Admiral wasted no time. There had been, he said, a wireless report from the Norwegian Resistance in the port of Bergen: three heavy German ships were believed to have left the port earlier that day. Their course was unknown; they could be heading down for a German port, or they could be steaming towards the North Cape to intercept the British convoys for Archangel and Murmansk, or, more likely, they could be on course to pass below Iceland and out into the Atlantic to spread havoc among the convoys coming through from Halifax, Nova Scotia. Currently there was no information beyond that single coded transmission picked up in London and passed at once to the Admiralty and the War Cabinet. As a result of it, all home commands had received their orders: the main Home Fleet under Admiral Sir Bruce Fraser flying his flag in the battleship *Duke of York* was under orders to leave Scapa Flow and move easterly. All available ships in the Forth and Clyde were to proceed to join the main fleet at sea, the destroyers to act as the extended escort to back up a force depleted by sinkings, by dockyard refits and by the ever-present need for boiler-cleaning after too many weeks spent constantly at sea or with steam at four hours' notice when in port. Escorts were perennially short; the demands of the convoys were insatiable. When the orders had come through from the Admiralty, the weather locally had been clear and

6

the fog to the north had not been expected by the meteorologists to extend so far south. But the Admiralty, recognizing that the German force would be just as discommoded while the fog lasted, had decreed that the fleet was to raise steam and sail as ordered so as to be in the vicinity of the Germans when the fog lifted.

'It won't be an easy passage,' the Rear-Admiral said unnecessarily, 'but you'll have to do your best – and I know you will. Good luck to you all.'

The commanding officers were fallen out; there were loud comments that the difficulties of the passage would begin long before the ships weighed anchor: the first problem would be for them to find their own ships, but the Rear-Admiral had covered that. They were told by the raised voice of the Chief of Staff that a drifter had been laid on in Albert Harbour to take them all to their ships, dropping them one by one. The Scottish drifter skippers, the Chief of Staff said, most of them drafted in from Stornoway and other places to the north, could navigate blindfold and they had learned to know the Tail o' the Bank like their own back yards. The lurid swearing, only partially understandable, of the drifter skipper as he nosed a little later out of Albert Harbour didn't entirely bear this out; and it was just over an hour later when Cameron at last climbed to his own quarterdeck to be met by his First Lieutenant.

Hastings' face, dimly seen in the shaded blue light from the quartermaster's lobby, was one big question mark. Cameron gave a brief grin at the sight of it, though there was no humour in the situation. He said, 'We go to sea immediately, Number One – or rather, we stand by to proceed in rear of the line as the other ships move out, the cruisers first. It'll all be done by radar and sound signals.'

'Aye, aye, sir. And the orders?'

Cameron said, 'There's no need for secrecy within the ship . . . you can pass the word, Number One.' He took a deep breath, already visualizing something of the murderous days that might lie ahead, the slaughter and the heroism. 'The *Attila*'s out.'

V

THE *Attila*. So well-named, by all accounts –
Attila the Hun, who had laid waste Thrace and Illyria in the
fifth century, who had marched on Gaul with an army three-
quarters of a million strong and although defeated on the
Catalonian Fields had soon recovered to lay waste northern
Italy and threaten Rome itself. Attila, who had spread the
supremacy of the Huns from the Caspian to the Rhine, was a
fitting enough name-source for Hitler's newest battleship. Of
some 45,000 tons, she carried a main armament of nine 16-
inch guns together with twelve 6-inch and a massive array of
anti-aircraft weapons. Although very heavily armoured she
was capable, it was believed, of close on thirty knots of speed.
She easily outclassed all the latest British battleships: *King
George V*, *Anson*, *Howe*, and the *Duke of York* herself. It
was not so long ago that the *Prince of Wales* of the same class
had succumbed to a Japanese air attack in the South China
Sea, which had left a sense of unease at the apparent
vulnerability of the new construction.

A ship like the *Attila* could wreak havoc with Britain's
battle fleet; if she ever got within range of a convoy it would
be a case of wholesale destruction of ships and men. The
country stood in urgent need of all the cargo-carrying space
available – and it was never quite enough. As the Battle of the
Atlantic continued on its relentless, bloody way, it was ever in
the minds of Whitehall and the war leaders that the oil and
food reserves could be measured in days rather than weeks.

The word went round the *Glenshiel*'s decks like wildfire:
the *Attila* had got away to sea under cover of the fog; and as if
in indication of something extra big she was believed to be
accompanied by the heavy cruisers *Recklinghausen* and
Darmstadt.

As Special Sea Dutymen were piped to their stations and
the cable party was mustered on the fo'c'sle, the gunner's
mate, Petty Officer Lindsay, stared balefully into the fog from
alongside 2 gun-mounting. 'Dunno what they expect my pea-
shooters to do,' he remarked to Leading Seaman Maloney.

Maloney grinned through the wool of his balaclava. 'Never

called 'em that before, you haven't, GI.'

'Never been called upon to penetrate about twenty bloody feet of armour, have I? And don't tell me *you* have, Maloney, cos we all know that.'

Maloney wiped the back of a hand across his nose but said nothing. Maybe he did have a big mouth at times, but he was a Royal Fleet Reservist and he'd been in the last lot and why not teach those who hadn't a thing or two? Maloney had been in a battle-cruiser at the Dogger Bank and had seen what big guns could do, but he took the GI's point all right, not that the *Glenshiel* or any other of the destroyers would be called upon to attack the big stuff, they were just the escorts and, Maloney reckoned, a sight safer than the poor sods aboard the battle-ships and cruisers would be if they came inside the *Attila*'s range and engaged. The whole thing would be fought out between the big boys and it would be just bad luck if the destroyers caught a projy. Maloney was reasonably phleg-matic about the prospects; his own view was that the perishing fog was the bigger hazard. They'd probably go and pile up going through the boom, or on the rocks by the Cumbraes, or go straight up the arse of their next ahead as they groped their way through the blankness. But that Cameron, he was a good ship-handler, and the navigator, who was RNR, one of the professionals even though he was just a subby, had already shown himself to be shit hot at his job. Sub-Lieutenant Millard, late of Canadian Pacific, junior Fourth Officer of the *Duchess of Montrose*, had had his share of navigating through fog off the Newfoundland Banks and he was no stranger to the Clyde. They'd get through all right. The Navy usually did, by guess and by God, bungling through and coming up trumps, impro-vising when needs be. . . . The Nazis were almost too efficient, Maloney thought as he waited for the others to come down from the forebridge, efficient in an automaton-like sort of way, and rigid with it. He hoped the *Attila* was as rigid as. . . .

Maloney jumped a mile as the blast of a steam syren broke the fog-bound silence, just off their port quarter. Dimly something moved, a deeper shadow in the night's murk – the flagship of the 27th Cruiser Squadron, probably, leading the force out. CS27 had entered just the day before, and the cruisers were on a pierhead jump as well.

There was a shout from the forebridge: the skipper. 'Number One?'

Lieutenant Hastings answered from the eyes of the ship. 'Yes, sir?'

'Shorten in, Number One. Third shackle on deck.'

'Third shackle on deck, sir.' The First Lieutenant passed the word to the shipwright at the centre-line capstan as the slips were knocked away. There was an electrical whirr and a thump and clatter on the steel deck as the links of the starboard cable came home up the hawse-pipe to be washed down by the hoses before they descended into the cable locker. From the forebridge Cameron strained his eyes through the fog, watching with his navigator for the shaded blue stern lights and fog buoys to come up ahead and tell him how many ships had moved past.

Millard said, 'Three gone, sir.'

'Yes. That'll be cs27 out of the way, Pilot. What do you reckon the chances?'

'We'll be all right, sir.' Millard sounded as though there was nothing in it. 'A straight run from the boom to the Cumbraes, and then wider water down to the Mull of Kintyre.'

'All those western islands, Pilot.' The orders were to proceed north for Cape Wrath and then move easterly across the Scottish coast to the Pentlands to come up in the wake of the Home Fleet. 'Maybe it'll clear by then. We can but hope!'

'Yes, sir.' More ships came past and were counted off. As the last went by the orders were called down to the fo'c'sle to weigh and hold the anchor at the waterline, ready for letting go if required while the ship was in restricted waters. Leading Seaman Maloney, in charge of the hosing-down party, looked over the side as the flukes of the anchor broke surface. He could just about see the hook as no more than a disturbance in the water, a bit of curfuffle as it broke through, but he fancied there was a slight lifting of the fog, not enough to help very much but it was a good sign.

He caught the eye of one of the hostilities-only ordinary seaman, name of Aldridge, what Maloney thought of as a wet streak. Aldridge had been an actor, or so he called himself, until the cruel Navy had yanked him off the stage and away from his boy-friends. He didn't seem happy at sea. Maloney

10

said with unkind satisfaction, 'There we are, then. Nearly away.' The sudden vibration as Mr Bream, below in the engine-room, obeyed telegraphs and put his power through to his shafts, confirmed Maloney's prognostication. 'All set for the bloody *Attila*. You haven't seen what war's like yet, my lad – but you will. Talk about blood and guts!'

'It's not very nice, to say that,' Aldridge said. Maloney sensed rather than saw a pout. He moved suddenly and his sea-booted foot trod hard on Aldridge's toes. Aldridge gave a shrill cry that sounded like 'Ooh!' and this was heard on the bridge.

'Stop that damn racket!' Cameron called down. This was no time for unnecessary sounds. In fog, the ears were as vital as the eyes. Petty Officer West, PO of the Fo'c'sle Division, repeated Cameron's order close to Aldridge's earhole, a hiss of menace.

'Bloody little twit, what you going to do when we meet the *Attila*, for God's sake, eh?'

'Shit himself,' Maloney said. He looked ahead as the *Glenshiel* moved outwards, heading for the boom running across from Cloch Point to Dunoon. As junior ship of the destroyer flotilla, *Glenshiel* was last in the line: no danger of being rammed from astern, which was something. Maloney felt impelled to remark on this. 'First time I ever been glad to be arse-end Charlie . . . oops, sorry, Mr Aldridge, shouldn't have said that word in your hearing. . . .'

vi

IN Bergen earlier, the Resistance had been unlucky. After Olav Gjerde had passed his message and left, Ivar Haaland shut up his workshop and carried a bag of tools and some wood along to a ramshackle van parked near the entrance to the alley. He drove towards the outskirts of the town, made a couple of calls, then came back a little way into the town, parked his van again, and walked to the railway station. Here he took a train for the town of Voss some seventy miles to the north-east of Bergen; and on arrival made for a small house just outside. He was admitted by a man named Thorstein Kleppe; within ten minutes the signal

11

for London had been encoded and transmitted. So far, so good.

But the good luck could not hold.

It was the sheerest chance, the sheerest luck for the Gestapo that the transmission was picked up and pin-pointed by the radio detectors. From that moment the Gestapo in Voss moved swiftly; Ivar Haaland was about to leave again for Bergen when the black uniforms and shiny-peaked, high-crowned caps arrived with guns. Haaland and Kleppe were forced back into the house and a search was made: even though the transmitter had been dismantled after the message had been passed, it took no time for the Gestapo to find it.

The questioning began: what had been transmitted, and to whom?

Both men refused to answer. The Gestapo officer, who so far had no reason to connect the Resistance men with Bergen, grew angry. He smashed the barrel of his revolver into Kleppe's mouth, knocking out three teeth. Blood poured from a badly split lip, but still no answers came. He then attacked Ivar Haaland, an old man who was no longer strong, lifting a knee and jabbing it hard into Haaland's crutch. The old man doubled in agony, only to have his head sent upwards and backwards by a wicked blow from the Gestapo officer's fist.

'You will answer!' the German shouted, his face dark with fury.

'No.'

'You have committed an offence against the Reich for which you will both die. This you know. Why make death harder for yourselves, why be fools?'

'We have our honour,' Ivar Haaland said simply.

The Nazi gave a jeering laugh. 'Such honour!'

'We are not Quislings,' Haaland said. 'We fight for Norway. We are prepared to die for Norway. We know the penalty. And we shall not speak.'

The officer nodded to his companions. 'Into the car,' he said. Kleppe and Haaland were seized, taken outside and bundled into the staff car. At Gestapo HQ in Voss there were more sophisticated methods of interrogation.

2

SAFELY passing the shoals of Rosneath Patch off the Gareloch, *Glenshiel* made the turn to port to pass through the anti-submarine boom thrown across the Clyde; the boom defence vessel was just visible as a squat lump. In spite of the intense cold, Cameron was sweating. He said, 'Well done, Pilot.'

'All in the day's work, sir. Anyway, it's lifting a little now.'

Cameron nodded. They could just pick up the dim blue of the stern light of *Glenorchy*, their next ahead. Beyond that they could see nothing; constant reports from the radar cabinet were keeping them on course for the Cumbraes. They moved dead slow, feeling their way. It would take them an hour or more to pass the Cumbrae light. The fog wreathed, its chill fingers clammy on exposed flesh, the syrens sounded their prolonged blasts every two minutes when the patchy fog thickened. Special Sea Dutymen were still at their stations, the cable party still stood by on the fo'c'sle, ready with the starboard anchor underfoot. Lieutenant Hastings stood ready in the eyes of the ship, staring ahead, acting as an additional lookout. Petty Officer West moved up and down keeping an eye on the hands, having a quiet word now and again with the shipwright at the centre-line capstan, the man who would have to be nippy in throwing off the brake if there was a sudden order from the bridge to let go and bring the ship up should they look like hitting something – always assuming the something was seen in time.

In the wheelhouse below the forebridge the torpedo-coxswain was on the wheel: Chief Petty Officer Stace, one of the few members of the ship's company who was neither a reservist nor a hostilities-only, had a face like a hatchet, very thin, very sharp. Now that face was tensed up in total concentration: the response to orders down the voice-pipe had to be immediate or he could be responsible for piling the old crate up and that would never do.

Chief PO Stace was young for his rate and had ambitions in the service; he wanted to make warrant rank and then maybe the wardroom in the fullness of time. Lieutenant Stace, RN, had a nice ring to it, very nice. While he concentrated, Stace chain-smoked, turning the wheelhouse into a denser fog area. His smoking was so automatic that he could reach for another fag without thought, without losing anything of his concentration as he lit the new from the old and then stubbed out the dog-end in an empty round-shaped tin of fifty Players hanging from a rivet-head in the bulkhead on his right-hand side. Even so, from time to time home thoughts penetrated and had to be thrust down, hard and savage. There was someone back home in Chatham whom Stace would much like to murder, the man his wife had gone off with, a commercial traveller, a bloody civvy, sheltering under a reserved occupation because he happened to travel in food and kept the Home and Colonial Stores stocked up – or something like that. Stace had suspected something the last two or three leaves, but the word had come, the final confirmation, only a few days ago, the day after the *Glenshiel* had come in from a North Atlantic escort. The letter that said Mavis was off and away, that she was sorry but she loved Bert Cockshutt – talk about a prat-like name! She wanted a divorce. Mrs Cockshutt. Well, she wasn't going to get it. Stace was adamant; and he wouldn't even ask the skipper for compassionate leave to go home and try to sort things out. He had a strong gut feeling it wouldn't make any odds in any case and he wasn't going to crawl and plead, not he. Chief petty officers on active service brushed off commercial travellers like fleas.

Stace, when that letter had come, had a fleeting thought that maybe he'd asked for it, or the service had asked *for* him. The Navy was his life and home had always come second in his restless urge for advancement. Stace was real RN, very pusser,

14

and he ran the house like a ship, everything done properly, no excuses, efficiency insisted upon. Meals – everything – punctual, on the dot. He couldn't help it; it was second nature to Stace, brought up hard in his boyhood and put through the Navy's training mill at the *Ganges*. Mavis hadn't liked it; she moaned about it in a quiet sort of way, not wanting to anger him, but stating her viewpoint, which he considered a kind of insubordination. Women weren't there to argue the toss. . . .

Panic stations.

Millard's voice smote into Stace's ear: '*Engines to Emergency Full astern, wheel hard-a-port*!'

The response was instant, Mavis forgotten. 'Emergency Full Astern both engines, sir. Wheel hard-a-port, sir.' Stace spun the wheel in big, capable hands while the telegraphsman wrenched over the handles of the engine-room telegraph, twice for the emergency signal, and bells rang. 'Wheel's hard-a-port, sir.'

No acknowledgment from the bridge. Stace waited for the crash, lit another fag, went mentally through the routines for coping with a bottom ripped to buggery by jags of rock, or for dealing with a fo'c'sle twisted to Kingdom Come on impact with the stern of the next ahead. Damage Control Parties, collision mat – you had to have your mind ready and not be caught on the hop. But this time, nothing.

Millard's voice again: 'Stop engines. Wheel amidships.'

'Stop engines, sir, wheel amidships – '

Thick and fast. 'Both engines slow ahead . . . port ten . . . midships. Starboard five . . . midships . . . steady!'

'Steady, sir. Course one-eight-two, sir.'

'Steer one-eight-oh.'

'Steer one-eight-oh, sir.' Stace moved the wheel a fraction. 'Course one-eight-oh, sir.'

'Right,' Millard said. What the sod had happened? A moment later Cameron's disembodied voice came; the skipper always explained things himself whenever he could.

'Cox'n . . . we're clear now.'

'Glad to hear it, sir!'

'We lost the stern-light from *Glenorchy* – when the fog thickened for a moment – avoiding action, just in case. That's all. Fog's patchy now. Tell the engine-room, please.'

'Aye, aye, sir.' Stace nodded to the OD acting as telegraphsman; the rating picked up the sound-powered telephone to the engine-room – the skipper would be needing his eyes ahead. Ordinary Seaman Nye passed the word to the warrant engineer.

'Bloody hell,' Bream said from the starting platform, wiping sweat from his face. In the wheelhouse Nye caught the note of recent agitation and grinned briefly to himself. Down there, Mr Bream and his black gang were pretty close to the bottom plating. Out in the open, on the fo'c'sle, Leading Seaman Maloney had spotted some skulking: Ordinary Seaman Aldridge had moved aft of the centre-line capstan, right back to the break of the fo'c'sle, putting all the distance he could between himself and a possibly crumpled bow. Maloney moved for him, sea-booted feet sliding on the fog-wet deck plating.

'Get for'ard, you.'

'But I –'

'Don't bloody argue, you poncy little brown 'atter, or you'll get something up your arse you *won't* like.'

Aldridge made a squeaky sound and moved for'ard. Maloney followed up behind, grabbed his arm and hissed, 'We're all in this together, right? If we'd gone up *Glenorchy*'s backside it wouldn't have made no difference where you was, you'd have had to do your share. Got it?'

'Yes.'

'Yes Leading Seaman Maloney.'

'Yes, Leading Seaman Maloney.' Aldridge's tone was sulky.

'Right! When you're worth condescending to, Ordinary Seaman bloody Aldridge, I'll allow you to address me as Killick – like the *men* do.' Maloney put two fingers on the left-hand sleeve of his oilskin, in the vicinity of his leading hand's badge, the fouled anchor from which the sobriquet of 'killick' was derived, now covered by as much warm clothing as Maloney could scrape together. 'For now, just jump to it when I say.'

Aldridge nodded and moved farther for'ard. Leading Seaman Maloney could be more dangerous than a shattered fo'c'sle when he put his mind to it. Half a minute later Petty

16

Officer West came up alongside Maloney and jerked a thumb aft. Maloney scowled but took a few paces to the rear with the PO.

West said, 'I won't be telling you again, Maloney. No more bleeding bullying, all right?' The PO's voice was hard and his stare direct. 'Aldridge may be a nancy boy but we have to suffer what God or the Drafting Jaunty sends us, right? Bullying I will *not* have.'

Standing just for'ard of the capstan, Ordinary Seaman Aldridge was aware of the reason for the unheard exchange and did a little gloating: Maloney was getting a right bollocking and not before time. Last time out with a convoy, Aldridge had considered appearing at Captain's Request-ment on return to harbour to state an official complaint, but had been dissuaded by the daddy of the lower deck, Able Seaman Higginbottom, who by popular legend had sailed with Noah in the Ark, and had very likely been responsible for putting it aground on Mount Ararat. Higginbottom was a Fleet Reservist, a perennial AB with three good-conduct badges – which made him Stripey to the ship's company – and likely never to be rated leading seaman. He was happier anyway in a quiet number; he acted as petty officers' messman, which brought plenty of perks. Stripey Higginbot-tom, unlike most Stripeys, was a lean man to the point of being cadaverous, and very tall. He was like a beanpole to look at, but a beanpole with its head screwed on and plenty of wily experience gleaned from a long seafaring life that in fact stretched back to before the last war. He'd actually served as a boy aboard the famed *Dreadnought* and had even, from a distance admittedly, set eyes on the even more famed Lord Fisher, Admiral of the Fleet and a right bad-tempered one at that. And Higginbottom had positively not advised making a complaint.

'Skippers,' he'd told Aldridge, 'don't like moaners. No one does. Complaints only gets a proper 'earing if they're justified, what yours isn't in my opinion, lad. You're a lousy bloody cack-'anded matloe and it's a leading 'and's job to sort you out an' see you don't sink the boat. That's what the skipper'll say, you mark my words – '

'But honestly, Maloney's – '

17

'Don't bloody interrupt your legal adviser. Skipper, 'e'll give you a flea in your ear and after that Maloney'll make your life a proper misery – see if 'e don't. Just keep your trap shut and try to act like a seaman and Maloney'll get tired of gettin' on to you. It's 'uman nature . . . and Maloney's not a bad bloke if you treat him right.' Higginbottom had scratched reflectively at a rum-bulbous nose, rum being one of the perks pertaining to his office as PO's messman. 'Your civvy job's against you aboard a bleedin' ship, lad. Actor . . . it's not right, some'ow. Can't you bloody see that for yourself?'

'No, I can't!' Aldridge had snapped angrily, going red.

Higginbottom said, 'Hoity-toity, eh! Don't you take that tone with me, young feller-me-lad.'

Standing now on the icy, fogbound fo'c'sle, behind the oilskinned back of Jimmy the One as the *Glenshiel* continued slow for the Cumbraes, Ordinary Seaman Aldridge longed for the bright lights and friendships of show business. It all seemed a long time ago now, aeons away from the vile, wind-torn weather of Scotland, a place Aldridge detested with all his heart. The terrible discomforts of life aboard a destroyer, the heaving decks and the wetness below as well as above, the rough men with whom he was forced to associate, the constant belching and breaking of wind along the stuffy messdecks, the crude jokes, the snide looks and comments about actors and nancy boys, the dangers from sea and foe – all that for days and days on end, not to mention seasickness on a stomach empty because the food was too appalling to contemplate: warmed-up corned beef and spuds, figgy duff, revolting thick tea with condensed milk, and then back into some dim Scottish port or harbour like Scapa as often as not, or maybe the Forth or the Clyde like this last time; a little better when you went ashore, but not much. The Scots didn't like Sassenachs and probably it was a good thing you couldn't understand half they said. And the whole place seemed to lie for ever under a blanket of snow, both fresh and hard-trodden till it was like concrete; perhaps they had such a season as summer but Aldridge had come to doubt it. And he didn't like mountains, saw no beauty in them at all. They merely oppressed him with their snow-covered vastness and their eerie silence broken only by the wind's howl. He preferred the ambience of the stage and the happy, easy lack of formality of theatrical lodgings. Of course, there was the occasional rift, the clash of temperament, anxiety-making rivalries and the hysterical outbursts of leading ladies and so on but they were a sight better than sailors and ships, a sight better than the bloody Clyde in fog. . . . Aldridge caught his breath as Jimmy the One suddenly vanished.

Gone overboard?

Should he cry out, or what?

He was about to utter an alarm when he realized that the fog had thickened again and Jimmy was wrapped in it. Just as he realized that, the vibration from the engines, low and gentle at their slow speed, ceased. The skipper had put the telegraphs to stop; they lay ghost-like, the syren now sounding two long blasts with one second between.

ii

IN Voss neither Haaland nor Kleppe had answered any questions. The Gestapo were brutes and behaved as such: blows were rained on the two men and when that had no effect other measures were tried: long matches were thrust beneath fingernails and lit. The agony brought sweat but no speech. Next the burned finger-ends had the nails withdrawn, one by one, with pincers. Still the men refused to talk.

As it turned out, they didn't need to; all the torment had been in vain, all the guts unnecessary. Investigation by another Gestapo department revealed the information that one Ivar Haaland, well known as a working carpenter in Bergen and suspected of having connections with the Resistance, had been missing from his workshop since early that morning. Haaland had not even revealed his name, nor had Kleppe; but two and two were put together and the officer was withdrawn from the interrogation for a message to be passed to him.

When he went back in he said, 'In Bergen there is a woman . . . not young. Elise Haaland. She has been arrested by the Gestapo. Under certain circumstances she might be released.' As he spoke, he observed both men closely. Ivar Haaland's face told him what he wanted to know: his identity.

19

'You are Haaland, the woman's husband. And you come from Bergen, where there are warships . . . there is now no need to tell me the rest. Later there will be more questions about the Resistance in Bergen.'

The Nazi left the room, his face white. He had been a long time getting at the truth, perhaps too long. Herr Himmler didn't suffer inefficiency and now much might be at stake, so he lost no time in passing the word through to Berlin: it was virtually certain that the outward movement of the great battleship *Attila* and her cruisers had been seen despite the prevailing fog and reported by the Resistance to the British Government and its leader, Churchill.

When this news was received by Grand Admiral Raeder there was a certain amount of consternation at an early revelation but no more than that: it had always been recognized that sooner or later the passage to sea of the *Attila* could not help but become known to the British Admiralty via its reconnaissance aircraft or a sighting by a warship at sea – perhaps by the armed merchant cruisers of the Northern Patrol off the icy shores of Greenland. Nevertheless, because of this unexpectedly early leak, certain redispositions had now to be made. The *Attila* was currently under orders to steam north-west to clear Shetland and the Faroes and then to head due west across the north of Iceland before turning south-westerly through the Denmark Strait. It had been believed that the British would not expect a German battleship to approach the North Atlantic by this route, and that her sudden appearance to confront the puny escorts of a big HX convoy coming through from Halifax would have a devastating effect.

Now there must be a change: the route via the Denmark Strait was too long: the *Attila* must be brought to action against the convoy sooner, before the British could make their own dispositions effective, before a chase developed.

Raeder's Chief of Staff made a tentative proposal. 'Should not the *Attila* be withdrawn back to base – temporarily, Herr Admiral, until – '

'No! Most certainly not. This convoy is vital to the enemy war effort and if we delay our chance is gone. The strike must be fast, Wünche – it is a question of re-routing only, and of a direct course at high speed to attack the convoy farther out in the Atlantic.'

'But the British heavy ships, the battleships from Scapa Flow – '

'They cannot sink the *Attila*, Wünche. The *Attila* is known to be unsinkable . . . the *Attila* is in a sense the very embodiment of our Führer's own strength, purpose and dedication . . . the flagship of the Third Reich. Heil, Hitler!'

iii

'How do they know she's bloody unsinkable?' Maloney asked rhetorically on the *Glenshiel*'s fo'c'sle. As the destroyer lay with her engines stopped, he and Petty Officr West had been discussing earlier radio boasting of Lord Haw-Haw about the mighty *Attila*. 'No one's ever fired at the sod yet, have they? Never bloody been to sea, except from the builder's yard to bloody Bergen. Ship's company won't even be worked up yet.'

'Doesn't stop bloody Hitler, mate. The bloke's infallible. Sun shines out of his arse, doesn't it?' He broke off. 'Aldridge!'

'Talk about tact and juxtaposition,' Maloney murmured. 'What's bloody Aldridge done now, eh?'

'Feet,' West said succinctly. Maloney looked. Aldridge was standing with a foot each side of the starboard anchor cable. Some people never learned, not even when they had a sense of self-preservation as strong as Aldridge's. West said, 'Come on, you bleedin' brain-soft twerp – stand away from the cable, cos if we let go you'll be in danger of havin' your equipment carried away – cable bloody *jumps* when it runs out!'

Aldridge gave a high sound and moved aside to stand by the guardrail. A half-minute later the patchy fog cleared again and on the bridge Cameron passed the order for dead slow ahead as *Glenorchy's* stern light and fog buoy came up. Not long after that there came a period of greater clearance and Millard pointed out the light on Toward Point, fine on the starboard bow. They were coming up to the entry to Rothesay Bay, and now the Cumbraes were not far ahead. Once they passed the narrows, much of the strain would be gone, at least for a while. It was a clear run from the Cumbraes to the great rock of Ailsa Craig, and then the turn to starboard into the North Channel between the Mull of Kintyre and Rathlin Island to head below the Mull of Oa towards Skerryvore and the Minches.

By some miracle the fog cleared further as they passed the Cumbraes and left the Sound of Bute to starboard. Ahead, the *Glenorchy* could be seen clearly now, and beyond her the wakes of the rest of the 24th flotilla: *Glenaffric* and *Glenfinnan*, the latter in the lead with Captain (D) in charge. Away ahead of them would be the ships of the 27th Cruiser Squadron – *Leicester*, *Stafford* and *Monmouth* with their 8-inch turrets, County Class cruisers with high freeboards, poor gun platforms in anything of a sea, and virtually unprotected sides. If they should meet the *Attila* without the support of Fraser's battleships there would be savage slaughter, but the Navy had to make do with what it had and keep smiling while it did so.

'The buggers left us nearly naked,' Cameron said suddenly.

'Sir?' Millard sounded surprised.

Cameron said, 'Just thoughts, Pilot. The pre-war politicians who wouldn't re-arm in time, wouldn't build enough ships.'

'Short-sighted lot. . . .'

'All except Churchill and one or two others. If it hadn't been for Churchill, we'd have gone under long ago, and I don't mean just the way he's fighting the war.' Cameron was silent for a while as the great mass of Arran Island loomed on the starboard bow. A blue-shaded Aldis began flashing from ahead, a speed signal reported to Cameron by the Yeoman of Signals.

Cameron said, 'Half ahead, Pilot.'

'Half ahead, sir.' Millard passed the order to Stace in the wheelhouse. The vibration increased and a bow wave started.

'Secure the anchor now, sir?'

'Yes,' Cameron answered. He called down to the First Lieutenant on the fo'c'sle, then spoke to Millard again. 'Course for Ailsa, Pilot – you know the rest.'

'Yes, sir.'

'There's something else for you to know. I'll be speaking to the ship's company later, but you may as well have it now.' Cameron took a deep breath. 'FOIC told all commanding

22

officers the score. The *Attila*'s believed not to be out just to play games or turn her engines over – not out just to shift to a German port, either. There's a very hush HX coming through from Halifax, Nova Scotia – or as hush as any convoy can ever expect to be. Big stuff, Pilot. A hell of a big troop lift – Yanks. Two divisions, no less, with attached transport and support corps. Not to mention ammunition and tankers.'

'And the *Attila* – '

'Someone's got to get to the *Attila* before she reaches the convoy. Currently they're nine hundred miles west of Cape Farewell. It's a fast convoy, of course . . . eighteen knots. That puts them about five days from UK.' Cameron paused. 'There's something else: the Queens – both of them, *Mary* and *Elizabeth*.'

'Surely not in the convoy?'

'Hardly.' The great Cunarders used their speed as their protection; they were too fast to be put into the convoy system, too fast for the other ships, too fast for the escorts mostly. Speed and zig-zags were the better bet. Cameron went on, 'They're carrying the greater part of the troop lift, Pilot – coming across independently, four days later out of New York and taking a different route for the Clyde. We hope the Nazis don't know about them . . . but no one can be sure.'

3

No one could be sure – except inside Germany. The security had been intense on both sides of the Atlantic, in Washington and the departure port of New York, in Whitehall and the Western Approaches and all other Naval and military commands. But there was pessimism in plenty; it was impossible to disguise the sailing of the world's two biggest and most prestigious merchant ships, impossible to disguise the embarkation of two American divisions. New York had its spies and although in strict accuracy no one could, as Cameron had said in repetition of FOIC's words, be certain, equally no one in fact doubted that news of the sailings would have reached Germany before now.

This, the planning took into account.

Normally the attacks when they came – at any rate on the convoy itself – would have been by U-boat and, as the ships neared Scotland and came within the range of the German bombers, by aircraft. Now there was the new dimension of the break-out from Bergen. The *Queen Mary* and the *Queen Elizabeth* could not this time rely on their speed or the zig-zag pattern: the moment they were sighted by the *Attila* they were doomed.

In the Admiralty's Operations Room the staff officers were at the posts they would not leave until the ships were safely into the Clyde and the *Attila* had been either brought to action or had retreated to Bergen or Trondheim or a German or French port – in all conscience Hitler had plenty of choice now that he had spread the Nazi web over most of Europe and

24

Scandinavia. There was a determination in the Admiralty and the War Cabinet that the *Attila* would not survive to venture out again; any number of air attacks had been made on likely ports in the hope of putting the battleship out of action before she could go to sea. There had never been any certainty as to exactly where she had been berthed; her camouflage had been too good for the aerial recce crews and the Resistance had, oddly in retrospect, been silent on the matter until a report – earlier than Ivar Haarland's message that the *Attila* had moved out – had come through that she had been identified in Bergen although dressed up, as it were, with bits of false upperworks, wooden, grey-painted removable structures that had concealed her outline and given her the appearance of the *Tirpitz*. That had been only twenty-four hours before Haaland had reported the outward movement; another air attack, a heavy one, had been planned . . . and that alone, if it had been leaked, could have accounted for the move.

But the Chief of the Naval Staff was no believer in such a theory: the convoy out of Halifax and the huge American troop lift were both too much to be a coincidence. CNS walked up and down, hands behind his back, face anxious as he looked at the wall maps showing the dispositions of the Fleet in their home bases, the flags moving out across the spaces of sea as the warships moved, in accordance with orders, to the east of Scapa Flow.

'Weather?' he snapped.

'Clearing still, sir. But it's around yet and could come down again.'

'So the bugger could vanish again. We're going to assume the obvious, that she's heading direct for the vicinity of Cape Farewell. After that, a degree of uncertainty sets in: either she makes for the estimated positions of one or other of the Queens and leaves the HX convoy alone – or she goes for the more positive position of the convoy first. Imponderables, imponderables, always blasted imponderables! She may well have a difficulty in finding the *Mary* or the *Elizabeth* – at any rate we have to hope she will – but she can hardly miss the HX.'

The Admiral went on with his pacing, backwards and forwards, deep in thought, assessing, assuming, trying to see into the enemy mind and come up with the right counter-stroke. That convoy was vital in itself and never mind the two big liners filled with troops. The convoy was bringing desperately needed war supplies in ships that could not be quickly replaced should they go down; and there were the crews too. Seamen could not be trained quickly: the masters and mates and engineers aboard the merchant vessels all had a long training behind them.

Yet there was something special about the *Queen Mary* and the *Queen Elizabeth*. Prestige ships in peacetime, they were no less so in war with their Cunard-White Star colours of red and white and black replaced by dull camouflage to break up their enormous outlines. And if now they and the US troop lift should succumb to the immense gun-power of the *Attila* and her consorts, the effect on the American people as well as the British would be catastrophic. Of course, the Nazis would be well aware of this. To them, those ships were probably the greater prize; and if they attacked the convoy first, then their own position would be known for sure and they would no doubt find it more expedient to retreat and make at full speed back to base. And yet again, there was that broad and easily locatable HX convoy steaming at its comparatively slow speed for the Clyde; together with its escorts, its well-spaced columns covered very many square miles of sea. The Chief of Staff summarized the gun-power available to the German raiding force: to the *Attila*'s nine 16-inch and twelve 6-inch guns had to be added the main armament of the *Reckling-hausen* and the *Darmstadt*. Between them the heavy cruisers carried sixteen 8-inch guns together with twenty four 4.1-inch HA armament.

It was a lot to counter with a depleted battle fleet. *Royal Oak*, *Prince of Wales*, *Repulse*, *Hood*, *Barham* all gone; others in distant waters, unrecallable in time. Time was so short, the *Attila*'s break-out had caught the Admiralty unawares. . . .

And that damnable, obliterating fog. It would be too late now to locate the *Attila* to the north-east – that should have been realized earlier, the needle-in-a-haystack element seen for what it was. Half the trouble, the Chief of Staff reflected, was good old Winnie, all the dogmatic, ill-tempered orders. . . . Winnie had come in person to tell them what to do and had insisted on the Home Fleet being moved north-east to pick up the Nazis in their own waters and teach them a lesson slap bang on their own doorstep, but it obviously wouldn't do now.

With reluctance the Chief of Staff took up a telephone that connected him direct with the Prime Minister. It was answered immediately: did Winston *ever* sleep? The Chief of Staff put his views with insistence.

'Something of a compromise, sir. And a change in the orders to Fraser. I suggest his heavy ships close the area south of Cape Farewell, while CS27 and the destroyer flotilla from the Clyde are ordered to search to the eastward behind the main battle fleet out of Scapa.'

ii

As *Glenshiel* made her northing towards the Minches, the Petty Officer Telegraphist read a w/T message in cypher, originated by the Admiralty and addressed to CS27 repeated 24th Destroyer Flotilla and all individual ships. The cypher was sent down to the doctor, whose far from onerous medical duties when not in action allowed him to act as cypher officer. Surgeon Lieutenant MacNamara had turned in, and turned out again sleepily and reluctantly to dig out the decyphering tables from the safe in the Captain's office. Dealing with cyphers was always a slow job and one he detested, except insofar as when something was in the air he was the first to know about it. This time, when he read the preamble about changed orders, he hoped they were for Londonderry where he lived; but no such luck. Not that he'd really expected it, but all men lived in hope in this bloody war. When he had the message down in plain language he took it to the bridge and handed it to the Captain, who was still there hunched in a corner by the fore screen.

'w/T from Admiralty,' MacNamara said.

'Thanks, Doc.' Cameron took the message form and read it in the dim light from the binnacle. Looking up he addressed Sub-Lieutenant Millard. He said, 'Changed orders, Pilot. We don't join the main fleet – not yet, anyway. We're to search the area east from Scapa and report any sighting of the

27

Germans . . . Fraser's ordered south of Cape Farewell.' He looked ahead towards the ships in company. 'That means no alteration in our own course and route, Pilot.'

'Leaves us kind of lonely, too!'

'Not really. cs27's coming with us.'

'To meet the *Attila* . . .' Millard sounded sardonic.

'That's the ticket. Sort of, anyway. Depends how Captain(D) sees it, but to me it looks as if we're not expected to engage, just report.'

'Could come to the same thing, sir.'

Cameron nodded and turned back to his corner, where he stared out towards the dim shape of *Glenorchy*. The fog had cleared quite a bit now and that was some comfort; but he knew what was in Millard's mind well enough: even if they remained unseen after picking up the *Attila*, which was unlikely enough in all conscience, the fact that they had been, in effect, ordered to break wireless silence at sea held its own dangers. That transmission would be picked up by the German ships and the position of the transmitting vessel would be given away. No doubt orders would come through before long from Captain(D) for the destroyers to part company when they reached the search area and each comb her own sector; they would scarcely carry out such a search in company, thus only one ship need attract the attention of the Nazis. If it fell to *Glenshiel* to be that ship, that was just bad luck. And if he had to make the transmission, Cameron could only hope the main fleet units would get there in time.

He turned as the First Lieutenant came up the ladder from the iron-deck. He told Hastings of the changed orders and added, 'I'll speak to the ship's company during the morning watch, Number One.'

'Aye, aye, sir. Fog's clearing nicely.'

'Yes. There's a bit of wind coming up.'

'Let's hope the Jerries are still in it!'

Cameron nodded. 'The weather report'll be interesting when we get it.'

'No word about the *Attila*, I take it, sir?'

'Not a thing. I suppose we can assume the RAF recce boys are out, but if she's still in fog they'll be pretty useless – and so will we be, come to that.'

28

Cameron remained on the bridge throughout the night, unwilling to be below while his ship was in pilotage waters. The technique of keeping awake, practised through the years of war, had accustomed him to doing without sleep for long periods. As the weather continued to clear under the impact of a fresh wind coming down from the north, the land could be seen on either side: the island of North Uist to port, Loch Dunvegan on Skye to starboard as they headed into the Little Minch and continued on to pass between Shiant Island and Rubha Hunish at the outer entry to Kyle of Lochalsh. When later, steaming now by order from Captain(D) at twenty-five knots, they passed between the Butt of Lewis and Cape Wrath, turning to starboard off the latter to head for the Pentland Firth, they came into a stronger blow and breaking seas, a very different weather pattern from the fog's thickness. By this time it was well into the next day's forenoon and there had been signalling between the ships, confirming Cameron's belief that each destroyer would be given an area to search on its own. By this time also, the Petty Officer Telegraphist had brought the weather reports; the fog was dispersing all over and they would steam into increasing wind.

During the morning watch, just before the forenoon watchmen were due on deck to take over at the guns and in the lookout positions, Cameron had spoken as promised to his ship's company over the Tannoy, telling them of the changed orders and their own role.

He said, 'The main fleet's being thrown in to defend the convoy and the big troop transports from New York. That's the priority, obviously. I'm not saying it's being left to the cruisers and destroyers to despatch the *Attila* – joke! – but on the other hand we may find ourselves in action. I want every man to appreciate the facts. It's vital the *Attila* is picked up and shadowed into the guns of the battle fleet. You can all imagine for yourselves what the effect on morale would be if the *Mary* and *Elizabeth* went – and I don't need to remind you of the importance of the HX convoy either; men, munitions, oil fuel, food – the whole lot at risk of the *Attila* guns . . . a fast strike, then a dash for home. Because troopships are involved, the convoy's got an exceptionally

29

large escort – *Resolution* and *Revenge* in addition to the usual cruisers and destroyers, but you all know how old and slow those R class battle-wagons are. There's a carrier too – *Furious*, but she's a sitting duck for the main armament of any battleship.'

That was about all Cameron had to say for the moment; he would keep the ship's company informed of developments and in the meantime they were to be on the top line and fully alert for trouble. There was a buzz of conversation along the messdecks when the Captain had finished speaking. In the petty officers' mess Chief PO Ruckle, chief boatswain's mate, more familiarly known as the Buffer, gave it as his opinion that although the skipper hadn't said so in so many words, there was more than an even chance Captain(D) might, if the *Attila* was sighted, decide to go in and attack.

'What, with titchy little destroyers?' Petty Officer West said jeeringly. 'CS27 might use his cruisers, but that'd be suicide too.'

'Damage her,' Ruckle said, on the defensive. 'Just a bit. Enough to slow her down, say. Or maybe bugger up her steering.'

'Some hope! You'd never bring our bloody popguns inside her range, not before you got blown out of the hogwash anyway.' West scratched reflectively at an unshaven chin . . . one of the perks of being in destroyers was that you didn't have to be all that smart at sea, not like the big-ship Navy, all bull and yes, sir, no, sir. 'I don't reckon we'll pick her up anyway, Buff. Too much bloody sea, and she'll be pissing off flat out into the Atlantic now the weather's cleared.'

On deck amidships, Mr Tarbuck, Gunner(T) in charge of *Glenshiel*'s torpedo-tubes, was carrying out a routine inspection with his torpedo-gunner's mate, Petty Officer Clutch, like CPO Stace an active-service rating: nothing dug-out about Clutch, who'd come recently from the *Nelson* and always shaved at sea and wore a uniform pressed daily – when the exigencies of the service permitted – by Stripey Higginbottom under dire threat should the job prove poor. Clutch permitted himself a reflection on current matters. He

30

said, 'I reckon, sir, once the bugger's spotted she'll shove off for home, eh?'

Mr Tarbuck laughed. 'Not on your nellie, TI! Don't tell me the mighty *Nelson* would have run!'

'No, sir, not the *Nelson*.'

'Well, then! Same thing. Risk they take. If you go out on a mission, you stick to it – you expect to be seen some time or other, right? Bloody battleships, theirs and ours, they don't go to sea all that often . . . when they come out, well, it's for a purpose like this time and you don't drop back. . . .'

Tarbuck went on and on. Garrulous old sod, Clutch thought surlily, wishing he'd never opened his mouth – should have known. He'd not been shipmates with the Gunner(T) for long, but in the short space of time he had been, Tarbuck had yacked enough to fill the Bible and start a sequel. Tarbuck was an old-timer, went out on pension back in 1933 and in Clutch's view not only was he years out of date but had forgotten all he ever had known – which was why he had developed verbal diarrhoea: if you talked all the time you didn't leave room for questions you didn't know the answers to. Also, there was nothing *smart* about the Gunner(T); his appearance let the department down. If he hadn't currently been wearing a duffel-coat and an oilskin, both at the same time which made him look like a more-or-less animated rum cask, you would have seen the thin gold stripe of his warrant rank hanging three-quarters off his sleeve like a pennant at the dip, and you'd also have seen the remains of last night's wardroom dinner down the front of his monkey-jacket. It was a wonder the skipper didn't tell him to clean up a bit, enough to put the officers off their food it was. It had never been like that in the *Nelson*. The officers sat down proper, nice and clean . . . of course, if Tarbuck had been in the *Nelson* he would have been in the warrant officers' mess, not the wardroom. But destroyers didn't run to a wo's mess or much else either; it was all too free and easy for Petty Officer Clutch, who liked shine and gaiters and precise drill.

Tarbuck had stopped talking now and was delving into the tube mechanism, teaching himself how probably, and was covering himself with oil and grease and bird shit where a seagull had been. Not an officer's job: Clutch called out loudly for the LTO, Leading Seaman Pittman, another active-service rating with the non-sub rate of leading torpedoman, to send a hand to Mr Tarbuck's assistance. Tarbuck said he didn't want any assistance; he liked doing the job himself, kept his hand in . . . yack, yack. Petty Officer Clutch excused himself: things to see to, he said, in the gunner's store. He marched away along the iron-deck, arms swinging, left-right-left, jaw thrust out belligerently. Stupid twerp, Leading Seaman Pittman thought, wouldn't get his own lily-white hands dirty, oh no, leave it to poor old Tarbuck, who was as decent a WO as Pittman had ever served with. Pittman gave a loud laugh when Clutch did something daft with his goose-step on the wet deck and went arse over bollocks, slid a yard or two on his bum and fetched up under the splinter shield of Number Three gun aft.

Clutch, two piss-pots high as Pittman put it, got to his feet, cheeks red and angry, and faced for'ard.

'Stop that!' he shouted.

'Sorry I'm sure, TI.'

'You better be. Laughing – that's insolence, so watch it. Next time you'll be up before the OOW, all right?'

iii

BY some curious quirk of the weather, the *Attila* and her cruiser consorts were still enfolded in the fog and had been ever since stealing out from Bergen the day before. The reports from the meteorologists indicated that the fog was clearing to the west and the ships would find better visibility before long. But Vice-Admiral Fichtner, commanding the force from his high admiral's bridge aboard the *Attila*, was in no particular hurry to emerge from the fog's security; nor was the battleship's captain, Captain Sefrin. Urgent cypher traffic from Berlin had told them that their passage out from Bergen had been observed and reported to the British Admiralty – and this, of course, was why their route orders had been changed from an approach through the Denmark Strait to a direct approach south of Iceland. In the meantime the longer they could remain hidden in the fog, the more

32

distraught the British would become, Fichtner thought. He said as much.

'When the British become worried, Captain Sefrin, they do foolish things.'

'Yes, Herr Admiral, that is true.'

'And as for us, we have the speed in hand – so much faster than the British battleships. There is no immediate need.'

Sefrin nodded, pondering his Admiral's words about the British and their reactions, their foolish reactions. This, Captain Sefrin believed, was on account of Churchill of whom such horrifying stories had been reported from London by agents of the Reich. Churchill, it was reported, continually saw red and his gory appetite became worse, it would not let him rest and it affected his judgment . . . he gave stupid orders and he harassed his Naval and military commanders into doing stupid things. As likely as not – had not his Admiral just inferred so? – something stupid would be done this time if the German squadron remained hidden from the sight of Churchill. To forecast what Churchill would in fact do was impossible; those who were themselves sane could never predict what such a man would do. A vision came suddenly to Captain Sefrin of the entire British fleet delving busily into the fog. All Churchill's ships would smash into one another and they would sink or lie helpless while the *Attila* stole out still unseen with no one left to stop her as she steamed towards the British convoy. . . .

Fichtner asked, 'What are you smiling at, Flag Captain?'

Sefrin said, 'Thoughts of the madman Churchill, Herr Admiral.'

Fichtner grunted. 'Do not underestimate him.' Nothing further was said; Fichtner stared out into the thickness, thinking his own thoughts of war and death at sea. He would, without question, do his duty for his Führer and the Reich but he would genuinely regret the forthcoming slaughter of so many brave British seamen, to say nothing of the soldiers embarked in the troopships, Americans coming across the North Atlantic to pull Winston Churchill's chestnuts from the fire. But it was the seamen who principally occupied Fichtner's mind; seamen were seamen whatever their nationality, and also the British seamen were mostly pure Aryan; one did not count the black men and the Chinamen who manned many of the merchant ships under Aryan officers. It would not be a pleasant task, to fire his great guns at unprotected hulls and bring agonizing death to men who sailed the seas just as he did, but the war had to be won and the *Attila* was going to play a very great part in winning it. A few days before moving out from Bergen, Vice-Admiral Fichtner had been recalled to Germany and had been granted an audience with Herr Hitler himself at Berchtesgaden; in front of Grand Admiral Raeder, the Führer had personally charged him with his duty for the Reich.

'The *Attila*,' the Führer had said, staring fixedly at him and flourishing a field marshal's baton, 'is the pride of the German fleet, and carries the very flower of the German Navy as her crew. She will achieve splendid things, she will write a page into the long history of the Aryan people and will be remembered and spoken of with bated breath in future centuries, and your name will go with her, never to be forgotten. . . .'

The Führer had said a good deal more, having worked himself up to full patriotic spate and begun to foam a little with spittle at the corner of his mouth. After a while they had been joined by Reichsmarschal Goering in a sky-blue *Luft-waffe* uniform, a fat man full of jokes and good humour but in Fichtner's view a showman and a buffoon, who had been full of his aircraft and had tended to be superior about the *Attila*, which made Vice-Admiral Fichtner more than ever determined that the great battleship should live up to the Führer's expectations.

Now, from his bridge, he looked down towards the guns. He was almost unable to see them; the fog was certainly very thick. But to know they were there was enough, to know that the batteries were manned for action, that throughout the ship men were already at their stations to support the guns, the sole purpose for which every warship went to sea. Navigators, engineers, doctors, accountant officers and their staffs – cooks, stewards, storemen, electricians, shipwrights and all the rest – they were ancillary to the guns, those great steel shafts that could throw death and destruction for many miles across the sea and could hit their targets, thanks to the wonderful intricacies of fire control, even when they couldn't see them.

Steaming at dead slow speed, the *Attila* moved on through the fog, her course directed north-westward. Two hours later her radar reported a contact.

4

By now the 24th Destroyer Flotilla had reached its allotted area of search and the individual ships had broken away to carry out the sector searches visually and by radar. The gale had blown itself out and the fog was persisting to the east. From the *Glenshiel*'s bridge Cameron looked towards a thick, impenetrable fog-bank, obscuring the horizon to starboard.

He said to his Officer of the Watch, 'Looks at though it extends all the way to the North Cape!' He took up his binoculars again. There was no point in steaming into the pea-soup. All he could do was to hover on the fringe and hope for a sight of a battleship's fighting-top looming over the murk below – either that, or her bows thrusting out from the fog-bank into clear visibility and a sight of the British destroyer on watch. If and when either of these two contingencies occurred and the watching ship identified the *Attila* beyond a doubt, then the orders from both cs27 and Captain(D) were precise: the sighting vessel was to report immediately by w/t, using plain language, turn away at full speed and carry out distant shadowing routine, reporting thereafter as necessary.

Cameron had discussed these orders with Hastings and Millard. The big question was, what would the *Attila* do when she knew she had been spotted? Would she turn for home, or would she continue on for her obvious target? That remained imponderable; and there was as much disagreement on the bridge as there had been on the messdecks: Hastings believed the German would run for port and live to fight another day.

Both Cameron and Millard disagreed. The *Attila*'s chance was now, not in the future. It was seldom enough that a major convoy was heading across the North Atlantic at the same time as the *Queen Mary* and *Queen Elizabeth*. It had never happened before; it would probably, almost certainly, never happen again.

'You could say this sort of thing was what she was built for,' Cameron said. 'What else can she achieve? The days of pitched fleet battles are over – they died with Jutland. The only other alternative would be to spend the rest of the war in port, scared to come out in case she was seen! That can't be what Adolf had in mind for her. I think now she's out she'll go for the main chance, spotted or not.'

'And meet the whole Home Fleet?' Hastings asked.

Cameron shrugged. 'I say again – old ships, Number One. Floating coffins. Not enough gun-power, not enough speed, not enough armour. They looked fine at the Spithead reviews back in 1935 and 1937. But did you ever read the reports after the *Royal Oak* was sunk? Poor old crate was hardly sea-worthy, patched together with sticking-plaster and half the electrics didn't work. I reckon the *Attila* would go through them all like a dose of salts – except perhaps for the flagship. *Duke of York*'s bang up to date right enough, but you know as well as I do the German gunnery has always been better than ours. We have to face that – or Fraser does!'

Hastings nodded. What the Captain had said was true enough; Hastings' father was a rear-admiral(E) holding an Admiralty appointment under the Engineer-in-Chief; and often enough he had done some head-shaking over the fitness for battle of the Home Fleet's capital ships, the older aircraft-carriers included. No doubt fortunately, the British public believed that all was well with the Navy, that nothing could get through the ocean battle-line, blithely unaware of its obsolete nature in so many cases. . . . Hastings dismissed it from his mind. They would face the consequences, and know their future, in the Nazis' own time, and for now there was much for a first lieutenant to see to about the decks. First lieutenants, ships' nursemaids in effect, never had time to stand about talking. Hastings went down the starboard ladder to the iron-deck, feeling the intense cold of the northern winter bite into his bones through his duffel-coat. He shivered: give him the Med every time! Going aft, he encountered the torpedo-gunner.

'What-ho, Torps. How's the tubes?'

Tarbuck gave a hollow wheeze. 'Mine or the boat's?'

'Bugger yours, Torps –'

'They're on top line, little beauties, all ready to drop and run.' Mr Tarbuck closed one nostril with a thumb and blew vigorously down the other, over the guardrail. 'Think we're going to need 'em, do you, Number One?'

'You never know,' Hastings answered tritely, 'But somehow I doubt it.'

'Just checking, eh? No bloody need to.'

'Just checking,' Hastings confirmed with a grin, 'and I do realize how bloody efficient you are, Torps, but I have my duty to do as well as you, all right?' He was about to go on his way aft to climb to Number Three gun platform when he heard Cameron's shout from the bridge wing.

'Number one!'

Hastings turned. 'Sir?'

'Radar reports a contact starboard – three ships.' As the First Lieutenant ran for the bridge ladder, the action alarm sounded throughout the ship, the urgency of the rattlers bringing the off-watch men doubling out with their steel helmets, running for their action stations, pulling on duffel-coats as they went. Hastings reached the bridge; all the bridge personnel were looking out to starboard, towards the fog-bank which was as thick as ever, watching closely through binoculars for the first sign that the Germans were there.

Cameron said, 'It's got to be the *Attila*, Number One.'

'Three ships . . . sounds like it. How far off, sir?'

'Ten miles, bearing green four-five.'

'Slap abeam. Will you break wireless silence, sir?'

Cameron shook his head. 'Not yet. We have to be sure. They *could* be merchant ships, or other German Naval units.' He was sweating now in spite of the intense, clammy cold. He had two alternatives in fact: he could wait so as to get a sighting, wait to be certain as he had said to Hastings; or he could make what he considered a wholly warrantable assumption, send his report by wireless, and then turn away at full

38

speed, out of the range of the German guns when the *Attila* emerged into clear visibility, and carry out his shadowing orders at a safe distance. That his presence would be known by now to the enemy could be taken for granted; the German radar would be at least as efficient as his own. It would be prudent to keep his command intact.

Reports came through in a steady stream from the radar cabinet: the contact was closing their course very slowly but, as *Glenshiel* continued on her track, drawing aft. Millard, action Officer of the Watch, kept an eye on his course as well as on the fog to starboard. When using his binoculars he found himself gripping them like a vice. Neither he nor any of the ship's company had ever before been so close to action against a battleship, and they all believed along with Cameron that they now had the *Attila* and her cruiser escort on their tail. Millard knew what would happen if the German fired a salvo before they were out of range: they would vanish like the *Hood*.

Cameron said, 'Port twenty, engines to full ahead.'

'Port twenty,' Millard repeated down the voice-pipe. 'Both engines full ahead.'

The destroyer heeled sharply as the coxswain put the wheel over. Cameron said, 'We'll see her just as clearly from a safe distance, Pilot. Safer distance, anyway!'

Millard nodded, breathing out hard, blowing out his cheeks in a measure of relief as Cameron passed down his intentions to the engine-room. Sounds of moving equipment came up from below, things sliding about to the degree of list. Below on the starting platform Mr Bream all but slid into the arms of his Chief ERA. Downs said, 'Whoops-a-daisy, sir.'

'Grease on the bloody deck,' Mr Bream said. 'Get it seen to.'

'Aye, aye, sir.' Downs did sod all; Bream was just being an officer. Upset dignity had to be accounted for. There was always grease or oil on the deck of any engine-room and in a few minutes' time, if what the skipper had just told them was right, there could be a bloody sight more, mixed with blood and guts. Down here, they were rats in a trap; engine-rooms, if they didn't blow up or catch fire first, didn't take long to flood and there was only one way out, a narrow way at that,

39

for the whole complement of the engine-room and boiler-room. As the ship steadied on her new course, Downs wiped a handful of cotton-waste across his face. It didn't do to think about what might happen; and at least they were now pissing off in the right direction.

In the wheelhouse Chief Petty Officer Stace held the ship on 270 degrees – due west. She was thundering along now, flat out, and everything shaking and vibrating, a terrific sensation of sheer power as 1450 tons of steel hurtled along at more than thirty knots. Like Chief ERA Downs, Stace wiped his face clear of sweat. It could have been a close shave; and before long it was going to be closer.

On the bridge Cameron took the continuing radar reports: the contacts were drawing away, not unexpectedly, and were now on the port quarter. Summoned by the Captain, the PO Telegraphist was on the bridge. Cameron said, 'I'm assuming it's the *Attila*. I want the message ready, an immediate transmission when I give the word.'

'Yessir.' The PO Telegraphist had his message pad and pencil ready.

Cameron said, 'From *Glenshiel* to Admiralty – '

'Admiralty, sir?'

'Yes. They'll pass the orders to C-in-C Home Fleet and the others – CS27 and Captain(D). I don't want to address ships at sea and alert the Germans as to our strength.' Cameron paused, collecting his thoughts and phrasing the message. '*Attila*, *Recklinghausen* and *Darmstadt* observed emerging from fog in position . . . get that from the Navigating Officer, and I'll give you their course when I've assessed it. The message continues: Propose maintaining contact out of German range. That's all. When you get the word, make that in plain language, prefixed Most Immediate.'

The PO Telegraphist raised his eyebrows a little at the use of plain language. Cameron, seeing this, added, 'Orders, Larkin. We'll have been spotted by then, seen for what we are. The moment they pick up our transmission they'll know what it is. Speed of reception and understanding at the Admiralty is what counts and there's nothing to be gained by wasting time in decoding.'

40

He took up his binoculars again and watched with all the others for the first emergence from the fog's obscurity.

ii

THE earlier report from the *Attila*'s radar had been given to Captain Sefrin, who passed it immediately to Vice-Admiral Fichtner.

Fichtner asked, 'Only one echo, one ship?'

'Yes, Herr Admiral.'

'Has there been a transmission from her?'

'No, Herr Admiral. Nothing has been intercepted.'

'H'm. What size?'

'Small, Herr Admiral, and moving on a northerly course.'

Fichtner pondered, pulling at his beard. 'Fast, and alone. Not a merchant ship, I think – but no transmission, that is strange. One would assume she has picked us up on her radar as we have her – but no matter. I believe this is the first contact with the British Navy. This is not unexpected, of course.'

'No, Herr Admiral.'

Fichtner walked up and down the admiral's bridge for a turn or two, frowning. What to do? Why, perhaps nothing at this stage. Already the flagship and the cruisers were at action stations and there was nothing to be done until they were actually spotted visually. . . . Fichtner was projecting himself into the mind of the invisible captain, who if he was indeed of the British Fleet might well report to the Naval command at any moment, but on the other hand might prefer to await a positive identification. If he, Fichtner, had been in the British shoes he would have waited rather than rush in with a possibly false report that would serve only to confuse the issue when eventually an enemy really was sighted. So if he opened fire now, on the radar bearing, blind through the fog, he might inhibit that message with a lucky fall of shot. Or he might sink a neutral . . . but in any case he could by no means be certain of a hit, however excellent his guns and however great the accuracy of his radar bearings upon which the guns would go into action. Not certain . . . and all he might achieve might be to alert the other ship, confirming his presence before he needed to.

There was a better way.

'Captain Sefrin,' he said, 'we shall display to this ship, which I am convinced is British, a masterly inactivity! We shall remain longer in the fog, which extends far to the north – if the meteorological reports and my own seaman's sense are at all accurate. You will please alter your course northwards, Captain, and have the *Recklinghausen* and the *Darmstadt* informed by lamp.'

'Yes, Herr Admiral.' Sefrin clicked his heels together and gave a tight bow from the hips.

'One more thing: I wish to speak to the ship's company. I shall tell them I believe the British are now close. In the meantime, Captain, please see to it that the main armamant is directed continuously on to the radar bearing. If we should move into a patch clear of the fog, which is always likely, and bring the British ship in view of us, then I shall open fire as soon as the identification is positive.'

Like some terrible leviathan the *Attila* began to swing on to her new course with the ships in company following suit as the executive, read hazily through the swirls of fog, was passed by lamp. Like the fog earlier in the Clyde, conditions were patchy for the Germans, and the ships had had brief visual sightings of one another during the voyage from Bergen; but it had been an unnerving experience for all the commanding officers and navigators. Had the *Recklinghausen* or the *Darmstadt* come too close to the *Attila* and caused her damage, the Captain responsible would be pilloried upon his return to Germany. So they had stolen on by use of the radar and the booming syrens, also largely by guess and by God, hearts and minds projecting ahead for comfort, eager for the splendid sight of the great *Attila* steaming fast through the British convoy lines with all guns firing, then turning to come back again and bring about more destruction before altering course towards the troop-packed liners from America. Aboard the flagship Vice-Admiral Fichtner remained on his bridge, damp from the wreathing fog, surrounded by his staff officers, receiving the reports as the juxtaposition of his squadron and the lone British ship changed. The fact that the distance was opening and the other vessel's course had altered was of little account: Fichtner knew that from now until he had sunk his adversary she would remain in distant contact, that he would be shadowed continuously and it would not be long before the British sent out their aircraft. This was for the time being unavoidable but it was to be regretted. If it had not been for the troublesome Norwegian Resistance, he would have had high hopes of closing the convoy very much nearer before being picked up by the British. There was, however, one comfort: the flagship's wireless receiving room, keeping a continuous watch on possible transmissions, reported utter silence on the part of the invisible vessel. Thus far, Fichtner was preserving his secrecy vis-à-vis the wider world and the British Admiralty.

Hands clasped behind the back of his greatcoat, the Admiral paced his bridge.

iii

'BUGGER all,' Petty Officer Clutch said with a sniff. He was standing by the depth charges aft, rising and falling on the balls of his feet, hands clasped behind his back like the German Admiral as he talked to Petty Officer Tremlett, PO of the Quarterdeck Division. 'Probably pissed off, shouldn't wonder.'

Tremlett grinned. 'Think they're scared of us, do you?'

'I didn't say that. They won't want to be seen, stands to reason. Or it may not be the bloody *Attila* after all.' Clutch paused, looking down at the curfuffle below the destroyer's counter, foam like Niagara Falls and a streaming wake cutting a wide swathe across the surface. The curfuffle had in fact eased. The skipper was reducing revolutions.

'Going to hang about, are we, d'you reckon, TI?'

'Likely. Tell you something, though. That line of fog looks like it's breaking up. There's a wind coming up – see it on the water, do you?'

Tremlett looked astern. The surface, hitherto flat calm but with quite a swell, was starting to ruffle, and it was true enough the fog-bank looked different, less solid, more sort of swirly. Then, just a moment later, he saw something and said, 'Christ!'

'What?'

Tremlett reached out an arm. 'Look, TI! Starboard quarter . . . three sets of masts and fighting-tops – ' He broke off; Clutch was already moving for'ard along the deck, shouting out a warning to the bridge, an unnecessary one for the emerging German squadron had been seen, drawn well north by this time. Cameron ordered the revolutions up again to the maximum, and held his westerly course. Millard was staring aft through his binoculars. He said, 'They're on a northerly course, sir.' Then he added, 'Turning now. Turning back, towards us – and we have our identification now. It's the *Attila*, all right.'

Cameron had the telephone to the w/t office in his hand. 'Make the signal right away,' he said to the PO Telegraphist, and thrust the instrument at Millard. 'Give the w/t our position, Pilot, and make it fast as you can.'

Millard was passing the latitude and longitude when a ripple of white smoke and a number of bright flashes were seen along the *Attila*'s beam. She had opened fire on the turn, while her broadside was presented to the British destroyer. All along the decks men flung themselves down flat, an instinctive reaction to what was coming. Cameron felt frozen, as if turned to stone. There was nothing he could do now but wait – wait and hope that their speed would carry them clear.

5

THE projectiles came for them with a roar like an underground train entering a station. With Cameron, all hands waited for what might be the end. In the wardroom, now turned into an action dressing station, the Surgeon Lieutenant and his sick-berth attendant waited for a shell to penetrate and blast them into the next world. If that didn't happen, they would be very busy within the next few seconds coping with casualties – that was what MacNamara was thinking, but not so the SBA, who believed that if there was a hit anywhere at all they would all be goners. Destroyers couldn't be expected to stand up to 16-inch projies, after all.

On the bridge, Cameron felt the wind of the heavy shells passing overhead a fraction of a second after one, dropping short, had gone into the sea some four cables astern. The sea rose in a waterspout, a high column that broke and dropped back, and then the sea erupted all around them as the rest of the shells took the water, the resulting spouts drenching the decks with spray.

'Close,' Cameron said, 'but not quite close enough.'

'They will be next time,' Millard said in a shaking voice. 'That was pretty good for a ranging shot!'

'I think we're nearly at their extreme range,' Cameron said.

'Well, we'll soon know. One thing, we're a small enough target – ' Millard broke off as there was a whine from the sound-powered telephone to the wireless room. Standing nearest, he answered, then listened. He swore vividly. Then he looked upwards and said, 'Right, PO.' He turned to

Cameron. 'W/T, sir. They can't get the message away.'

'Why the hell not, for God's sake?'

Millard pointed upwards. 'That's why, sir. Aerials shot away . . . and we never even noticed.'

Cameron followed the pointing finger. The fore topmast stood bare of all its clutter, W/T and radar, all gone. The whole lot had been taken, sliced off as though by a bacon cutter as one of the *Attila*'s shells passed overhead. Cameron stared helplessly as another ripple of fire came from the distance. This time the fall was well short as the *Glenshiel* continued heading away at full speed. Below, Mr Bream was giving her all he'd got, the engines moving so fast that he reckoned that if this was kept up for long they'd go and shear the holding-down bolts. They had all felt the reverberations as the shells had smacked into the water, much too close for Mr Bream's liking.

There was a lot of relief around when the bridge reported they were moving out of range, but no one expected them to get away with it for long, unless the skipper was really pulling out. Then the news went round the ship that the transmitting aerials had gone for a burton, likewise the receiving aerials and all the rest of the gubbins that kept them in touch with the outside world and enabled them to see in fog. That, in Mr Bream's view, just about did it. If the skipper had been unable to report the presence of the bloody Huns, then it was likely he was going to attempt to hang about until the telegraphists had rigged a jury aerial or whatever. Talk about suicide. He certainly wouldn't be losing visual contact with the *Attila*, not having once picked it up, and that was a different matter from just carrying out distant shadowing, which could be done largely by radar, Mr Bream reckoned, admittedly not knowing much about it, with the boat nicely out of range of the big stuff.

It was a dicey situation; and where, Mr Bream wondered, was the bloody RAF? Knowing the *Attila* was out, knowing her approximate area, surely the RAF would be in the vicinity, ready for when the fog cleared?

ii

CAMERON was watching the German ships through his binoculars. There had been no more firing; the

46

Attila and her consorts were hull down now and appeared to have turned once again for the north.

'What d'you think she's going to do, sir?' Hastings asked.

Cameron shrugged. 'It's anyone's guess, Number One. She could be meaning to go hell-for-leather towards the convoy while she has the chance, before the Fleet catches up with her – she won't know Fraser's already on his way.'

'They'd make that assumption, though.'

'Perhaps. We just don't know. She could have called it off, I suppose.'

'Making tracks for Trondheim?'

'Could be.' Once again Cameron swept his binoculars all around; the sea was empty of all ships except their own, steaming at full speed on a northern course to maintain distant contact so far as possible with the German squadron. Stace, still at his action station in the wheelhouse, caught the eye of Chief PO Ruckle, who had looked in whilst checking round the deck. Ruckle said, 'What I don't understand is why the Jerries didn't go a bit farther with us. They could've sent a cruiser in, eh?'

'They could, yes. Be thankful they didn't!'

'I am. But why?'

'Jerry mind,' Stace answered briefly. 'Maybe they believed we'd have transmitted already – natural enough if they did. Maybe some poor bloody Jerry sparks is being keel-hauled at this very moment for not having picked up our transmission.'

Ruckle pushed his steel helmet to the back of his head and dealt with an itch. 'If they thought we'd transmitted – '

'There'd be no point in lingering, would there, Buff? They'd do what they *are* doing – piss off out of it fast and get lost again. It's not easy to pick up a ship at sea, you know – not even something the size of the perishing *Attila*. And don't forget, as it happens we're the only poor sods who know where she is anyway!'

'Where she was, you mean, 'Swain.'

Stace laughed. 'Right!' Where she was.'

Ruckle said, 'Let's hope we can get those aerials made good, eh? Not much use shadowing even, not without that lot.'

Above on the bridge Cameron was watching the efforts of a leading telegraphist and an electrical artificer to rig a jury aerial and get something working; they didn't appear to be having much success, and the PO Telegraphist had come to the bridge to explain why. He was greatly embarrassed and fearful at having to do so.

'Shortage of spares, sir.'

Cameron's face tightened up but he held back the angry retort: every man was entitled to offer, not an excuse, but an explanation. 'How's that, Larkin?'

'My own fault, sir. I'm sorry, sir. Didn't check when I took over. There's an outfit that's no use to us, sir – sent up from Pompey a while ago, should have gone to a ship with a different type of installation . . . and there's been stuff pinched, sir, the proper spares what were lying around.'

Cameron felt his fists clench on the bridge rail: they felt as if they wanted to strangle someone. Larkin had joined the ship as replacement for the previous PO, killed in action whilst escorting the last-but-one convoy. That action had resulted in enough superficial damage to put the *Glenshiel* into dockyard hands on the Clyde for almost a week. It was just as they had been on the point of sailing to rejoin the flotilla when Larkin had reported from Portsmouth, a pierhead jump for him but that was no excuse. Cameron said, 'Shipyard workers again?'

'I reckon so, sir. Buggers'd nick from their own grandmothers.'

'As you should have known.'

'Yessir.'

'There's been plenty of time since, come to that. I don't need to tell you, you've put the whole operation in jeopardy. That's not an attribute of a good PO in charge of a department.'

'I'm sorry, sir.' Larkin fidgeted, face like a beetroot.

Cameron sighed. 'All right, Larkin. Do the best you can; get some sort of contact going. I'll speak to you again later.'

'Yessir.' Larkin saluted and began the climb up what was left of the mast. Cameron turned for'ard and stared down at his fo'c'sle as the bow cut fast through the water, cleaving the wind-blown sea and sending a heavy bow wave back to join the wake.

The tasks and responsibilities of a commanding officer seemed to be without end, by no means confined to the handling and fighting of his ship. There was the domestic side, the disciplinary side, and Cameron was no lover of the business of Captain's Defaulters, which was where Larkin must inevitably end up. Discipline had to be maintained and must be seen by all hands to be maintained; men charged with responsibility must not be allowed to get away with it or the result would be a rotten ship's company and general slackness all round.

Larkin's sin of omission had been no less than appalling, in a war situation an act of criminal irresponsibility that showed him to be unfit for his rate. The only punishment was, and had to be, disrating; this was in fact outside Cameron's own jurisdiction to inflict and would require ratification by warrant applied for through Captain(D). There was no doubt that a warrant would be forthcoming, and Larkin would, by regulations, be given the opportunity to opt for a court martial – but Larkin wouldn't do that. He would accept the Captain's punishment. Larkin was no pusher and the wonder was that he had ever been rated PO. It would be a kindness to other ships to which he might be drafted if he was broken. But Cameron detested the thought of breaking any man, of putting him down to work under men who had been his juniors in rank.

And there was another side to Larkin, as Cameron knew from Millard, who was divisional officer for the communications branch: Larkin had serious family problems – an old mother who lived with him in a too-small house in North End, Portsmouth, and was adding her own barrage to Hitler's bombing insofar as she was driving Larkin's wife round the bend. Larkin's wife was herself something of a nagger and leaves were hell. But that wasn't all by any means, and the nagging itself could be excused since the wife had had one operation after another and although she got remissions from time to time was basically dying of cancer, which Larkin knew. He also knew that his eldest boy, still at school in the village he'd been evacuated to, kept undesirable company, was in constant trouble with the police for playing truant and had been caught shop-lifting just before Larkin had joined *Glenshiel*.

It was enough to make a man pre-occupied. But it was still, in Naval terms, no excuse.

Cameron straightened from the bridge rail. The matter must be put out of mind for now. Hastings was still there, sweeping the horizon through binoculars. Cameron said, 'If we can't make contact, Number One, there's no real point in shadowing so far as I can see. Agree?'

'Well, yes, sir . . . but Larkin may do the trick yet.'

'True. But the better bet would be to break off while we have the chance, and make visual contact with Captain(D) or any of the others, and let them do the reporting. That's more urgent than sitting on *Attila*'s tail like arse-end Charlie.' He turned to Millard. 'Pilot, lay off a course to the search area nearest ours, all right?'

iii

BOTH the w/T and the radar remained out of action and during the afternoon watch, with the wind increasing and the German squadron now completely out of contact, another untoward event occurred to worry *Glenshiel*'s Captain. Petty Officer Larkin, no doubt anxious as to what was to happen to him, was all thumbs and shaking as though with palsy as he tried his best to repair both the aerials and his own standing with the Captain – and with the ship's company, to whom word of the scandal, and it was nothing short of that, had spread.

His problems made Petty Officer Larkin clumsy, and he lost his grip – literally. There was a sharp cry from aloft and Cameron, swinging round, saw the body falling. There was a nasty crump from just aft of the forebridge and then silence. The leading telegraphist and the EA went down fast. The Buffer, moving past the torpedo-tubes on the starboard side, saw what had happened and called out to the captain of Number Three gun to send a hand for the Surgeon Lieutenant, then doubled along the deck towards Larkin.

He went down on his haunches for a quick examination, and called up to where Cameron was looking down over the after bridge screen. 'Bad I reckon, sir. He's unconscious, and there's a leg all twisted under him.' Ruckle clicked his tongue. 'Talk about cack-handed!'

'Leave him till the doctor gets there,' Cameron called down. 'See he's not moved in the meantime, Chief.'

'Aye, aye, sir.' Ruckle steadied his heavy body against a stanchion; a nasty roll was beginning as the wind grew strong. MacNamara was quickly on the scene with his SBA, the latter carrying a Neil Robertson stretcher. MacNamara, clicking his tongue like the Buffer, straightened Larkin out with expert hands and saw him strapped into the stretcher and carried below to the tiny sick bay with its two sick berths and room for very little else. Ten minutes later MacNamara went to the bridge to make his report to the Captain.

'He's in a bad way, sir. Should be got to hospital soonest possible – '

'Hospital!' Cameron gave a humourless laugh and swept a hand around the cold, grey horizon. 'Out here, Doc?' He sighed. 'Let's have the details.'

MacNamara said, 'Right leg broken, ditto left arm and three ribs. Penetration of the right lung. I don't like his breathing or his colour. He's very deeply unconscious.' He paused. 'That's not all, I'm afraid. The skull's fractured . . . not necessarily a serious thing in itself, but I suspect deeper injuries.'

'Brain damage?'

'Almost certainly,' MacNamara said. 'The prognosis i poor. Again I say, hospitalization – '

'For God's sake! It's all you medicos ever think about – get 'em into a base hospital!'

'That,' MacNamara said, 'is just not fair.'

Cameron laid a hand on the doctor's shoulder. 'I know it's not, really. But there's no bloody hospital! Do your best – I know you will – and if we raise one of the cruisers and the weather's suitable for a transfer at sea, I'll have him sent across. How's that?'

MacNamara shrugged. 'Not good enough, I'm afraid. I doubt if any cruiser would have the resources – I'm not sure, but as I say, I doubt it.' MacNamara was RNVR, not long qualified and very new to the Navy. His SBA was even newer, half a dog-watch . . . as for Cameron, he had no idea of the medical and surgical capacities of cruisers. The doctor went on, 'If he doesn't get to hospital he's likely to die on us, sir.'

'I say again – no hospital.'

'Quite. I do realize that. 'I'm just telling you the position as I see it.'

'Yes, of course.'

'There's always Rosyth. That's the nearest place with full Naval hospital resources – or civilian hospitals in the Moray Firth, or Aberdeen. . . .'

'Save your breath, Doctor. I can't return to port without orders, you must know that, and meanwhile I can't communicate.' And for that, Cameron thought sardonically, Larkin had only himself to blame. 'Even if I could raise Captain(D) it's obvious he'd never detach us just on account of one man.'

'One man's a life,' MacNamara said. His thatch of red hair, capless, blew up in the strong wind. Beneath it his face was angry, rebellious. 'All this . . . it's too damn hidebound. There's medical expertise and resources waiting, and God knows we're just one tiny bloody boat against the *Attila*, with the whole Home Fleet not far off – '

'Yes. I know.' Cameron spoke quietly in contrast to the doctor's rising tones. 'Mac, you and I, we're in the same boat as regards the RN. Don't forget I'm RNVR as well. Perhaps we don't always see things so clear-cut as the regulars. But there's nothing hidebound about the absolute necessity of stopping the *Attila*. Think about all those other lives . . . and the *Glenshiel*'s a link in the chain that may save them – *will* save them if the *Attila* can be brought to action. Keep that in mind, Mac, and go below and do what you can.'

He turned away towards the bridge screen. MacNamara's mouth opened but he said nothing further. He gave a resigned gesture towards Cameron's back, caught Millard's eye for a moment and read support for the Captain. War was war and single lives couldn't be allowed to sway its conduct. Maybe that was right, but to MacNamara it was a wicked thing that a man should perhaps die when he could be saved. There might just about have been time, with luck, if Cameron had ordered an alteration of course and a dash at speed for Scotland. MacNamara turned away and went down the ladder, back to the sick bay.

52

Cameron thought about the conversation after the doctor had gone below: he shared MacNamara's concern but knew there was nothing else he could have done. And doctors could be wrong: they really didn't know a lot about the human head. Larkin could improve. Or maybe to die might be a better way than disrating and dishonour, and all those family problems. . . . He would be reported as died in the execution of his duty and Mrs Larkin would get a pension, a larger pension than if her husband had been disrated first, probably, though Cameron wasn't too sure about the Admiralty's outlook on war pensions. It was one of the things you didn't think about since you never expected it was going to be you who bought it. Cameron brooded on Larkin's misfortunes. The whole thing couldn't be blamed on Larkin: Sub-Lieutenant Millard, communications divisional officer in addition to his duties as navigator, should have checked on Larkin . . . come to that, he himself as Captain should have checked on Millard. That was the way it went: each rank checked on the next and everything, in the final analysis, was written into the Captain's account.

iv

THE ship had reduced to second degree of readiness and was steaming in two watches, rolling heavily now, with solid water coming over the bow to drop like thunder on the Blake slips and bottle-screw slips, on the centre-line capstan and the links of the cable, down the hawse-pipes to swill over the close-stowed anchors, and to rush on aft to drench the crew of Number One gun and drop like a waterfall over the break of the fo'c'sle. Every man on watch was drenched to the skin and would remain so unless the galley and the engine-room could cope with the drying-out problems. The messdecks used by the seamen and stokers were as wet as the men themselves, with water swilling about and surging on the roll up against the lockers. Things were a little better in the petty officers' mess, but not much. There was a filthy cold fug that caused Petty Officer Clutch to complain bitterly when he came in on relief from deck duties and shouted for the messman.

'You – Higginbottom!'

'Yes, TI?'

'Up off your fat Higginbottom,' Clutch said, making a stale joke, 'and bring us a cup of kye.'

'Coming up,' Higginbottom said. After so many years in the Andrew he was used to potty jokes about his name, but that Clutch, he didn't make jokes like other people did, there was always a nasty sound in his voice that took away the joke part and replaced it with a sting. Stripey Higgingottom, whose bottom was far from fat anyway, prepared the TI's cup of cocoa, making sure he got himself one as well, and carried it from the pantry into the mess itself where Clutch was sitting on a settee still with his wet seaboots on and spread across the fabric. Bugger all the other inmates of the mess, Higginbottom thought, so long as *he*'s all right.

Clutch took the cup with a grunt, stirred the contents, sipped and complained. 'Storing away all the sodding sugar for your own use, Higginbottom? Shove some more in, pronto – *move yourself*!'

Higginbottom did so, muttering in a low voice once his back was turned to the TI. Torpedo-gunner's mates weren't usually such ullage as that Clutch – unlike gunner's mates, they more often than not had a softer side to them, like their own torpedoes that went off with a friendly plop rather than a bloody great bang like the guns. But Clutch was a proper sod, the sort that took the shine off the job of petty officers' messman. Higginbottom carried the re-sugared cup back to the TI who took it again and kicked irritably at a cap lying on the settee.

'Caps, they should be on the hooks,' Clutch said. 'Whose is this?'

'PO Larkin's, TI.'

'Larkin, eh. Arse over bollocks, and cracks his skull open.' Clutch kicked again at the cap. 'On the hook, Higginbottom.'

Higginbottom picked up the cap and hung it with the others on a row of hooks fixed to the inboard bulkhead of the mess. Clutch, he knew, didn't like Larkin. Larkin wasn't a seaman PO; Clutch seemed to think only seamen had the right to be petty officers. Engine-room artificers were Clutch's real bugbear and he wasn't alone in that – given the rate of PO almost as soon as they joined and without the training to carry it and behave like petty officers, a lot of men didn't go much on them. But Clutch went further and reacted against everyone who wasn't a seaman. Telegraphists were technicians, not much better than tiffies. And now Clutch had something to bite on; what PO Larkin had done, or rather what he had failed to do, was common knowledge throughout the ship and, with his personal view of non-seaman rates, Clutch evidently felt he wasn't letting down a fellow PO by criticizing him to a junior rating, if anyone so elderly as Stripey Higginbottom could be considered as a junior. . . .

Clutch said, 'That Larkin asked for what he got.'

'He's pretty bad, TI.'

'So?' Clutch stared, eyes wide.

'Doesn't seem right, to talk like that about him, TI.'

Clutch lifted his feet clear of the settee and sat bolt upright, his mouth a thin, hard line. 'Watch yourself, Able Seaman Higginbottom. What's it to do with you?'

'Nothing, TI. Only PO Larkin's always been all right to me, and –'

'Gives you sippers, I don't doubt. That's an offence in itself as well you know. And don't talk to me about old service customs, right? They don't always hold.' What he meant, and what Stripey Higginbottom didn't need telling, was that unofficial customs could always be used against those indulging in them when someone of a nasty frame of mind wanted so to do. 'People who don't do their job shouldn't be in this mess. Chances are, Larkin *won't* be much longer. That's if the skipper does *his* job. All right, Higginbottom?'

'If you say so, TI.'

'I do, and that's that.'

'But look –'

'I'm looking, Higginbottom. At you. Want to stay as messman, do you? Or do you fancy being sent back to work part-of-ship – eh?'

'I'm happy here, TI,' Higginbottom said uneasily.

'Right! Soft number. Plenty of others'd like it just as much as you and maybe be better at it. So watch it and don't bloody argue, Able Seaman Higginbottom.'

Higginbottom had a number of things he'd have liked to say

55

to Clutch, one of them being that the TI wasn't God, wasn't even president of the mess with the right to kick out the messman – that honour fell to the 'swain, and Chiefy Stace was a good bloke and always fair. But Higginbottom didn't say anything – what was the use? No one could talk to Clutch, not even his messmates, without him shouting the odds and flattening all opposition just by being obstinate in his belief that he was always right and no one else was. So Higginbottom just turned his back and looked busy, straightening things and clearing away some cups and plates used by the other petty officers as they'd come off watch for a missed-musters meal. He was dead sorry about Larkin; they'd had a yarn or two – Larkin wasn't the sort to stand on his dignity as a PO and Stripey Higginbottom was just about old enough to be his dad anyway. So he knew a thing or two about what was on Larkin's mind and, like Cameron although he didn't know this, he was half inclined to think the PO Telegraphist mightn't wish to recover and that he could be better off if he didn't.

v

So far no other ship had picked up the *Attila* and her cruisers; thus there was no word of the Germans' whereabouts in the Admiralty. The HX convoy from Halifax, warned by cypher of coming events, was now approaching a point well to the south of Cape Farewell, whence it would drop down on the Bloody Foreland in County Donegal to pass across Lough Swilly and Lough Foyle for Rathlin and the approaches to the Firth of Clyde. *Queen Mary* and *Queen Elizabeth*, on their separate courses across the Atlantic from New York and warned, like the convoy, of the danger ahead, were as yet to westward of the convoy and farther south. While the main units of the Home Fleet stood northward to put themselves between the *Attila* and its targets, other ships from the Western Approaches command would leave Liverpool to meet the independently-routed liners off the Bloody Foreland.

On the high bridge of the *Queen Elizabeth* Sir James Bissett, the Cunard – White Star commodore, paced unendingly, weary from lack of sleep but determined to be at the seat of command if the *Attila* was sighted.

No longer a young man – Bissett had first gone to sea in the old windjammers, beating into the westerlies off the pitch of Cape Horn for Chilean ports and thence Australia – he was well accustomed to responsibility. But this time the responsibility had become a nightmare: so many thousands of fresh American troops aboard, the vast majority of them youngsters going to their first war assignment, and the Nazis chose this moment to send out their prestige battleship – against Britain's prestige liners. Bissett's mind, as he paced his bridge, watched by his staff of Officer of the Watch, quartermaster, telegraphsmen and messengers, went back over the years of peace and the very different passengers the Cunarders had carried then. Politicians, lords and ladies, Mrs Simpson who was to marry the King, ambassadors, writers and actors, industrialists, all very wealthy people in the first class. Important people, people whom even the liner's Master had to deal with tactfully and politely though the iron fist of discipline, extending to the wealthiest when necessary – some passengers travelling first class, a nice distinction from first-class passengers, never learned how to behave themselves decently and had to be corrected – was always there in reserve.

A high responsibility?

'Yes, of course,' Bissett had answered when the Officer Commanding Troops had put the question to him. 'But none of them was ever, in my view, a responsibility to compare with carrying your GIs. War's war – and I salute them all, every man. Paid a pittance to endure overcrowding and discomfort that even the steerage would have complained of in peace-time . . . a pittance to go to war. I'm glad I don't have to go to war!'

The American had grinned at that. 'Why, dammit, Captain, you're at war now!'

'Yes. But I meant the land war. Mud and foot-slogging and being sniped at. At least the sea's clean.'

But it won't be, Bissett thought now, if the *Attila* gets a sight of us. The sea will never feel clean again if they get the *Elizabeth*. Blood and fire, the screams of mangled men, the terrible rasp of twisting, tortured metal, the surge of the

57

Atlantic along the alleyways, filling the engine-rooms and boiler-rooms, the stores and offices, galleys, cabins and lounges as the great ship settled. . . . Sir James Bissett, who held the rank of Commodore RNR, had been a lieutenant in the earlier war against Germany and had been in action against the Kaiser's fleet. He knew what it was like when a ship went down.

And there was nothing he could do against the *Attila*. He'd been aware of that from the moment the Admiralty's cypher had been broken down. Nevertheless, he had called a conference attended by his Staff Captain, Chief Officer, Chief Engineer and other heads of departments together with the OC Troops and his staff officers to talk about what could be done. It amounted only to the measures to be taken after being hit: very negative but inevitable. Constantly from the Ambrose Light the whole ship had been exercised in boat drill, abandon-ship procedures, fire drill and so on, and the military knew, or should know by now, the details of the intricate system of watertight doors and fire doors throughout the ship. But despite the best of leadership, both British merchant service and US Army, it was going to be a monumental task to clear the survivors away into the boats under fire of those monstrous Nazi guns.

6

THE weather was appalling now, a sheer
misery; it was as though nature itself was conspiring against
them. The seas heaved, great rising walls of water lifting to
starboard and then sliding beneath the small destroyer to lift
her to the murky heavens and then drop her back into the
depths. The *Glenshiel* rolled heavily and from time to time
her upper deck was invisible from the bridge as green sea
swirled from for'ard to aft, bringing horrible conditions
below. The seamen's messdeck beneath the fo'c'sle was
already awash with some eight inches of water slopping from
side to side and carrying with it all manner of personal flotsam
that had escaped being crammed into the lockers. Caps,
socks, scraps of paper, cigarettes, a huge pair of underpants
that belonged to Slim Backhouse, the fattest man aboard at
some seventeen stone that was mostly stomach.

Above it all Ordinary Seaman Aldridge lay inert in his
hammock, wishing he could die. Aldridge didn't give a hoot
for the *Attila*, except that if she was sighted Leading Seaman
Maloney would have him out of his hammock on the instant
and he didn't believe he had the strength to reach his action
station. His stomach heaved drily; all he could do was retch
horribly and bring up bile, which was all that was left now. He
was too far gone even to try to fill his thoughts with the better
time before he'd been called up. All he could do was lie there
and watch the deckhead, close above him with its cork-
insulated paint and its rows of pipes and electric cables and
ventilator shafting, watch it roll to port and then back to

starboard while he stayed still. Still, that was, at times: hammocks when slung properly fore and aft didn't respond to the ship's roll, but they did respond to the pitch. Every now and again, when the destroyer went into a pitch and stood first on its head and then on its tail, Aldridge had to hold tight to a projection in the deckhead to stop himself being thrown out, and the jerk of the hammock-lashing was sick-making and terrifying.

The destroyer seemed filled with noise, too: the shriek of the wind, the crash of the sea dropping on to the fo'c'sle, the banging of deck gear, smaller tinkling sounds as mess crockery broke free of its stowage and smashed. And every now and then on the pitch a judder that ran through the whole ship as the screws lifted clear of the water and raced dangerously.

In the engine-room itself, Chief ERA Downs took the full brunt of the judder along with the rest of the tiffies and the black gang in the boiler-room. Downs was in charge for the present: the warrant engineer had got his head down in his cabin, snatching an hour or two while he could, before the Nazis came on his tail. Bream had been watch on, stop on for too long and was not far off being a zombie from lack of sleep, and Downs had persuaded him to rest. Now, he believed he might have to get Bream back.

'Them bloody shafts,' he said to no one in particular. The racing wasn't doing them much good. The *Glenshiel* was no longer in the first flush of youth, far from it. Much more of that furious judder and something was going to give. . . . Downs moved about the greasy deck plates with difficulty and a long-necked oil can, giving a shot here and there just in case. There was nothing Chief ERA Downs couldn't cope with and he knew it, but that Bream, he'd create hell if he wasn't there when anything went adrift.

Downs turned as Stoker PO Munro came through from the boiler-room, wiping his hands on the inevitable bundle of cotton-waste. 'Hullo there, Stokes,' Downs said mechanically.

Munro wiped the cotton-waste across his nose. 'Heard the buzz, Chief?'

'What?'

'The buzz,' Munro said more loudly.

'Yes, I heard that. What bloody buzz?'

'*Attila*'s gone back to Bergen.' There was a grin on Munro's face.

Downs pushed his oily cap to the back of his head and stared. 'Now where the ruddy hell did *that* originate?' he asked.

Munro shrugged. 'Dunno. Galley wireless. . . .'

'Well, I hope it's right! Sounds like wishful thinking to me. Buzzes! Old enough to know better than believe 'em, you are, Stokes.'

'I never said I believed it, Chief.' Munro went back towards the boiler-room and his oil-fired furnaces, thinking about buzzes, something no ship was ever free of, war and peace alike – only more so in war when you were always waiting anxiously for the buzz that said you were booked for a spell in port and a nice drop of leave. Buzzes burgeoned, spreading like the ground elder his garden in Basingstoke was never free of. God alone knew where they started; usually the Captain's steward got the blame, not without reason. It was like the old first war army chestnut, the message passed by word of mouth down the line from the colonel: *Send reinforcements, we're going to advance*, which had metamorphosed into *Send three and fourpence, we're going to a dance*.

His mind on past buzzes, Stoker PO Munro did what the Chief ERA later referred to as a Larkin: his feet slid from under him as the ship seemed to fall down the side of a mountain and he crashed heavily on to his right arm. He swore afterwards that he'd heard the crack.

Downs moved for him. Munro was swearing, a sustained stream of bad language, and his face was white with pain. 'Arm's bloody broken. At a time like this an' all. How do I bloody swim if our number comes up, eh, tell me that!'

Downs said, 'No worry. You'll be all right if your stupid buzz turns out right.' He used the sound-powered telephone to the forebridge and reported, asking for medical assistance.

ii

Now the snow had come. It had come suddenly and blindingly, bringing the visibility down as badly as the fog. In a way it was worse; the snow was blown viciously along the

61

tearing wind, making it blizzard conditions. The bridge personnel could scarcely face it, could barely open their eyes. Cameron had gone below an hour earlier, to grab a little sleep, like Bream, while he could. Hastings had taken over. Now the Captain would want to be on the bridge, had to be called in accordance with Standing Orders.

Hastings went to the voice-pipe to the Captain's sea cabin. 'Captain, sir. Bridge.'

'Yes.' Cameron's response was instant; no sleep at sea was deep; however tired a man was he was still subconsciously on the alert.

'Snow, sir. Heavy. Visibility down to half a cable.'

'Engines to half ahead, Number One. I'll be up.'

'Aye, aye, sir.' Hastings snapped back the voice-pipe cover and passed the orders to the Officer of the Watch, Sub-Lieutenant Poole. In the wheelhouse the quartermaster spoke to the telegraphsman and the orders went to the starting platform below. Cameron reached the forebridge, his face showing anxiety. Even half speed was risky. In the heavy seas that were running beneath the snow-storm, in the rearing crests, the radar, even had it been working, would have been completeiy unreliable and the same would be true of any ship that might lie across their track. Collision was always possible but there was also a risk in reducing speed too far in seas such as the destroyer was faced with, the risk that you might lose steerage way and then broach-to, to come broadside to the sea and be thrown right over to turn turtle.

Hastings, wrapped in duffel-coat plus oilskin, thick scarf, balaclava and woollen gloves, shouted over the noise of the weather. 'We're not making much through the water, sir.' Broaching-to was on his mind as well.

Cameron said, 'We're all right, Number One. I've weighed the risks, don't worry! I have to think of the rest of the flotilla. They could be anywhere, they could be close. For that matter, so could the Germans. Or our cruisers.'

Hastings nodded. The area was big enough in all conscience, big enough for the *Attila* to lose herself for as long as she wished, but there were a devil of a lot of warships concentrated in it, and there was always something out on the world's oceans that seemed to draw ships together like a

62

magnet, almost as though they were human and needed company in the loneliness of the sea. Hastings said, 'I still think the *Attila*'s beat it for home,' in repetition of earlier guesses that in fact had been responsible for the Stoker PO's buzz.

'We won't bank on it,' Cameron said. He had huddled into a corner by the bridge screen and was trying to peer over the glass dodger, strain his eyes into the freeze of snow that lashed at him. 'What's the word about Larkin, do you know, Number One?'

'No, sir. Nothing further. Shall I call the sick bay?'

'No, leave the doc in peace. He's got his worries – he'll let us know if there's any change.' Cameron was thinking that if they should happen to sight one of the cruisers of CS27 they might be able to raise her by signal lamp and pass the word of their sighting of the German squadron for what use that might be after so much time had elapsed, but they certainly wouldn't be able to do anything about Larkin in the sea that was running. A whaler wouldn't live five minutes and even if it did it could never go alongside with a sick man to be hoisted clear. In fact the chances of passing a signal were doubtful – the very sighting of a ship was currently doubtful, unless they were close enough to collide; if they missed a collision, both ships would be lost again in the snow long before there had been a chance to use the signalling projectors.

The day itself was darkening now, darkening towards evening; the blizzard continued. This was like the Russian convoys; the whole ship, decks and upperworks, was white with the snow, and ice was beginning to form in the exposed positions, turning the upper deck and the fo'c'sle into skating rinks. Ice lay along the gun-barrels, over the torpedo-tubes. In danger of sliding on his arse, Mr Tarbuck was giving the tubes a look over, along with his LTO, Leading Seaman Pittman, who could see no point at all in doing so: no one was going to have a need for torpedoes while this perishing weather lasted and when it eased everything would unfreeze and dry out.

The Gunner(T) seemed to sense this. He shouted above the howl of the wind, into Pittman's ear, 'Can't leave 'em on their own, lad. They wouldn't like it.'

Pittman said, 'Bloody hell, they're not human!'

'What was that?'

'Nothing, sir.' Pittman looked at the elderly warrant officer's face, blue and pinched with the freezing cold. There was something like a father's love in that worn face, or maybe a mother's, as though old Tarbuck had given birth to the tin fish nestling with menace in their tubes. The reassurance of his presence. . . . Tarbuck must be half-way round the bend under the strain of war. But somehow Pittman felt humbled. He, Pittman, had to be where he was, on watch by the torpedo-tubes, but there was no reason for the Gunner(T) to risk a slide on the deck and a fatal toss into the hogwash – other than his barmy parental concern. At least it was preferable to Clutch's acidity. . . . Mr Tarbuck, Pittman thought as he tried to feel his fingers through thick woollen gloves, was of an older Navy than he himself remembered, a different Navy in many ways, a Navy in which the ship had been every man's first concern, not just something you went to sea in and were thankful when you got back, something that provided you with a career, a ladder to climb if you wanted to and enough pay to keep you in beer and duty-free fags. In Tarbuck's Navy men had really loved their ships and had finally swallowed the anchor with real regret, leaving a way of life and real friends behind. There had been old bosuns and such who had passed hour after hour of their off-watch time doing unpaid-for things for the ship – making tiddley, intricate turk's heads out of rope, tending the boats' paint-work and brasswork, proud of their particular niche in the ship. Old Tarbuck, he wouldn't have seemed at all odd in those days, mooning about his tubes in brass-monkey weather with Hitler's pride and joy lurking somewhere out there in the snow.

Or was she? Pittman had also heard the buzz that had reached Stoker PO Munro and he half believed it. The *Attila* was too valuable a ship to take risks with. True, she had to be used some time and there was a lovely target waiting for her, but that Hitler might not want her to steam slap into the Home Fleet and by this time he must know Fraser was out for the kill. And in the meantime, where was the rest of their own flotilla, and the cruisers? The *Glenshiel* must have passed through the other search areas by now, and there hadn't been a smell of the other units. Perhaps they'd been recalled; the *Glenshiel* wouldn't know that, thanks to Larkin. In Pittman's view, the skipper had every excuse to turn about and piss off home if he'd felt inclined; ships without wireless or radar were a right danger to themselves and everyone else.

iii

THE HX convoy to the westward was currently in better weather: no snow, though heavy seas were cutting across a deep-water swell, and it was cold. The laden tankers, the ammunition ships and the hired transports butted into curling crests as the night came down. The order had come from the convoy Commodore to increase the distance between the ships and between the columns. In heavy weather there was always the risk of collision among merchant ships whose officers were not so familiar with station-keeping and sailing in close company as were the officers of the warships: and the escort always had a hard task, the destroyers weaving in and out of the columns, chivvying and exhorting while the cruisers, and in the case of this fast and vital convoy the battleships and aircraft-carriers, stood clear and majestic, keeping watch for the enemy, for the thin trails of water streaming from the periscopes to warn, if they were seen, of imminent U-boat attack.

On this occasion they were not afraid of U-boats. For one thing the weather was far from suitable for such an attack; for another, the U-boat packs would most probably stand clear and leave the convoy's destruction to the *Attila*. The officers and men of the convoy and escorts had never known such tension as now ran along their decks. Experienced men for the most part, they knew that they faced something worse than had threatened any previous group of ships making for UK across the North Atlantic. Other convoy routes had been the object of surface attack by German raiders, cruisers and auxiliary cruisers, even the pocket-battleships *Admiral Scheer* and *Deutschland*, but the *Attila* was something different and there could be almost total annihilation once she got among the ships or stood off and opened her bombardment outside the effective range of the elderly British battleships.

There was a feeling, not of despair exactly, but of resignation as the men aboard the merchant ships watched the Naval escort vanish into the darkness, the cruiser screen ahead and astern, the battleships on the beam of the columns, the aircraft-carrier HMS *Furious* watchful astern with her squadrons ready for take-off, the destroyers now withdrawn from the columns to take up their stations as the extended screen ahead, a screen that spread its protective umbrella right across the convoy's line of advance and out to port and starboard.

There was still no news.

Earlier that day the last cypher had been received from the Admiralty, addressed to the convoy Commodore and the Rear-Admiral commanding the escort aboard the battleship *Revenge*. That cypher had said simply: *No contact since leaving Bergen.*

That was the sum total of all they knew.

The Rear-Admiral, pacing his bridge, as Vice-Admiral Fichtner had been pacing his, tried to project himself into the mind of the German commander, attempting to make some estimation of what his adversary might do. Rear-Admiral Horsted, then a captain commanding the battleship *Royal Sovereign*, had been present at the Coronation Review of the Fleet at Spithead in 1937; and he had had aboard as a guest the then Captain Fichtner, who had been a naval attaché at the German Embassy in London. Fichtner had struck him as a decent man, unassuming, almost no Germanic bombast, but shrewd enough and a dedicated seaman. Horsted had kept off the subject of Herr Hitler and his rise to power and Captain Fichtner for his part had made no attempt to raise it. There had been no discussion of such things as *Lebensraum*, territorial demands in Europe, the German youth movement, the Nazi Party or the about-to-blossom Third Reich. Horsted had been unable to assess Fichtner's feelings about the Nazis but he believed the German to be a man who would stand clear of any political involvements so far as he would be permitted. Fichtner had struck him as first and foremost a

66

seaman and there had been no Anglophobia. The German officer had saluted with the rest when His Majesty the King had steamed past the Fleet, visible to all as he stood on the bridge of the *Victoria and Albert*. Fichtner had been visibly moved by the sight of England's somewhat diffident monarch in the uniform of an Admiral of the Fleet, the man who all the world knew had never wanted the job but was determined to make a resounding success of it. . . .

'Which he damn well has,' Horsted said aloud as the skies darkened over the convoy.

'Sir?' Horsted's Flag Captain had heard. Horsted told him his thoughts and of what had been his personal regard for Fichtner.

'That may be so, sir. But he'll do his duty – won't he?'

'Yes, I don't doubt that. It depends *how* he does it.'

The Flag Captain laughed. 'Same as anyone else would. By opening fire!'

Horsted nodded. 'Yes, but that doesn't cover it all. Fichtner has a human side. Or had. Times change, of course, and men with them, though not usually after middle age. Also, we weren't at war in 1937. But he did something that impressed me, something that I suppose made me remember him particularly. Perhaps it wasn't much but it did give a clue, I think, to his character and outlook.'

Horsted paused, frowning into the darkening distance of the sea until he was prompted by his Flag Captain. 'Yes, sir? You've aroused my curiosity.'

Horsted laughed. 'Good! Well, as I say, it was little enough really. But after the high jinks were all over, my wife and I lunched Fichtner at the Queen's Hotel, and afterwards he said he wanted to have a close look at the Naval war memorial on the common. He took some time going round it all, looking at the names, and it seemed to sadden him. After that we crossed over to the sea wall and strolled round past Southsea Castle, and there we came across an old man – very old, and who had obviously been a seaman. Quite a character . . . blue jersey, peaked cap, white beard and carrying a pack draped with the Union Flag. Fichtner, who spoke good English, stopped to talk to him. They got on like a house on fire, talking of old times.'

'The old chap had been in the last war, sir?'

The Rear-Admiral nodded. 'Yes – fought at Jutland. So had Fichtner. Oh, they talked a lot – the old fellow had been in sail, in the merchant service – the Cape Horners. Fichtner admired him, shook him by the hand and said something to the effect that real seamen had gone out with sail. Then the old man asked him if he thought there would be another war. Fichtner said he hoped not. He respected the British and he respected any man who went to sea, and he had hated sinking ships in the last war. He hoped he would never have to do it again. The old man said, "But you'd carry out your orders, sir?" and Fichtner said, "Yes, but with humanity."'

Horsted fell silent. The Flag Captain said, 'I wonder just what he meant by that, sir?'

'Hard to say – guns don't tally with humanity. Perhaps we shall find out.'

iv

DURING the night, Larkin died. The doctor came to the bridge himself to make the report to Cameron, whom he found still huddled into his duffel-coat in a corner of the bridge, staring into the driving snow. In a sense the news was a relief: Larkin hadn't faced a happy future and now he wouldn't need to be hauled up at Defaulters. His family would never know that he'd proved a weak link; not, that was, unless the *Attila* was lost beyond recall and the full report from *Glenshiel* revealed the facts, as it would be bound to, and the Admiralty demanded its pound of flesh. Dead flesh now but that wouldn't necessarily inhibit Their Lordships, land-bound and comfortable, not facing filthy weather out at sea however much responsibility they carried. . . .

MacNamara said, 'You look all in. Hadn't you better get some sleep?'

'I will, later. Don't worry about me.'

'But I do. No one can go on for ever, you know.'

'It won't be for ever,' Cameron said irritably.

'You know what I mean.' The doctor sounded dead tired himself: he'd stayed by Larkin all the way through, absenting himself only to deal with Stoker PO Munro's arm. 'You are my medical responsibility – '

'I'm my own responsibility.' Cameron spoke sharply but at once regretted it: the doctor was doing his job. He reached out and laid a hand on MacNamara's shoulder. 'Sorry. I didn't mean to sound narked. But I'm needed on the bridge . . . or the Admiralty thinks I am. *I* know that my officers can cope – but that's not the point.' He hesitated. 'It's the same for you too, isn't it? You don't pack up in the middle of an operation or whatever.'

'No. It's not quite the same thing, but I get the idea. Now I'm going to do something I should have thought of earlier, but I was tied up with Larkin – '

'Do what?'

'Send my SBA up with a couple of Benzedrine tablets. They'll make you feel bloody awful later on, but they'll keep you going through the night at least.'

'Oh, balls to drugs, Doc!'

'Doctor's orders,' MacNamara said, and turned away down the ladder. It took him some time to reach the door in the after screen that gave access to the ladder down to the wardroom; the deck was more iced-up than ever and to move along it was potentially lethal. MacNamara, no seaman, clung fast to anything that offered a hand-hold. When he reached the door, he began to struggle with the clips, half-frozen hands slipping and muffing the job badly. An oil-skinned figure materialized from aft by the depth-charges and a voice said wearily, 'For Christ's sake. Let me, sir.'

'Who's that?'

'Clutch, sir. Torpedo-gunner's mate.'

'Ah. Well, thank you, Clutch.'

Clutch pulled back the clips and held the door ajar against the weather. 'Right, sir. In you go, pronto.' He cleared his throat. 'That right, sir, Larkin's a goner?'

'Yes, I'm afraid so.'

Clutch gave a grunt, a sound that almost said Larkin had had no business to die and avoid his deserts, which was in fact what he was thinking. When the doctor had gone through, Clutch clipped the door down hard and moved for'ard with difficulty along the ice, carrying out his upper-deck rounds as petty officer of the watch. Seas still bloody high and no hint of a let-up. He went on thinking about Larkin. The body would be lying down below in the sick bay, presumably, ready to be sewn into its canvas shroud and dropped overboard, only it couldn't be, not in this sea. Come back inboard like a bad penny, like as not – *thrown* back inboard, to go splat against the tubes or guns. That meant they'd have to keep him aboard, a corpse when going into action, a bloody jonah to give them all the heebie-jeebies before they met the *Attila*. Good for morale, was that!

Clutch, whose dark, jowly face had a hint of the warlock about it in accord with his superstitious nature – he never walked under ladders, always threw spilt salt over his left shoulder, never took a third light for a fag, touched wood whenever he made an indiscreet utterance that might anger fate – Clutch continued towards the break of the fo'c'sle, feeling savage. Corpses and parsons – they went together aboard a ship, omens of ill luck, the one white and bloodless, the other black and sinless. Clutch had heard yarns that many of the old-time captains had refused the services of a chaplain because of the effect the man's presence might have on the ship's company. . . . Suddenly there was a flash of flame from the thickness dead ahead and something took the fo'c'sle and exploded in a tangle of bodies and fragmented metal. Just in time Clutch threw himself flat and slid on the ice towards the port-side guardrail.

7

THE SBA had been on his way up the bridge ladder when the explosion came. Sheer shock loosened his grip and as the destroyer heeled sharply to a sea he plunged, hit a stanchion that broke his back, and vanished into the turbulence on the starboard side. On the bridge there was shock as well, but Cameron reacted on the instant.

'Wheel hard-a-starboard, engines emergency full astern!'

Sub-Lieutenant Poole, white-faced and shaking, passed the order down. No one could be sure of what was happening, but certain facts were plain enough: Number One gun had gone, probably along with all its crew, seemingly ripped out from its trunking, and Number Two gun's barrel was twisted up like a cow with a crumpled horn. There was screaming from the fo'c'sle, long-drawn sounds of human agony, as Cameron rammed his thumb against the alarm rattler button. Hastings was already coming up the ladder. He called out, 'What was it, sir?'

'A bloody gun, Number One, but I don't know any more than that. Meanwhile I'm taking avoiding action.' Cameron had pushed Poole away from the binnacle by this time and was taking the ship himself. Behind the First Lieutenant, the navigator reached the bridge and stood looking bewildered. There was nothing to be seen, no ship responsible for the gunfire. Then, a couple of seconds later, something showed, fine on the port bow as the way came off the destroyer. A black shadow, no more; in a sense it was just a cutting-off of the direct assault of the snow as though a wall had been

71

suddenly and miraculously erected to shield them.

Cameron ordered the wheel to port to check the swing of his stern, and then amidships.

The *Glenshiel* juddered and lurched. Now they were close to the apparent wall, dangerously close, and from high above their heads a searchlight suddenly pierced through the darkness, bringing up the slicing, driving snow in its brilliant beam, picking out the fo'c'sle and its wreckage and then moving aft to illuminate the bridge. There was a brief pause and then, as the *Glenshiel*, still moving astern, was scraped down the side of the unknown ship, close-range weapons started up, raking the destroyer's decks. Without waiting for orders, the *Glenshiel*'s Oerlikons opened, firing up and back at an indistinct target that was now fast disappearing into the murk astern and could be pin-pointed only by the blaze of the searchlight. Cameron put his engines ahead again.

The whole thing had been over in not much more than a minute.

Cameron found his body, inside his duffel-coat, damp with sweat. He said, 'Close shave, Number One.'

'Very close, sir. Who d'you suppose she was?'

'No idea. Not one of ours; they'd have recognized us as British when that searchlight came on.' Cameron found that his hands were shaking – the effect of shock. 'Must have picked us up on their radar, decided we couldn't be German since they'd have known the dispositions of their own ships, and just took a pot shot.'

'The *Attila*, then?'

'It seems likely enough, Number One. Her, or one of her cruisers. It's all guesswork, but I wish to God we could communicate the guesses!'

'You mean –'

'I mean if that was the *Attila* or any of the German squadron they're not behaving as expected. We're heading due north, and whoever that was, was on a reciprocal of our course, or as near as dammit. So what's the *Attila* doing heading south? Back to base after all – or doing what she can to confuse the issue before she turns and heads out for the convoy?'

'No point in confusing the issue when she can't be seen,' Millard said from behind Cameron.

Cameron gave a short laugh. 'I suppose that's true, Pilot. Radar . . . but radar doesn't exactly identify ships by name!' He paused; the sweating had passed now and he shivered with the clammy cold it had left behind. 'Something tells me we're on a wild-goose chase. What d'you think, Number One?'

'I'm inclined to agree, sir. We're pretty useless if we can't make contact with anyone. The telegraphists . . . they've done their best, but Larkin's. . . .' Hastings didn't go on with what he'd been about to say. Larkin was dead and there was no point now in labouring his shortcomings. Cameron sank his head on his folded arms momentarily, then resumed staring through the glass screen. The First Lieutenant left the bridge to carry out a survey of the damage sustained and get reports of casualties; Cameron thought about the useless w/t and radar. It was really inconceivable that they should have gone to sea with a virtually nil list of relevant spares and he was going to get the grandfather of all rockets from Captain(D) when they made contact, if ever they did, and a worse one, a more basic and lasting one, from the Admiralty. Would they consider him still fit for command? Not if he was the commanding officer responsible for losing the *Attila* and allowing the convoy and troopships to come under attack. In no time the word would spread throughout the fleet and he would be too discredited to be allowed the responsibility of leadership. The fact that his communications department hadn't even been able to rig up a makeshift, short-range aerial was devastating; and the German shell that had taken out the aerials had done something to the electrics, as had later been discovered, and there was internal damage to the transmitter. Again, no proper spares. Even had the telegraphists been able to repair the aerial, the set was kaput.

The First Lieutenant was quickly back on the bridge. 'Ship's intact, sir. Only damage is to the for'ard guns – nothing left of Number One gun, Number Two useless – and the capstan, what's left of it. But the cables are all right and the slips and stoppers are holding.'

'Casualties, Number One?'

'Fourteen, sir. Ten men from the guns' crews, all dead. SBA missing, believed gone overboard. The GI bought it when – '

'Lindsay? Dead?'

'I'm afraid so, sir. The close-range weapons got him. Also two men on the after guns, wounded. The doctor's seeing to them and I gather there's nothing serious. Oh, and the TI's badly bruised and has some skin burns from a slide across the deck.'

Cameron said bitterly, 'Just one brief encounter, Number One. Just one brief bloody encounter.' His voice hardened. 'I'm pulling out. Doing what I should probably have done before now. Pilot?'

'Yes, sir?'

'I'm altering south-west. Have you a dead reckoning position?'

'Guesswork, sir – '

'Intelligent guesswork I trust, Pilot. Fix us as near as you can, and lay off a course for the Orkneys. Unless I can pass a VS message to a ship or aircraft before we get there, I propose to enter Long Hope in Scapa.'

ii

THE rumours began to spread as soon as the different motion told all hands that the *Glenshiel* was altering course. The skipper was heading for home; alternatively the skipper had somehow or other picked up the spoor of the *Attila* and had gone round the bend with the thrill and meant to attack single-handed and cover himself and all of them with glory – those that lived to tell the tale afterwards anyway. Stripey Higginbottom thought that if it was true the ship was heading homewards, it was a bloody pity the skipper hadn't altered in time to save Larkin. If he'd altered soon enough they might just about have got Larkin in and aboard the hospital ship. Now, with Larkin dead – and Higginbottom reflected again that the PO Telegraphist might not be sorry to be dead – his missus was going to have a dog's life looking after his terrible old mum all on her own, and that tearaway kid too. But Higginbottom didn't really believe the skipper was heading home – too good to be true, was that. And in any case he couldn't detach himself from the search force without orders.

He was surprised when the Tannoy came on and Cameron put them all in the picture as to his intentions.

'The ship,' Cameron's voice said throughout the destroyer, 'is on course for Scapa. We're useless without communication, and unless we make visual contact before we get there, I shall return to port to pass word of the *Attila*, which I now believe is steering south.'

That was all. It settled the buzzes but it didn't still the speculation along the messdecks when the morning watchmen were relieved and went down to breakfast. Some thought Cameron was dead right in the circumstances brought about by Larkin – and a destroyer with half her main armament gone wasn't much use anyway. Others thought the skipper was crazy to pull out on his own initiative and that he'd get himself clobbered by King's Regulations, the Articles of War, and the Fighting Instructions, all bumph, but bumph with a very hefty bite wrapped up in it. However, as Mr Tarbuck said in the wardroom, they might at least come clear of the snow as they made their westering. He made the remark to Sutcliffe, one of the RNVR sub-lieutenants, who was sprawled on the settee, relaxing after a spell in the director.

'Scotland,' Sutcliffe said.

'Well?'

'Snow. If it's snowing anywhere, Torps, it's bound to be snowing all round Scotland.'

'Well, let it, I'm not all that bothered, son. 'Cept my fish don't like it all that much.'

'Pity you didn't fire one off at that German.'

'Yes,' Tarbuck said regretfully. 'Just give me the chance, that's all. Did I ever tell you about the time I fired off a dummy fish against the old *Empress of India*, second battle squadron in the Med, back in 1923? When I was torpedo-gunner's mate aboard the – '

'Yes, Torps, you did.'

It made no difference; Petty Officer Clutch wasn't the only one aboard the *Glenshiel* to have experienced verbal diarrhoea . . . but Sutcliffe was tolerant of the old sea-daddy, who reminded him in a way of his own father, also garrulous in life but now dead. Colonel Sutcliffe, late the Punjab Light Infantry, had married when in his fifties, a woman much younger than himself and had had progeny; he'd also had a long memory and Sutcliffe junior almost felt he had served himself on the North-West Frontier of India, bringing the Pax Britannica to the warring tribes in the name of the Queen-Empress, Victoria the Good. He'd heard so much about the Army that when war had come he had joined the Navy, starting on the lower deck at the age of nineteen and advancing to an RNVR commission. The same as the Captain, only Sutcliffe never expected to get a half stripe himself . . . while old Tarbuck nattered away about the battleship era of the twenties, Sutcliffe thought about Father, not his own, but *Glenshiel*'s. There was an element of hero worship. The Captain was everything he would like to be: efficient, confident without being brash or overbearing, fair, and very far removed from someone like Petty Officer Clutch, who was all gate and gaiters and made it quite plain that he didn't like RNVR sub-lieutenants. Clutch, Sutcliffe had found, could get a remarkable degree of expression into his tone and his hard-looking, five-o'-clock-shadowed face. He'd had a bit of a barney with him after returning to the Tail of the Bank after their last convoy run; Sutcliffe, Officer of the Day in port with Clutch as his PO, had required the services of the duty hands, that small part of the duty watch on stand-by for particular tasks as they arose. He had told off the bosun's mate of the watch to make the pipe, Duty Hands Lay Aft.

Clutch had hastened along, face forebearing, arms swinging in tune with his feet, left-right-left and halt.

'Now then, sir, what's all this?'

Sutcliffe had looked astonished. 'What's all this what, TI?'

'Duty 'ands, sir. What've they bin piped for?'

Sutcliffe had pointed down at a stores lighter lying alongside the starboard quarter. A number of cases lay ready for bringing aboard, stacked on the lighter's hatch cover. 'Wardroom stores to come aboard.'

'Stores, eh.' Clutch had done a little tooth-sucking, staring at the single wavy gold stripe on Sutcliffe's cuff. 'Not the duty 'ands, sir. There's a store party detailed.'

'I see. Does it really matter, TI?'

'*Matter*, sir? Course it matters! Duty 'ands, they're for use after 1630 hours, sir, once the ratings 'ave shifted into night clothing, not half-way through the forenoon watch.' Clutch had risen and fallen on the balls of his feet, like a bobby easing his corns in a shop doorway. 'Usual ship's routine. Any ship I ever served in . . First Lootenant'd have had the Officer of the Watch by the short hairs if he'd piped the duty 'ands 'stead of the store party – '

'I take your point, Petty Officer Clutch.' Sutcliffe had been obstinate. 'But I've piped the duty hands and it's the duty hands I'm going to have.'

'I see, sir. Yes, sir. Some officers, sir, won't be told. But they learn, sir.' Clutch had said no more, but he'd lurked about by the quartermaster's lobby with an expectant look on his face and his lip curling slightly. And no one had answered the pipe: the duty hands didn't consider themselves as such while working part-of-ship – not until after Clutch's stipulated 1630 hours, and in the end Sutcliffe had had to pipe the store party and Clutch had gone on his way almost hugging himself. Sutcliffe had been mortified but on reflection grew philosophical about it; he should, of course, have known, but it had so happened that whilst on the lower deck himself he'd never been detailed as one of the duty hands and he simply hadn't thought. It had been a lesson but Clutch, though delighted at being proved right, had been offended at being argued with by a wavy sub and wasn't going to let that sub forget it. . . .

And now when a knock came at the wardroom door, it was Petty Officer Clutch. Standing there, he said, 'Mr Tarbuck, sir.'

Tarbuck broke off his story in mid-sentence. 'Hullo there, Reg. What's up now, eh?'

'Nothing up, sir.' Clutch's gaze travelled over the reclining Sutcliffe and then moved away with something like a shudder.

'Now the GI's gone, sir . . . do I take over his duties as well as my own? I'm the only PO near enough qualified – West and Tremlett, they've only got a seaman gunner's non-sub rate.'

'I know. Not up to me. First Lieutenant and gunnery officer.'

'Just thought I'd mention it,' Clutch said, and looked again at Sutcliffe, who happened to be Number Two to the gunnery officer, an RN lieutenant named Lyon. 'Perhaps Mr

Sutcliffe'd care to mention it to Lootenant Lyon,' he added, speaking to Tarbuck.

'Mr Sutcliffe will indeed,' Sutcliffe said. 'I thank you for your offer to assume extra duties, TI. Very kindly meant, I'm sure. But Leading Seaman Fox happens to have the non-sub rate of director layer and is a very capable hand – and we haven't all that many guns left anyway.'

Clutch's face was furious. 'Leading seamen, Mr Sutcliffe, are leading seamen, not petty officers. And director layers, they're not gunners' mates.' Excusing himself to the Gunner(T) he turned about and marched out of the wardroom. Sutcliffe didn't know whether he'd won that round or not, but he certainly didn't want Clutch continually on his tail around the guns. As the TI left the wardroom Sutcliffe had noticed that he was moving somewhat stiffly and he remarked on this to Tarbuck.

Tarbuck said, 'Got shaken off of his feet by that shell. Doc says he's got a skinned arse like a monkey . . . tore himself across a rusty metal splinter.'

'I'm sorry to hear that,' Sutcliffe said politely.

iii

THE battleships of the Home Fleet with their cruisers and the destroyer escort forming the protective screen were now in clear weather, beneath more-or-less blue skies with cloud scudding fast across. The sea was running heavily, with breaking crests, but here there was no snow though there was a heavy bank of dark cloud lying away to their east, low on the horizon.

Aboard the *Duke of York* the Admiral, like everyone else involved, was awaiting reports. Nothing at all had been heard of the *Attila*; Sir Bruce Fraser was beginning to think the whole thing had been a figment of someone's imagination. Shadows in the fog, moving out from Bergen . . . it had all been based on that radio message from the Resistance. All honour to brave men – but they could be as mistaken as anybody else.

Fraser, his eyes red and sore from lack of sleep and the constant use of binoculars, turned to the Master of the Fleet, his staff navigating officer.

'How far off Cape Farewell, Commander?'

The answer was pat, immediate. 'Cape Farewell bearing 287 degrees, sir, distant three hundred and ten miles.'

Fraser laughed. 'Brilliant! X-ray eyes, or have you just worked it out?'

'The latter, sir. Noon sight, and a good one.'

'And the convoy – and the Queens?'

'We should pick up the HX in two days' time, sir.'

'That's guesswork this time?'

'Yes, sir. We can't be certain of their speed.'

'Never can, with convoys.' Ships broke down, in so many cases old and overworked engines just couldn't keep up the strain, and then it was the convoy Commodore's decision whether to slow the convoy for a while, whether to detach a destroyer to stand by, or whether to leave a lame duck to the mercy of the North Atlantic and the enemy. Fraser reflected dourly that it was often a case of the relative importance of the lame duck. No commodore would leave a tanker or a troopship, or an ammunition ship come to that, but he might decide to leave one carrying a general cargo or even foodstuffs. The British public could always pull in its belt another notch, but you couldn't do without the means of war. It was always a case of the greater good. 'As to the Queens. . . .'

'We just don't know, sir. Law unto themselves.'

'Just as well. If they confuse us, they're bound to confuse the enemy. Not that we're anything but confused ourselves, in regard to the confounded *Attila*.'

Fraser looked down at the guns along his fo'c'sle: the turrets with their 14-inch barrels, moving this way and that, laying and training on imaginary targets as the Fleet Gunnery Officer carried out his constant exercises . . . the sea spurting up through the hawse-pipes on either side or coming green over the fo'c'sle-head as the battleship dipped under and rose again to fling the water aft like a horse shaking out its mane. The fighting efficiency of 35,000 tons of metal, racing for the convoy at her full speed of a little over twenty-eight knots. Not fast enough, perhaps; certainly not as fast as the *Attila*, nor was the flagship as heavily gunned. But the *Duke of York* was not alone and the total gun-power of the Home Fleet was greater by a very wide margin than that of the vaunted *Attila* and her consorts; it was even money the Germans had turned for home.

iv

Away ahead in the HX convoy there was in fact a lame duck causing a good deal of anxiety to the Commodore and the senior officer of the escort, Rear-Admiral Horsted in the *Revenge*. A deep-laden tanker bringing aviation spirit to Milford Haven at the south-western tip of Wales had suffered an engine breakdown and was wallowing in heavy seas. Her master had reported that he expected to be disabled for some hours. The weather was too bad to pass a tow and Horsted could not delay the convoy: the urgency now was to get the HX into the Clyde before the *Attila* turned up in the vicinity. There was a chance that the tanker, the *British Star* of the British Tanker Company, would be able to catch up – a chance, but no more than that, since she had little speed in reserve above the speed of the convoy.

Horsted said abruptly to his staff signal officer, 'Make to the Commodore, you are to proceed without *British Star*. I shall detach a destroyer to stand by her.'

'Aye, aye, sir. Which destroyer, sir?'

Horsted said, '*Icarus*. Inform her and *British Star* accordingly, please. And then make to both ships: *Regret the exigencies of war. Good luck go with you to journey's end.*'

Horsted looked across towards the convoy, at the heaving, weather-worn ships struggling home in the face of deadly threat. The *British Star* might well be the lucky one after all, if the *Attila* concentrated, as she would, on the main convoy and the huge troopships somewhere to the west. On the other hand, as she dropped down on the Northern Irish coast to make the North Channel after repairs had been completed, she would be virtually at the mercy of the prowling U-boats and the long-range Nazi bombers. The *Icarus* would be little enough protection; but Horsted knew he couldn't spare any more of his force.

Aboard the hired transport *Orion* of the Orient Steam Navigation Company, Commodore Sir Arthur Lewis-Bryant,

RNR, received the Rear-Admiral's signal with an expression-less face but with a slight tic at the corner of his mouth. He was well enough aware of the dangers of a lone tanker in the North Atlantic, left to wallow restlessly without power and then to move into the zone for almost inevitable attack. He caught the eye of the convoy signalman on his staff.

'Make to *British Star*,' he said. '*Will be thinking of you all the way home.*'

'Aye, aye, sir.'

The *Orion*'s First Officer, Officer of the Watch on the bridge, was standing beside the Commodore. He said, 'They'll be all right, sir. They'll be met by escorts from Londonderry.' He was thinking that few people aboard were aware that Lewis-Bryant's son was a cadet aboard the lame duck.

v

ORDINARY Seaman Aldridge knew that he was lucky to be alive. If it hadn't been for a call of nature coming at the right time, he wouldn't have been, since his station when in second degree of readiness, which was the state the *Glenshiel* had been in when the shell had struck so suddenly out of the snow, was as a loading number on Number One gun for'ard. He'd been sitting in the heads with his trousers down when the gun had disintegrated and all its crew – except him by the grace of God – with it. He had come out of the heads at the rush when all hell broke loose above his head: the ship might be going down. He'd just cleared the heads when the alarm rattlers went. Feeling his whole body shake and his stomach turn to water he had gone out on deck and, making an effort, had climbed the ladder to the break of the fo'c'sle, which was when he'd seen the carnage in the beam of the searchlight probing through from the blackness on the port side.

He'd gone down the ladder, seen the TI lying against the guardrail and looking as if he were about to slide into the water; the TI had appeared to be dead – events proved that he wasn't, only temporarily dazed, but the dead look had been good enough for Aldridge, who had left him to it and gone aft as being the safest place currently. The whole ship's company had been caught on the hop and there was more than a degree of confusion, and no one seemed to notice an OD scurrying out of harm's way. Not till the next morning, when they had turned for home and come thankfully out of the snow-storm at last, and Leading Seaman Maloney had ticked over that only Aldridge had escaped from Number One gun.

Maloney bore down upon him, face truculent, as he stood shivering in his duffel-coat at his new station on Number Three gun aft.

'How come the Lord chose *you*, you little git?'

'What d'you mean . . . Leading Seaman Maloney?' He'd learned that much by now.

'You know bloody well what I mean,' Maloney said. 'You of all people! Skulking. If you'd been there, you'd be in little pieces. Where was you?'

Sulkily Aldridge said, 'In the heads.'

'Heads, eh? Shit scared.'

'I had permission from the Captain of the gun.'

'Did you now? That's neat, that is.' Maloney thrust a belligerent face close to Aldridge's. 'Who's to say – now – if you didn't? Just tell me that.'

Aldridge went red and began to stutter. 'I – I told you, I h-h-had permission . . . it's not fair to – '

'Don't bloody whine at me, you little brown 'atter. *Actors* . . . God give me strength to endure! I dunno. What you staring at, may I ask, when I'm bloody talking to you?'

Aldridge was looking out over the port quarter. He pointed. 'I think we've caught up with the Home Fleet.' He sounded very much relieved; the *Glenshiel* had been a lonely ship for too long. Maloney turned, as relieved in fact as Aldridge. Then he stiffened as he saw the dark, distant shape that was emerging from the thick weather; he grabbed up the sound-powered telephone to the bridge.

To Aldridge he said, 'That's not the Home Fleet, you little twerp, it's the bloody *Attila*!'

8

THE yeoman of signals had seen the battleship at the same moment and had reported. In the after part of the ship Maloney had just got the handset to his ear when the alarm rattlers sounded. Cameron spoke to the engine-room himself after telling the Officer of the Watch, Lieutenant Lyon, to hold his course.

'*Attila* on our tail, Chief. Give her all you've got.'

'Aye, aye, *sir*,' Chief ERA Downs answered, feeling a surge of disturbance in the depths of his gut. He ran for a handwheel and was turning it, sweat pouring from his face, as Mr Bream came down at the rush.

'*Attila*, sir,' Downs said.

'God Almighty. In clear weather, too.'

'Just our luck.'

'Never mind. We'll earn a place in the history books when this lot's over.' The warrant engineer watched his dials and gauges as the revolutions increased and the destroyer shuddered around him, vibrating from the thrust of her spinning screws like some devilish contraption in a fairground. Any minute now . . . if those monstrous shells took the old *Glenshiel* she would open up like a sardine tin. They wouldn't have a hope, none of them would, least of all him and the others down here in the engine-room. Suicide, that was what it was, being an engineer. Bloody fools the lot of them, should have joined the Army. Mr Bream found himself thinking, since there was nothing else he could usefully do for the present other than stand by for orders from the bridge, of his missus and that last telephone call from Gourock. It was a good thing she didn't know what was right behind him now. She'd bust a gut at the mere thought and no blame to her for that. The missus was a worry; she was no longer young and resilient and they'd been together for a hell of a long time and she depended on him for everything. When she got the telegram from the Admiralty to say that her old man had been vaporized by the *Attila*, well, he just didn't see how she would cope. Of course, she had friends in Pompey and many of those friends also had husbands or sons at sea and they would understand only too well and could be relied on to do what they could for a widow. Mr Bream had been on leave when the *Hood* had been blown up in the Denmark Strait, and he well remembered the shock reaction from the whole of Pompey, a town that had known the old battle-cruiser from her birth and where many of her company had lived. Three survivors out of a complement of fourteen hundred and nineteen officers and men. That had been a monumental catastrophe and the very size of it, the very number of families affected, had in some odd way helped each individual to bear it. When the *Glenshiel* went it would be just one small episode in a long war, and so much the worse for people like his missus.

Negative thoughts: Mr Bream gave himself a brisk shake and was trying to think of something else when the sudden roar and shatter of an explosion came from somewhere up top and the engine-room seemed first to be pressed down deep into the water and then to lift right up into the air. Lights flickered, went off, came on again and Mr Bream found himself lurching like a drunk from side to side of the starting platform.

Then he was called on the voice-pipe from the bridge: it was the Captain speaking. 'How is it, Chief?'

'Rocky, sir. Rocky . . . but I think we're intact. What was the bang?'

'Direct hit – not the big stuff, secondary armament. Slap through into the starboard quarter, right under Number Four gun. Let me know at once if you get any sprung plates, Chief.'

'Aye, aye, sir.' Bream replaced the cover of the voice-pipe. There was a shake in his hands. He passed the word to his Chief ERA and they made an inspection. Everything seemed all right; they'd had a slice of luck, or thought they had until they found

84

the twisted metal overhead. The deckhead seemed to have buckled and the upper ladders had a crushed look as a result, a sort of telescoping. And it looked as if the hatch from the engine-room to the alleyway up top had caught the blast. Downs sent an ERA up for a look-see and when the man came back his face was white. Buckled was right, he reported. Their exit was blocked.

ii

MOST of the blast had in fact gone downward but Number Four gun aft had been unseated and its barrel twisted into a knot. There had been a lot of metal splinters and blood was dripping from the wreckage, along with strips of raw flesh, some of it blasted on to the torpedo-tubes. Fire had broken out below and Hastings was there with the fire parties and damage control parties. Lyon, Lieutenant RN, sat like a spare hand in the director with his director layer, Leading Seaman Fox, having taken up his action station on leaving the bridge when the rattlers had sounded. Only one gun left now, and that a mere popgun against the *Attila*. The thought occurred to Fox that they might as well be somewhere else, and he expressed it.

'Be more use if we joined the fire parties, sir.'

'It's a point. Fox. But they seem to be coping.'

'Yes, sir.' Fox said no more, just sat and reflected that they were about as much use as a whore at a wedding, but Lyon, he wouldn't shift to save his grand-dad from a mad bull until the skipper said so. Lyon was dyed-in-the-wool Dartmouth and hadn't much on top, no imagination. . . . He looked like a horse and had a laugh to match it: haw-haw-haw, he was always blasting off; you could hear him down in the wardroom when you were aft by the depth-charges, but he wouldn't be heard from there again – the wardroom was probably a shambles after that projy had hit. In the meantime the *Attila* had, for some totally incomprehensible reason, turned away. Fox didn't like to comment on that; to do so might tempt fate. But Lieutenant Lyon did.

'Funny!'

'*Funny*, sir?'

'The *Attila*. Must be scared of us.' Haw-haw-haw – Fox nearly said: Put a sock in it, you brassbound twit. Still, maybe at a time like this a laugh was better than a moan, all said and done. 'I wonder why?'

Fox said sardonically, 'Gone home to Mummy, sir, to tell her about the nasty British ship.'

'Haw-haw-haw! Quite a wit, Fox. And you may well be right, who knows?' Lyon reported to the bridge, just in case they hadn't seen the surprising development for themselves. Cameron answered; his conclusion was that the *Glenshiel* had friends in the vicinity. The *Attila*'s radar could be presumed to be working and in any case her fighting-top had a much longer view than was possible from a destroyer and she wouldn't be taking risks at this stage.

Lyon said, 'Great Scott, yes, I didn't think of that. Do we stay closed up, sir?'

'Until I order differently, yes. But you may as well come down from the director. With only one gun left, we're virtually in quarters firing already.'

'Aye, aye, sir. Shall I go to Number Three gun?'

'Lend a hand to the First Lieutenant, Guns, unless and until you're wanted elsewhere.' Cameron put down the handset, feeling that his gunnery officer needed a nursemaid sometimes. Good-natured and no hanger back from duty . . . but that wasn't enough and it was a surprise to Cameron that Dartmouth had failed to instil the little bit extra. Turning his mind away from Lyon, he resumed his watch of the horizons all around. The *Attila* had turned north again and seemed to be beating it back into the filth; and within the next fifteen minutes he saw that his deduction had proved correct. Two warship silhouettes came into view, hull-down to the north-west, coming in fast. Within the next minute the yeoman of signals had identified them.

'*Monmouth* and *Leicester*, sir.'

'Thank you, Yeoman.' Cameron pressed the switch on the Tannoy. 'Captain speaking. We have cs27 in company. For now, the *Attila* has turned away. She probably suspects heavier ships in company.'

iii

A ragged cheer had gone up as the word was passed and the two heavy cruisers closed towards the destroyer, exchanging signals. The cheering, however, was muted. Many more men had been lost, among them Petty Officer Tremlett, the Quarterdeck Division's PO, and Stripey Higginbottom whose action station had been on Number Four gun. The structural damage below had been heavy as well: as Leading Seaman Fox had thought, the wardroom was a fire-gutted wreck and contained more casualties: MacNamara was dead, burned almost beyond recognition, together with the wardroom servant and the Leading Supply Assistant and his number two, all members of the action stretcher parties. Another to die had been Sub-Lieutenant Poole, Action Officer of the Quarters on Number Four gun. That gun's ready-use ammunition had gone up with the rest and had scattered metal fragments about the decks. The superstructure was peppered with holes. A message had come up to the bridge from the engine-room that the engines were OK but the personnel were trapped. Cameron had sent the word to the First Lieutenant and as soon as the fire had been brought under control by the hoses Hastings went down with a shipwright to see what could be done.

He found the hatch buckled, twisted into the surrounding deck plating, and totally unopenable. He reported this to the bridge.

'There has to be something you can do, Number One.'

'Yes, sir – '

'Can you cut through?'

'We can try – we *will* try, of course. But we don't know what it's like the other side of the air lock, or do we?'

'The Chief reported his side buckled, Number One, remember?'

'Oh – yes, I do. Sorry, sir.' Hastings sounded harassed. 'We'll do all we can, sir.'

Cameron called the engine-room. 'We'll soon open you up, Chief, don't worry. But when we open up the air lock – '

'We'll have to turn the taps off right away now, sir – let the boilers die down, or there's danger of a flash-back.'

'Yes. All right, Chief, draw fires.' Cameron paused. 'I can imagine what it's like. Claustrophobic?'

Bream said, 'You might say so, yes. But this sort of thing, it's always on the cards. We all know you're doing what you can.'

'Keep me informed, Chief, and I'll do the same from here.' Cameron turned back towards the oncoming cruisers: cs27 was asking for damage reports. Cameron passed a concise summary, adding that he would be without power on his main engines, he didn't know how long for. He thought about the men trapped in the engine-room, just about the nastiest place in the ship to be when you couldn't get out of it and the enemy was known to be in the vicinity. But he didn't expect the German force to show itself again for a while at least. There was, however, an urgency to get the buckled entry straightened out as soon as the Chief reported the oil-jets shut off – not before: air locks were there for a purpose and with the jets going you couldn't open up both doors at once. From the fact that there had not yet been a flash-back from the boilers Cameron judged that the inner seal, though buckled, was keeping out the air. Flash-backs were nasty things: the updraught sweeping through the boiler-room would bring the flames backwards to scorch and sear human flesh. That was something to bear in mind after they had released the entry; and by now cs27 in the *Monmouth* was coming up to within distance of his loud hailer and asking about that very thing.

The voice came clear across the water: 'Are you fit to continue? Can you re-seal your engine-room and get under way?'

'I don't know yet, sir. I won't know until I see just what we have to do to straighten out the hatch.'

'Fair enough.' There was a pause. 'Sighting report's already been passed to the Admiralty repeated C-in-C Home Fleet. Your function's done, Cameron. You're not much use anyway, with only one gun left – no radar or w/t – and a currently defunct engine-room. As soon as you can move, lay off a course for Rosyth . . . I'll break wireless silence and ask for an ocean-going rescue tug to head for your current position in case you're still in trouble. All right?'

'I'm still basically seaworthy, sir,' Cameron called back.

'You may be.' The voice was short, crisp. 'You're for Rosyth all the same.' A gold-ringed arm waved briefly from the cruiser's bridge wing and the *Monmouth* began to turn away, heading for the north to continue shadowing the German squadron, waiting for them to make their re-appearance. Cameron fancied the snow was once again reaching out, coming down from the north-east and, as they lay helpless, would overtake them.

iv

THERE were mixed feelings throughout the destroyer now. Plenty of the hands were glad enough to be moving out of it, with honourable wounds to show the *Glenshiel* hadn't funked any issues. The weather was filthy again. The ship was wallowing horribly as she lay without way on her, a nasty motion that put even the old-stagers off their food; Rosyth undoubtedly had its charms by comparison and anyway nobody wanted to die. But there were plenty who regretted cs27's order. They had come out to fight and they felt frustrated at simply having been hit and nothing to show for it. Men had died and it was tough luck that their deaths should have been in vain, a real waste. Besides, to be in what promised to be one of the very few fleet actions likely in this war would have been quite something: free beer on the strength of it every time in port, and a yarn to keep their grandchildren enthralled in the fullness of time. To be in at the kill, the death of the *Attila*, would have been a heroic climax, for no one was in any doubt that the battleship was going to be given its chips once it had been driven into the arms of the Home Fleet. Likewise, if by some mischance this was not to happen and the Nazis got at the HX convoy or the Queen liners first, every man aboard would want to do his share to sink her afterwards.

Mr Tarbuck was one of those who was aggrieved at being withdrawn. He said so to Lyon, standing by his torpedo-tubes. 'It's not as if we was stripped of everything, sir.'

'What?'

Mr Tarbuck said, 'I've got my tubes, that's what.'

'Not much good, are they, Torps?'

Tarbuck stared, looking hurt. 'Not much good, eh. Torpedoes, they've done plenty in their time.'

'Well, perhaps. But they're not much good against, let's say, aircraft attack. Or the *Attila* come to that. Are they?'

'Not aircraft, no.' What Tarbuck wanted to say was, bloody ass, whoever suggested they might be? 'Against any battleship though –'

Lyon laughed his laugh, which irritated Mr Tarbuck as much as it did Leading Seaman Fox. 'My dear old chap, you'd never get inside *Attila*'s gunnery range and stay afloat for long enough to fire off your tin fish!' He walked away, still laughing – big joke, poor old Tarbuck, still stuck in the last war. Tarbuck watched the back of the horse's head making for'ard along the iron-deck and shook his own head sadly. You could never get through to the gunnery people, they were thick as a plank and thought of nothing but their guns, too dim to see that torpedoes could do a sight more damage than the pissy-arsed 4.7s carried by such as the *Glenshiel*. But Tarbuck did admit to himself that the gunnery officer had had a point insofar as there would be a certain amount of difficulty in getting inside the *Attila*'s bloody great gun batteries without being blown to Kingdom Come. . . .

In the meantime, the destroyer drifted helplessly, heaving around the ocean, with the snow once again lying everywhere like a shroud. Shroud was the word that came to Petty Officer Clutch as, with the Buffer, he organized a relieve-decks system to allow the hands to go below for meals and so on. Cameron was keeping the ship officially at first degree of readiness while the engine-room was out of action but had authorized men to stand down in ones and twos. Clutch thought of a shroud largely because the destroyer was so bloody quiet without the beat of its engines, an unusual state of affairs at sea, and without the noise of the ventilators of the forced-draught system.

Weird, that was what it was.

Needed livening up a touch. Clutch saw Ordinary Seaman Aldridge desultorily moving a broom about in a fairly useless attempt to shift snow from the quarterdeck aft, looking sick and bleak and his face all streaked with what

90

looked like tears, shivering like a castanet beneath his duffel-coat.

Clutch halted in front of the sad-looking rating, rose and fell on his heels, his short body lifting and dropping until the deck lurched and he had to look to his safety. 'Well, well,' he said. 'What a bloody object, eh?'

Aldridge managed a sick grin but gave no answer.

'What's up with you?'

'Nothing, TI.'

'Nothing, eh. Well, that's good that is. Look as if you're about to die. Been piping your eye, I see.' Aldridge looked blank. Clutch said, 'Crying. Bloody blubbing. Don't know what for. Going home to Mummy now, aren't we? Get all nice and tucked up in beddy-byes with a 'ot water bottle and Ovaltine. And bedsocks like as not – '

Suddenly Aldridge, his face flaming now, said, 'Shut up!' Clutch stiffened, thrust his face forward. 'Did I hear right, Aldridge? Did I hear you say to a superior officer, "Shut up"?'

Aldridge looked on the verge of collapse. He muttered, 'Sorry, PO. I didn't mean it.'

'Oh yes, you did.' Clutch was livid, the more so since he was in a somewhat cleft stick. Aldridge was due for the rattle, up before the Officer of the Watch, then First Lieutenant's report, then the skipper. You didn't tell a PO to shut up . . . but Clutch could get the back end of the rocket if he wasn't careful. Clutch was not a fool; he knew that what he'd been saying was not expected of a PO, could be called hazing, and Cameron was just the one to call it that. Of course, Cameron would have to inflict some sort of punishment on the OD but it would be token only, two days' leave stopped, which didn't matter a tinker's cuss at sea. But it would be Clutch who got the real blasting afterwards and a bad mark against him in the skipper's mind.

Aldridge spoke again, the words tumbling out. 'I never asked to join the Navy, never asked to fight the war, did I? It's not fair, I'm not used to the life . . . and it's all that bloody Maloney really, that's why – '

'Leading Seaman Maloney to you. Are – '

'Leading Seaman Maloney, then. I hate him. He's such a bully.'

'Are you,' Clutch asked in a raised voice, 'stating a

91

complaint by any chance? Because if you are, then let me tell you, it'll get bloody nowhere because. . . .'

'I'd like to – to bloody kill him! Perhaps I will if I get the chance.' Aldridge's fists were clenched, his body was shaking like a leaf. 'I can't go on taking it.'

Clutch stared at him, his gaze running up and down what he considered a streak of cringe, but cringe that could turn very nasty, the worm pushed too far. He said harshly, 'You've just uttered a threat, Ordinary Seaman Aldridge, against a leading 'and. I'll be dealing with you shortly.' He turned about and made his way for'ard to climb to the wheelhouse. He needed a word of advice from the coxswain before he took Aldridge to the bridge. Clutch had been by no means blind to Maloney's attitude. The 'swain would have some views, and with everyone concerned about that engine-room hatch this was not the time to bother the bridge with the frothings of ordinary seamen.

v

FROM the Operations Room at the Admiralty the orders had gone to the Home Fleet and to the 27th Cruiser Squadron. The latter was, along with the 24th Destroyer Flotilla, to maintain a presence north-east of Scottish waters and to re-establish contact with the *Attila*, reporting her movements as soon as they got a sight but avoiding action if possible. Cruisers and destroyers were in short enough supply and were not to be risked against much superior gun-power. Sir Bruce Fraser was now to move easterly with his battleships, keeping well ahead of the convoy in the hope of engaging the Germans well clear of the merchant ships. There was as yet no knowing what the *Attila*'s mean course might be, what her eventual intentions might be attack-wise. She had steamed north, she had steamed south, she had last been seen steaming north again. It was believed at the Admiralty that she might be altering her whole approach and intending to make for the waters north of Iceland and then drop down through the Denmark Strait. Minds went back inevitably to the fate of the *Hood*, caught in the Denmark Strait by the massive guns of the *Bismarck* assisted by the *Prinz Eugen*.

The *Attila* with the *Darmstadt* and the *Recklinghausen* made a more formidable force; and it seemed to the Chief of Staff as though the German Naval Command was fully confident that they could engage the British Home Fleet and go on to sink the ships of the HX convoy.

Fraser in the *Duke of York* was having similar thoughts. He had an immense respect for the German gunnery. Where the British gunners needed a number of ranging salvoes before they could even straddle their target, the Germans seemed to have an extraordinary ability to strike home with their first shot. The Home Fleet battleships were certainly much more heavily armoured against shells than the *Hood* had been, but an unlucky shot could still put them out of action. And they were slow, very slow except for the flagship herself. The old R Class battleships wallowed along, straining their engines to the maximum at not much more than twenty knots – the *Attila* could make rings round them.

In the ships of the convoy to the west of Fraser's battle fleet, the word had also come from the Admiralty that the *Attila* had been picked up. Well at sea now, she gave no appearance of turning back for her home port. She was out for a kill. The Convoy Commodore let his imagination rip, since to foresee what might happen was part of his job and in the mental vision of carnage he might see something that all his thought so far, all the thought of the OC Troops and their combined staffs, had not provided against. He saw the ships going sky-high under the impact of the German shells, the ammunition ships exploding in immense tongues of flame and thrown bodies, the tankers blazing beneath their palls of smoke and orange flame, the heaving sea itself ablaze with spilled fuel oil, the troopships with their bows thrust up into the air as they slid back beneath the water with men dropping like so much jetsam from the decks. Their one defence was the obvious one, the normal one when a convoy came under surface attack: scatter, and diversify the target. That would be ordered the moment the *Attila* was sighted, but it could be too late. When that order was passed, it would become a case of every ship for itself. Some would escape, many would not.

Sir Arthur Lewis-Bryant, pacing his bridge with the OC Troops, thought of the Queen liners under Sir James Bissett, and of the *British Star*, now well behind the convoy with her single destroyer escort. As if sensing his thoughts, the American officer said, 'They tell me your boy's aboard that tanker, Commodore.'

'Yes.'

'Too bad. It's an anxiety for you . . . to add to all your others.'

'Yes,' the Commodore said again. 'But the *British Star*'s in no different a situation basically.'

'You mean if we have to scatter?'

The Commodore nodded. 'All over the ocean – all of us. Each has an equal chance after that. No point in worrying.'

'I take the point,' the soldier said after a moment. 'God damn, Commodore, you people who go to sea for a living . . . sometimes you scare the hell out of me!'

Sir Arthur laughed. 'We've always fought something,' he said simply. 'That's all there is to it.'

The ships rolled on, heaving, lurching in their extended, bad-weather columns. There were times when the weather alone forced the convoys to scatter, but currently it wasn't as bad as that. Ahead, said the weather reports, conditions were easing – good enough news for the warships, whose guns would be more easily laid and trained on their targets from steady gun-platforms. There had been fog off the Clyde, extending both east towards the Bloody Foreland and west towards the Norwegian coast, and this was likely to come back as the winds eased. There had been snow, and this, too, was not out of the way yet. Pilotage would be hazardous as the convoy made its approach to the Northern Irish coast . . . it was always, the Commodore thought, a case of one damn thing after another.

But first, the *Attila*. And the weather affected all ships equally.

9

In his Berchtesgaden eyrie the Führer and his aspirations remained totally unaffected by considerations of weather. The *Attila* and her consorts had excellent radar equipment and could see through the fog. Snow was of no importance whatever and Herr Hitler brushed it contemptuously aside when Grand Admiral Raeder spoke of it.

'Pish, Admiral. If the *Attila* can see through the fog, then she can see through the snow.' Hitler was adamant, prey to no doubts at all. He had ordered; the *Attila* would obey. When Grand Admiral Raeder mentioned that the British Home Fleet was known to be at sea Hitler closed his ears to it. The British Home Fleet was a joke. All those ancient tin cans from an earlier war, mere left-overs preserved because they were almost all the British had, the British who fortunately had never properly re-armed in spite of warnings from Churchill. Ships of the Home Fleet were not capable of stopping the great *Attila*, mightiest ship ever to sail the seas, epitomizing the strength and vigour and splendour of the Third Reich. Already Hitler had been explicit on the point: the *Attila* was to reach her target, fighting through all opposition she might meet on the way. Those were the orders, the Führer's wishes, and he stressed the point to Grand Admiral Raeder.

'You already have my order, Admiral.'

'Yes. But I must –'

Hitler danced in the air, then thrust his arms rigidly down his flanks, clenching his fists and marching up and down the room a few times before turning on Raeder. 'You have my order! I shall brook no opposition! The British liners and the convoy are to be sunk. The *Attila* will sink them. There will be no mistakes! Any officer or man who fails to do his duty will be shot for cowardice. He will be made an example to all my fighting forces. There will be no shirking. You will convey my remarks in full to Vice-Admiral Fichtner for promulgation to all his officers and men.'

Grand Admiral Raeder gave a formal bow and a Nazi salute; the interview was at an end. Walking along the corridor Raeder espied a hefty female form approaching: Frau Eva Braun. For the Führer, the war could wait a little. The Chancellor of the Third Reich was said behind discreet hands to orgasm when he reached the peroration of a speech; the exchange that had just taken place had not, of course, been a speech but the excitement in the Führer's face had been intense and it was possible Frau Braun had arrived at an opportune moment. Speeding back to his command headquarters Grand Admiral Raeder reflected upon his Führer. The man was a boor, and often childish in his rages, a child that had been told it couldn't have a sweet. Churchill was said to be the same; both Britain and the German Reich suffered under tantrums. Perhaps all great men were like that. Charlemagne, Peter of Russia, Genghis Khan, Attila the Hun. *Attila* . . . a fine ship undoubtedly, but her company were not supermen, they were mere humans, and they were going to face heavy odds. There could be a tragedy; but one thing was certain, and that was that no man would turn from action when it came. Grand Admiral Raeder had no intention of transmitting the Führer's remarks about cowardice; to do so would be an affront, an insult to the brave. It could even undermine morale. Instead, Raeder would make another signal, one that sedulously and in his opinion wittily copied that of the great Lord Nelson before Trafalgar. *The Führer expects that every man will do his duty*. Raeder knew Vice-Admiral Fichtner well; he believed that Fichtner would read between the lines and understand. Indeed there was little doubt that he knew already that failure would lead to disgrace and a summary dismissal by Herr Hitler.

And Raeder was right.

The Grand Admiral's signal was received and decyphered aboard the flagship shortly after the British cruisers had been seen and by Fichtner's order the *Attila* had broken off the attack on the destroyer and faded back again into the seemingly eternal snows. Fichtner knew now that he had been reported, for his w/t had intercepted cs 27's message. From now on there was increased danger. The Führer had stated that the *Attila* was unsinkable and Fichtner had naturally not disagreed – one did not disagree with the Führer, that was axiomatic. The Führer considered that he alone would win the war by some strange mixture of screaming, strutting and having visions sent by God. But Vice-Admiral Fichtner knew, as would any seaman, that no ship was unsinkable. The British had said the great *Titanic* was unsinkable, and she had been despatched by an iceberg on her very first Atlantic crossing. So much for unsinkability; but Raeder's signal disturbed Fichtner, for it carried an obvious warning to himself and was equally obviously, in Fichtner's mind, the result of a recent tirade by Herr Hitler. Fichtner, as human as the rest of the ships' companies, was aware that he could make mistakes and expose the *Attila* to heavy broadsides if the British battleships should be permitted to close within the range of their main armament. . . . Fichtner turned to his Flag Captain.

'Captain Sefrin,' he said, 'there is a message from Grand Admiral Raeder – a fitting one.' He handed the message form to the Flag Captain. 'Please see to it that this is duplicated and pinned to all notice boards.'

'At once, Herr Admiral.'

'And when the weather is suitable for visual signalling, it is to be passed to the ships in company.'

It was an encouraging message; Grand Admiral Raeder was no mean psychologist when it came to understanding seamen. Necks craned throughout the flagship and there were words of approval and patriotism. The Führer was a very great leader and the Reich was supreme above all the world, fighting bravely for its life, for the life of the Fatherland, against the beast-like Russians, the British, the Americans and a bunch of evil Resistance men and women in the occupied countries. Fighting also against General de Gaulle,

97

that stiff-necked bastard, whom even the British didn't like. But Germany was going to win this war and the coming destruction would help to ensure the coming victory and send a shiver of fear, of terror, throughout the British Empire and North America.

Sounds emerged from Number Two gun-turret immediately before the tall superstructure with its many bridges. Singing . . . it reached the ears of the Admiral and for a moment tears pricked at his eyes and he became prey to strong emotion. '*Deutschland, Deutschland, über alles. . . .*'

'Captain Sefrin.'

'Yes, Herr Admiral?'

'The singing. It must stop. It is splendid but it is also foolish. It distracts . . . and every man must be fully alert as to his duty.'

ii

ABOARD the *Glenshiel*, Petty Officer Clutch had reached the wheelhouse and spun his yarn to Stace.

'Well, 'Swain?'

'Leave it, Reg. Skipper's got enough on his plate. So's Jimmy. So we all bloody have.'

'Discipline – '

'I know all that, Reg.' Stace did; discipline was his job. In the destroyers, the coxswain, senior rating on the lower deck, combined many jobs and one of them was that of master-at-arms, chief of the ship's police. 'There's a time and a place, and anyway Aldridge isn't responsible for his own utterances, he's that wet. Forget it.'

Clutch persisted. 'He uttered a threat, 'Swain. He knows I heard it – Christ above, he said it to me! Then there's telling me to shut up.'

'Yes. I don't excuse any of it, Reg.' Chief PO Stace was patience itself, and he knew Reg Clutch. Too rigid for destroyers, too bloody pusser. 'Any other man, any real normal man, I'd take it seriously. But Aldridge isn't the sort to listen to – don't mean what he says. And in addition, he's been driven up the wall by Maloney. Skipper's always fair. Maloney could get the shit and we don't want to see him lose his hook. He's a first-rate seaman and a good bloke when he's not sent round the bend by erks like Aldridge. I'll have a word with both of 'em – leave it with me, Reg.'

'But –'

'Look,' Stace broke in. 'You asked my advice. I've given it. My further advice would be to heed it, all right?'

Clutch banged ill-temperedly out of the wheelhouse and caught the snow down the collar of his oilskin. God damn destroyers. Aboard a battleship or cruiser the jaunty would have had Aldridge on the bridge on the count of three, doubling him up there and all, accompanied by King's Regulations and a nice long charge sheet. But, walking away aft, Clutch recalled his own earlier feelings, the reason why he'd gone along for advice before acting on his own: he might get the shit as much as Maloney. He had to swallow the pill and look happy; not that his had ever been looked upon as a happy face. Even his missus had said, once and once only, that if he looked in the mirror he'd see what turned the cat's milk sour.

iii

'NOT long now, Chief,' Cameron said down the voice-pipe.

'Thank God,' Mr Bream said. It had been a nightmare, the minutes like hours, the hours like weeks. At times he'd thought they would never ever get out, not till the *Attila* caught them up and used her own methods of can-opening. The skipper had mentioned claustrophobia earlier; Bream had felt he was already in his coffin, a steel one filled with steam pipes and oil-fuel injectors and bloody great shafts that if ever they started spinning again would grind him straight into the next world, like a coffee bean. With the boilers dead, the place was as cold as charity but Bream had been sweating like a whore in bed and so had the Chief ERA, up the twisted ladders by the air lock, doing what was possible to assist the hands working under the shipwright outside. The actual job had turned out to be not so bad as Downs had at first thought, but it had taken time and they'd had to be careful to make sure the air lock would work as such afterwards. Downs

99

reckoned some welding and canvas tamping would give it a seal and after that they would have to do their best and hope everything would hold together for long enough to pick up the ocean-going rescue tug and then make Rosyth in one piece. If the worst came to the worst they could always hang about, Downs supposed, and wait for the tug to find them, but they were going to be something of a needle in a haystack and the only certain way to reach the Firth of Forth was to get way on the ship again.

Which was how Cameron saw it. And the sooner the better; a ship wallowing helplessly in the sea was no one's idea of joy. No one liked being a sitting duck and this time there was an appalling sense of frustration that afflicted Cameron badly. The *Attila* was getting away with it, though with luck she might be picked up again by cs27 or another destroyer of their own flotilla, or RAF's Coastal Command once the visibility improved. They must already be flying out recces, surely, though with the RAF one never knew; they were a law unto themselves, or so the other two services believed, never there when wanted, swanning around in comfortable quarters on their airfields, downing pints in the mess or the local, making the grade with the women so that when seamen came back from sea they found all the best ones bespoken as it were. Of course it wasn't true and it wasn't fair; the Battle of Britain in the summer of 1940 couldn't be forgotten. But that was the way plenty of matloes and pongoes saw it. Hunched against the fore screen of the bridge, still in the blinding snow that was cutting visibility almost to nil, Cameron waited with growing impatience for Hastings to report the engine-room hatch serviceable and hoped that when they eventually came out to clear skies they would see some evidence of the search. All the time the HX convoy was coming closer to British shores; the whole area of search must be narrowing now – and that fact alone brought the danger closer. The *Attila* would not leave her attack until it was too late for success, and she certainly couldn't miss the convoy.

Cameron spoke without turning. 'Pilot, have you ever known it go on like this? The weather.'

'Not for so long, no. But I'm not familiar with the particular area, sir. The North Atlantic peacetime run –'

'Yes, I know. What with this and the fog . . . it's as though fate has it in for us this time. I always thought God was on *our* side!'

Millard grinned at Cameron's turned back. 'So do the Jerries. Must be confusing up there, sorting out requestmen! There's been enough prayer ascending. Wouldn't be God for all the tea in China. Talk about Solomon's troubles.'

The wisdom of Solomon was something that captains at sea needed as well. Petty Officer Clutch had a loud voice and some of it had come up the voice-pipe to the bridge at a moment when Cameron had been at the binnacle in place of Millard, watching his ship's head on the gyro repeater. He didn't like eavesdropping but he couldn't close his ears to it. Aldridge, he learned, had uttered threats against Leading Seaman Maloney and had told Clutch to shut up. Cameron had grinned to himself at that; he'd often wanted to use rather stronger language to the TI himself. Clutch would have asked for that, though that didn't excuse Aldridge. But much more serious was the threat. Cameron approved the coxswain's advice to Clutch and hoped he wouldn't have to hear any more about it, but it worried him that so much ferment must be going on inside Aldridge, who was a very weak link in the chain and who, like all weak links, would have a low breaking point. The hard physical conditions currently being suffered and the tension created by the clouded movements of the German squadron might tip Aldridge off balance and then God knew what the result might be. Ships, destroyers, had too many men crammed into them for enmities or grudges to be allowed to develop into psychopathic hates. Aldridge, the actor, might even see himself in some kind of role and might not take into account the consequences of acting it out.

Cameron gave himself a shake that ended in a shiver as snow went down his neck. He was being melodramatic. Stace would cope, no one better to do it. At the same time a word with Number One might be a word in time. Hastings could keep an eye lifting, and nip trouble in the bud, perhaps. Once they were under way again he'd speak to Hastings; and it would probably all die down in any case. It wouldn't be long before they entered the Firth of Forth, coming into the lee of the land between May Island and the Bass Rock to steam past

101

Inchkeith and on beneath the bridge and then, in the joy of shore leave being piped, Aldridge would relax and forget it.

Below on the iron-deck, by the torpedo-tubes, Petty Officer Clutch hadn't forgotten anything. He button-holed Maloney as the latter came past.

'A word in your ear, Maloney.'

'Yes, TI?'

Clutch said in a hard voice, 'That Aldridge.'

'What about him?'

Clutch paused before going on. It wouldn't do to tell Maloney of the threat in so many words; do that, and Maloney could bring it on himself and he, Clutch, might find himself accused of incitement or some such tripe; wardroom officers were like that sometimes, you had to be wary of them. So all he said was, 'Watch it. Right?'

Maloney stared back at him. 'Watch what, eh?'

'Like I said. Aldridge.'

'Little squirt. Liability, he is. Ullage.'

'Maybe.' Clutch thought about that 'shut up'. 'That's not the point. Lay off of him – for your own good.'

'Look, TI –'

Clutch wagged a finger in Maloney's face. 'I said, lay off of him. A wink's as good as a nod to a blind bloody 'orse . . . and what I just said, it's an order. All right, Leading Seaman Maloney?'

Maloney put on a baffled look, acting green, Clutch knew. Maloney was quite well aware he'd been chasing Aldridge. He wasn't going to admit it, but from now on he would know that Clutch's eye was on him and that ought to stop him farting in church as the saying went. Maloney went off scowling and Clutch carried on parading the upper deck, stepping warily in the snow and the forming ice, holding fast to the lifelines that had been rigged soon after the first snow-storm had struck. Clutch didn't particularly care what happened to Aldridge – he was just a hostilities-only rating and he could swing if he wished – but there was in Petty Officer Clutch an unexpected loyalty to the service and the men like Maloney who had made a career of it. He'd not want to see Maloney suffer because of a little twerp like Aldridge, either by getting a seaman's knife in his back or losing his rate because he'd gone too far himself.

It so happened that Clutch didn't like actors – any actors, not just Aldridge. Once, a number of years ago in Pompey, when he'd been an AB, he'd lost a girl to a bloke appearing in music hall at the Coliseum in Edinburgh Road, near the Royal Naval Barracks, a bloke who, oddly for an actor, wasn't a nancy boy. Clutch's girl, who'd worked in the Landport Drapery Bazaar in Commercial Road, had fallen for the bloke, a contortionist rather than a straight actor, which was probably why he wasn't a nancy boy, when Clutch had taken her for a coffee after the show in a café called the Live and Let Live in Queen Street, a place where there had been a nasty murder a couple or so years earlier, and the bloke had come in and got talking. Doris was quite an eyeful, huge tits and a waggling bum when she got up. Clutch had told him to piss off, which he did, but Doris made sure she saw him again and one thing led to another and the next thing Clutch knew was, she'd buggered off to Brighton with him, next stop on the tour. He never saw her again and shortly after had married Mrs Clutch, for which also he was inclined ever after to blame actors.

Moving aft, Clutch found Aldridge still where he'd left him when he'd gone up to the wheelhouse; only this time Aldridge was sitting on the deck with his back to the bulkhead and hanging on to a ringbolt to stop himself sliding over the side on the roll.

Clutch stopped. 'What's all this, then? Up off your arse, Aldridge.'

Aldridge obeyed. White-faced and sick, he asked tentatively, 'Wh-what's going to happen, TI?'

'About uttering insubordinate remarks to a superior officer. Well, we don't know yet, do we, Aldridge? Nor about the other charge. What do we *think* is going to happen, eh?'

'I – I don't know –'

'No. You don't. Maybe it won't come to that, and cos why? Cos we might for all we bloody know be steaming slap bang, or will be when we move, into them bloody Germans. If we are, you'll be spread like strawberry jam, like as not.'

Clutch moved on, mouth shut tight as a rat trap. Let the little bugger squirm for a while, do him good. There were always other ways of dealing with ullage than shoving them in the rattle.

iv

HASTINGS reported to the bridge. 'All right now, sir. It's not exactly a dockyard job, but it should hold.'

Cameron nodded. 'Well done, Number one –'

'Not me, sir. The shipwright and the damage control parties.'

'Yes, I know. You can pass my comments on to them.' As Cameron finished speaking the engine-room called him. Mr Bream reported all well below, and should he now flash up the boilers? 'Yes, Chief. Report when ready to proceed.'

'Aye, aye, sir.' Bream nodded to his Chief ERA, who held up a thumb towards Stoker PO Munro. Munro acknowledged and dodged through to the boiler-room. The fuel injectors were lit and inserted and a low roar of ignition started up, a happy sound for all hands.

Bream thought about Rosyth; they should be in port for a full due this time, what with the damage to the guns and all, to say nothing of the W/T and radar. Might be worth getting the missus up, though it would cost a packet if he had to pay for a hotel . . . might find cheap lodgings, perhaps, in Inverkeithing or across the Forth in South Queensferry. The Hawes Inn was a good pub, always a welcome to the Fleet though the landlord tended to grow a bit sick of the blokes that went in for the first time and, believing their wit to be original, enquired if the whores were in or out this evening. The missus could do with a holiday and a change of air, and the Firth of Forth was safer than Pompey – the Jerries had had their go at trying to bomb the Forth Bridge down and block the Fleet in, and they'd met with a conspicuous lack of success and seemed to have given up. Having had this thought, Bream furtively crossed his fingers. You never really knew what the buggers might get up to. And there was, in fact, another thought: the old *Glenshiel* might go in for a good deal more than what Bream meant by a full due. She might need a proper refit, and if that was the decision of the Admiral Superintendent of the Yard then her company would be split up and given fresh drafts – most of them, anyway. You didn't keep valuable men hanging round during a refit, and warrant engineers didn't grow on trees. It

104

would be typical of the Andrew if he was given a draft the very moment the missus stepped off the train at Waverley station.

When the steam pressure was up, Bream reported to the bridge. 'Ready to move, sir.'

'Right. Stand by main engines.'

'Stand by, sir.'

On the bridge Cameron glanced interrogatively at Millard. Millard said, 'Course 210, sir.'

'Right,' Cameron said again. 'Both engines half ahead, course 210.'

The order went down to Chief Petty Officer Stace in the wheelhouse. The ship came alive again. At any moment, Stace thought, or anyway once they were clear of the snow and the skipper could suss out his surroundings and found them empty of Jerries, they would reduce to second degree or even third degree of readiness. It all depended; and Stace was starting to forget the *Attila* now. Rosyth beckoned, and if he had a little time in port he might, just might, be able to re-establish some sort of contact with Mavis. She could have acted in haste and could be regretting Bert Cockshutt. He would get some leave and if he could sort Mavis out, well, they could stuff the *Attila*. There was a feeling of homecoming in the air now, and vague plans were being made throughout the ship. Ordinary Seaman Aldridge was thinking that if he got leave he might not come back. Desertion in wartime was just about the worst crime in the book but he might risk it. If he was clever, or lucky, they might never catch up with him. Even if they did, he'd be shot of the *Glenshiel*, and Maloney, and Clutch. Detention Quarters had a bad name – he'd heard that the Navy had taken over a part of Glasgow's Barlinnie Gaol to house Naval ratings from Scottish bases convicted of crimes meriting full-scale detention rather than cell punishment aboard or in barracks – but it couldn't be worse than bucketing around northern waters in a destroyer.

v

'Snow's thinning, sir,' Millard remarked on the bridge. The visibility was extending and within the next hour the ship had moved into clearer weather, though there was cloud, and still heavy overcast behind and to the north. The engines were put up to full. Cameron, the lookouts, the navigator and the yeoman of signals all swept the horizon with their binoculars; they were alone on a sea that still heaved around them beneath grey skies. Ten minutes later Cameron passed the word for the ship to reduce to second degree of readiness, which meant a two-watch system and some interrupted sleep for all hands during the rest of the passage. All that day *Glenshiel* steamed at full speed towards Rosyth and just after dusk Action Stations had been piped, the leading telegraphist came to the bridge, his face working with excitement.

'Captain, sir –'

'Yes, Hunter?'

'I reckon I can get the set working again, sir.'

'You – *what*? All right, I heard . . . talk about miracles!'

Hunter said, 'Sort of, sir, yes. EA made a repair on the electrics, and me, I've found some spares what PO Larkin evidently didn't know about, stashed away like in –'

'They're what you need?'

Hunter nodded. 'Yes, sir. Permission to go aloft, sir?'

'You bet! Fast as you can.'

The leading telegraphist left the bridge and soon after was up the foremast with two men and trailing wires, rigging a jury aerial. They worked throughout the night and by the time the hands were piped to breakfast next morning the w/T was back in service with, according to Hunter, a full capability to transmit and receive. This capability was restored just in time to bring Cameron a major headache: the *Glenshiel* picked up a signal in cypher from the Admiralty addressed Commander-in-Chief, Home Fleet and repeated CS27. When it was broken down, laboriously in the absence of MacNamara, by Sub-Lieutenant Sutcliffe, Cameron learned that the 24th Destroyer Flotilla had been brought to action by the *Attila*; and *Glenaffric*, *Glenorchy* and *Glenfinnan* had gone down and it was considered unlikely there would be any survivors.

10

It had become personal now: all the others of
their flotilla gone, and every man had had friends aboard the
three lost ships. They had been chummy ships for a long time
and over many North Atlantic convoys, remaining in company through the various changes of base; Scapa, Londonderry, the Clyde. There was a feeling of disbelief that they
could all have gone while they in the *Glenshiel* had been
wallowing around without power on the main engines in what
had turned out to be safety. There was something wrong
somewhere that it could happen like that.

Hastings, sent for to come to the bridge, asked, 'Any
mention of us, sir?'

'Yes,' Cameron answered. 'We're reported disabled and
heading for Rosyth as ordered by cs27.'

'No orders?'

Cameron said flatly, 'No orders. And so far no rescue tug
either. Missed us on the way, I suppose. Not that we need
her.'

'No, we don't, sir. Just a precaution by cs27 – '

'Quite.' As if by reflex action Cameron was using his
binoculars again. Bringing them down he frowned and said,
'How come they were all together instead of in their search
areas?'

Hastings knew the reference was to the flotilla. He
shrugged; probably they would never know the answer to
that. He said, 'One of them may have picked up the *Attila* and
transmitted and the others closed.'

Cameron gave a short laugh. 'I doubt it somehow, but never mind, it's happened. First blood to the *Attila*, Number One! Meanwhile we have the position of the Germans as reported by Captain(D).' The Admiralty signal had included that information, and no doubt it was being passed to the HX convoy and the independently-sailing Queen liners. 'How far off us?' he added, turning to the navigating officer.

Millard had the answer pat. 'One hundred and ten miles, sir, bearing 035 degrees.'

Cameron nodded. 'The *Attila*'s twisting and turning somewhat, it seems. No clear pattern to her course. We can be there in – what – four hours.'

Millard asked, 'To engage the *Attila*, sir?' He sounded sardonic. 'We – '

'To pick up survivors if any, Pilot,' Cameron snapped.

'If any, sir, yes. They wouldn't have a hope!'

Cameron didn't respond to that immediately. He turned away and stared ahead, his face bleak. Millard was right, of course. The sea was much too cold to sustain life for longer than a matter of minutes, but the destroyers might have got boats away. It all depended on how fast they had gone down. And the Admiralty signal had not been expectant of survivors. In the meantime he had his orders from CS27 to consider. They had not been countermanded and that was not surprising; a destroyer with one 4.7 left out of four was scarcely the vessel to send towards the *Attila*. But she could still pick up survivors – if there were any. One could never rule out all hope and in his view men's lives were more important than a blind adherence to orders when those orders were only taking them to safety, and to the plans of the land-bound brass in the Admiralty. . . .

'Aircraft, sir, bearing red one-five!' The sudden shouted warning came from the port bridge lookout, and all the binoculars swung to the bearing. There was plenty of cloud around and no identification could be made with assurance. Cameron reached for the action alarm and set the rattlers jarring throughout the ship, but when the aircraft had been identified they were seen to be British. The RAF was on the ball at last.

108

ii

By now the news of the *Attila* had been received by all ships affected. A sighting at last and a very positive one, and it was now being taken as certain that the German attack was going to develop. Aboard the *Duke of York* Sir Bruce Fraser intended to work on the assumption that the *Attila* and her consorts would indeed move north of Iceland and come down on the convoy by way of the Denmark Strait. If that was the case, then the Germans would move south thereafter to cut across the convoy's track before the ships began to close British waters. They had plenty of time in which to do it, and the Home Fleet had the time to intercept and bring them to action. But when action came Fraser wouldn't want the convoy too close; their safety lay in avoiding battle. After a brief conference with his staff officers the Commander-in-Chief detached a destroyer from his extended escort to steam at full speed towards the convoy and pass orders to Rear-Admiral Horsted in the *Revenge*: the convoy was to alter to the south-east and head for the Fastnet, making its approach to the Clyde south about via St George's Channel and the Irish Sea. This would increase the risk of attack by the French-based Nazi aircraft but Fraser considered the *Luftwaffe* a lesser evil than the devastating guns of the *Attila* should she manage to blast her way through the heavy screen of the Home Fleet battleships.

It was a big decision to have to make and it had to be Fraser's alone; he could not break wireless silence to ask for Admiralty approval nor even to inform the Chief of Naval Staff of his decision. The *Attila* would know the Home Fleet was at sea; but she would not know its precise position at any given moment and it was vital that that much secrecy was preserved.

The day happened to be a Sunday. Divine Service would be held as usual, conducted by the padre. Normally either Fraser or the Flag Captain would have read the lesson; today neither would leave the bridge, even though the Fleet was not yet at full action stations: Fraser saw no point in wearing out his ships' companies in advance, so that when action came they would already be tired. They would get enough warning to close up. So the Fleet was steaming in second degree of readiness, all armament skeleton manned with reduced shell-handling parties standing by at the bottoms of the great steel-lined shafts that led down to the magazines, the shafts that when action came would have the heavy hatches clipped down upon them so that if a ship was hit the magazines could be flooded by order from the bridge, and the rising water – and the drowning bodies of the seamen of the shell-handling parties – could be held fast inside the shaft. Fraser thought of the utter horror of being shut into a steel-lined grave, of the desperate heads rising on the water's surface to impact finally against the clipped-down hatch, and then to die. No theme for a Sunday sermon. Fraser glanced across at the Flag Captain, who would have to give the flooding order if the necessity arose. Each ship was the responsibility of its individual Captain; the Admiral commanded the fleet as a whole, not his flagship, which was a different matter, not always understood by laymen. If Captain Maconochie ever had to give that order, Fraser would be as sorry for him as for the seamen.

As the morning proceeded the *Duke of York*'s Executive Officer reported to the Flag Captain, who approached the Commander-in-Chief.

'Divine Service . . . have you any particular orders, sir?'

'Not orders, Maconochie. I don't presume to command the church! Ask the padre to pray . . . for every man that's going to be involved. That's all. Those who carry out the orders, and those who have to give them. A special prayer . . . he'll know what to offer up.'

Maconochie saluted and turned away. Sunday spread itself over the warring waters. Somehow Sunday, even at sea, was a different day. That difference could be felt and it was hard to put into words what the feeling was. It wasn't just the fact of Divine Service; something in the atmosphere perhaps, the sight of the padre in cassock and surplice, wafting like an angel before the wind along the upper deck, a garb that turned him from a mundane officer into a more identifiable man of God.

Away across the westward sea Sunday had come also to the *Queen Mary* and the *Queen Elizabeth*. So had Divine Service, attended by as many officers and men as could cram into the

110

great, lofty, once-ornate lounges. Like Sir Bruce Fraser, the Masters of the liners remained on their bridges. Normally the Master took the service, unless, in the vanished days of peace, some travelling prelate, a canon or dean or bishop but seldom a lowly parish priest, was asked to do the honours . . . today, it was in the case of each of the liners a chaplain of the United States Army who made his transatlantic supplications to Almighty God as the great eighty-thousand tonners drove through the North Atlantic at their maximum speed, a speed that made the chalices ring on the improvized altars. But in each ship the concluding hymn was British enough even if the massed voices followed the accents of their priests, and, bellowed out with a strangely passionate fervour, it reached the bridges, the familiar words of the British Navy's own hymn:

> *Eternal Father, strong to save,*
> *Whose arm doth bind the restless wave,*
> *Oh, hear us when we cry to Thee,*
> *For those in peril on the sea.*

iii

CAMERON had turned the *Glenshiel* on to a north-easterly course. The orders for Rosyth could go to hell. Currently he was skirting the filthy weather to the east and intended to alter again when farther north and move through the murk towards the position where he still hoped to find a whaler with survivors. Largely, it had been Mr Tarbuck, Gunner(T), who had made up his mind for him, though Tarbuck hadn't come to the bridge to talk specifically about survivors. Tarbuck, and never mind his humanity, was one-track-minded when it came to the ship itself. The only thing that really mattered when it was down to brass tacks was the fighting capacity of the old *Glenshiel* and that all boiled down to his torpedoes.

He said as much when he reached the bridge, puffing a little from the exertion of heaving his stomach fast up the ladder.

'Torpedoes, sir.'

'What about them, Mr Tarbuck?'

111

'Still got 'em, sir. The whole ruddy lot! Lovely, they are. And lethal, when fired off proper. Not so many of the older boats have bin left with their tubes, sir, more's the pity. But *we 'ave.*' Mr Tarbuck never minded teaching his grandmother; and the *Glenshiel*, where so many other pre-war destroyers had had their torpedo-tubes removed when they were hastily adapted for use as escorts and fitted out with HA armament, still carried her six 21-inch long-range torpedoes. Tarbuck brought out a hideous purple handkerchief and blew his nose: he knew his station in life. You didn't close one hole and blow through the other in front of the skipper. 'Do a sight more damage than the guns, they can.' It was a repeat of what he'd said earlier to Lieutenant Lyon; Tarbuck was a trier and he might persuade the skipper where he'd failed with a gunnery specialist. 'Weather's going to be thick again, if you're going back in to look for survivors.'

'So?'

Tarbuck said, 'Well, sir, if we could pick up the *Attila* and put some fish in her before she gets her gunsights on us . . . come at her out of the snow or whatever . . . well, we'd at least slow her down and give the Home Fleet a better chance.'

Cameron grinned. 'And you get a gong out of it!'

'Wasn't thinking of that, sir.'

'I know you weren't, Mr Tarbuck. Just a joke.'

Tarbuck grinned back. 'That's all right, sir. Got to have something to laugh at.' He paused. 'What about it, sir?'

'I'll bear it in mind,' Cameron answered, and that was just what he had done as he had altered course. The thought of stopping the *Attila* in her tracks was an intriguing one. If the *Glenshiel* could bring that off with almost all her main armament shot away . . . but he must never allow himself to think in grandiose terms of glory. That was not the way today's wars were fought. He had his ship's company to think about; but he had also to think of the thousands of men now steaming towards what might be destruction. If by some miracle he could close the *Attila* . . . but he wouldn't, in reality, have a chance. For one thing, although his w/T had been restored, he was still without radar. If he happened to blunder into the German squadron it would be by the sheerest quirk of fate and nothing else. And if he met them in clear visibility he would never get within range. It so happened that Lyon had told him of that conversation with the Gunner(T) and he knew Lyon was dead right. It was no more than an old torpedoman's dream, based on wishful thinking. Nevertheless, the torpedoes remained at the back of Cameron's mind as the *Glenshiel* headed north-east with all lookouts keeping a careful watch. During the next hour or so more aircraft of Coastal Command were seen distantly, quartering the search areas for a sight of the Germans. On more than one occasion Cameron had to make his signal letters in self identification, and to make the response in answer to the challenge of the day. When the RAF reported him, eyebrows were going to be raised at the Admiralty and he might well receive a signal ordering him to obey his previous instructions from CS27.

Meanwhile he would continue the search.

Below in the engine-room, Mr Bream was worried about his missus. The Admiralty might soon be releasing the news of the sinking of the rest of the flotilla . . . they probably wouldn't, not till after the *Attila* had been brought to action, but they just might and if they did his missus would have kittens on the spot. And likewise, when the *Glenshiel* failed to turn up as ordered in Rosyth – or when the ocean-going rescue tug reported that she had made no contact – then they might be written off as another ship lost and the next of kin might get those harrowing telegrams. Chief ERA Downs was a married man too, and Mr Bream discussed his shore-side anxieties with him.

Downs said, 'I'm not worried, sir. Them RAF blokes, they'll report a sighting.'

'I wouldn't bank on it,' Bream said sourly. 'Bloody Brylcreem Boys . . . mad as hatters they are, think the whole thing's a lark. Back at their airfields, they'll forget all about us, just another poor bloody destroyer bashing its innards out. . . .'

Bream wasn't the only one who was worried about the effect on the families. Aldridge, who had no girl-friend to concern himself with, was thinking of his mother, a widow living alone in Clapham. She'd cried buckets when he'd been called up and cried again each time he went back off leave. Each leave had been spent propping up Mum, and Aldridge

113

had been very attentive, never leaving her side and as sick himself at the thought of having to go back to the Navy. He liked being with his mother, liked shopping in Arding and Hobbs, taking her to coffee in cafés and that. She didn't do any war work; she had a heart condition and a doctor's certificate to prove it, and she lived on a small widow's pension from the Civil Service in which Aldridge's late father had been a member of the clerical grade working in the Ministry of Labour. If she got word that her son was in mortal danger, or close to it, there was no knowing what the effect might be. If he was killed, then she would go and do herself in, Aldridge was sure of that – or even if she *thought* he was killed, say if there was some mistake in the Admiralty's communiqués to the BBC. And then she could be said to have been killed by Lieutenant-Commander Cameron, who was disobeying orders in not returning to Rosyth. Aldridge, thinking himself into a real tizzy, let loose his feelings on Leading Seaman Pittman, PO Clutch's right-hand man on the torpedoes.

'Think we'll be reported missing, Killick?' It was safe to address Pittman as such; he wasn't Leading Seaman Maloney.

'Could be,' Pittman said off-handedly. 'So what? We *aren't* missing, not yet.'

'I was thinking about my mother.'

'Oh, I get you.' Pittman considered the point. 'I reckon they won't release any news back home, son. Give too much away to bloody 'Itler, that would.'

'You sure?'

'Course I'm not *sure*, I'm not the First Sea Lord. But it sounds like common sense to me.'

'Yes, but what about Lord Haw-Haw?'

'Lord Haw-Haw, eh.' William Joyce, otherwise the traitor Lord Haw-Haw who broadcast continually to Britain with his 'Jairmany calling, Jairmany calling', trying to spread alarm and despondency throughout Britain with his claims of sinkings at sea and disasters on land and in the air, was someone every serving man would dearly love to throttle. Haw-Haw had an uncanny knack of gleaning supposedly classified information and elaborating on it, keeping to some

114

strain of truth to give his lies authenticity, and if the Admiralty's signals had been picked up and the cypher broken, then he might at any moment gleefully and this time truthfully announce dire news of havoc caused to the 24th Destroyer Flotilla. Pittman went on confidently, 'I bet your mum takes that bugger with a pinch of salt, son.'

Aldridge made an indistinct sound that was neither assent nor dissent. It was considered not the thing back in Britain to put any credence in Lord Haw-Haw and Aldridge didn't wish to be disloyal, but he knew that his mother took in every single word William Joyce uttered and regarded it, in her pessimistic, defeated way, as gospel truth. Of course Lord Haw-Haw would have his gloat and his mother would react desperately. Even to the point of suicide. It was all too obvious.

He began to shake uncontrollably and his face crumpled. In a high voice he said, 'Why did Cameron have to go and disobey orders?'

'Captain to you, son,' Pittman said. 'The answer is, cos he wants to find survivors. So do I. I'm dead sorry if your mum's worried, but far as I know no one's mum's in command of a ship at sea.' He moved away for'ard, along the wet deck, still making use of the lifelines as the destroyer heaved to the breaking seas, the wind blowing his oilskin out behind him. At the break of the fo'c'sle he turned his head briefly and saw Aldridge staring towards the bridge, face as white as a sheet and the eyes looking funny. He appeared to be muttering to himself – or at someone on the bridge. Pittman didn't like the look of it. Aldridge had the aspect of being about to go off his nut, and they hadn't a quack aboard now to cope with him. Pittman thought it might be his duty as a leading hand to warn someone, but the thought went right out of his head in the instant it came in, when he heard the sudden scream of aircraft engines and then the action alarm sounded, strident, urgent.

11

EARLIER Cameron had spotted a distant, circling Focke-Wulf Kondor, a reconnaissance aircraft no doubt looking for the Home Fleet and the approaching ships of the HX convoy. It had been too far off to engage and for its part had shown no desire to come closer to the destroyer. Cameron hoped the RAF would spot it and shoot it down before it could report back to base, but once again the RAF had vanished and the next they knew aboard the *Glenshiel* was when a long-range bomber came in suddenly from dead ahead, flying low to rake the destroyer's decks with cannon fire before turning for a bombing run.

Bullets zipped and ricocheted, bouncing off bulkheads and decks. A body fell from near the searchlight platform, hit the iron-deck and went overboard, not to be seen again. Leading Seaman Pittman kept his head down, shielded by the after bulkhead of the fo'c'sle, then ran aft to his action station at the tubes where he found Petty Officer Clutch cursing like mad because his tin hat had been hit by a bullet that in glancing off had somehow sent the tin hat flying from his head into the water. As the German banked and gained height for its next attack, the ack-ack and the close-range weapons swung on to it and waited for it to come back in.

The barrage peppered the sky with smoke puffs as the 20-mm HA put an insubstantial curtain between the *Glenshiel* and the enemy. It came in regardless, and dropped a stick of bombs. They took the water a cable's length to starboard and sent spray flinging over the decks but doing no damage.

116

Cameron was twisting and turning the ship, making the target more difficult. Chief PO Stace in the wheelhouse listened to the racket of the ack-ack, the fast pumping of shrapnel towards the Jerry, the sharper clatter of the close-range weapons, Oerlikons, pom-poms, machine-guns, mounted in the bridge wings above him and amidships near the searchlight platform.

'Just the one bugger,' he said. 'Shouldn't be too difficult . . . given a bit of bloody luck.' The fact of action, action with the guns firing, was making him think of his friend PO Lindsay, gunner's mate, who'd bought it earlier. They were missing Tom Lindsay now; in action Tom had been everywhere at once, chivvying the hands when necessary but always cheery and encouraging, putting guts into them when they needed it. Not like Clutch, who was good at his job all right but got people's backs up and seemed to be for ever snarling like a bad-tempered dog. Always the same with smallish, thin men . . . Tom Lindsay had been big-built and where Clutch yapped Lindsay had roared – and only when it was called for. But no use thinking of the past. Lindsay was gone and that was all about it. Shut your mind to it till one day you got back to Pompey and met Lindsay's wife and kids and told them how Tom had died for his country and so on. That was, if you lived long enough yourself. . . .

Stace ducked instinctively as something took the bridge right over his head, the ship seemed to judder and flakes of cork insulation came down in a shower all over him. He heard shouts and screams and another impact on the port side, iron-deck he fancied, and the skipper calling for the fire parties. Then Cameron spoke down the voice-pipe, cool and collected. 'It's down, Cox'n. On us, partly.'

'All well up top, sir?'

'I wouldn't call it all well. But we're intact.'

Stace let out a long breath. For now it was over, but there was always another time in this bloody war. However, the old *Glenshiel* had done a bit of hitting back and that was good. Up top, Cameron wasn't quite so sanguine. The German aircraft had appeared to disintegrate as it had come in on its second run, a shade too low for its own good. A stream of bullets from the starboard Oerlikon had torn into it – Cameron had been able to follow the tracer all the way in – and must have hit some vital part. There had been a ball of flame and the next thing the bridge personnel had been aware of had been the aircraft's port engine dropping away and coming for them, coming in at an angle to hit the after bulkhead of the bridge itself before dropping like a blazing thunderbolt to the iron-deck below. The rest of the aircraft had gone on under its own momentum to crash into the sea astern and had then sunk like a stone. On its fatal path, the detached engine had taken the yeoman of signals, and his body was there still, what was left of it, spread bloodily against his own flag locker. Another quirk of fate: no one else had been touched other than by spurts of burning aviation spirit still left in the wreckage of the engine. Nothing serious.

Cameron put a hand on the shoulder of the Oerlikon gunner, an unlikely hero and one who wouldn't have been there at all if the First Lieutenant, as a result of the casualties earlier, had not had to reorganize his Watch and Quarter Bill. Cameron said, 'Well done. You saved the ship.'

The rating was Ordinary Seaman Aldridge. When the mess on deck had been cleared away the word went round the ship. Clutch's face was purple. He said in a grating voice, 'I don't believe it. I don't bloody believe it.' He looked as if he were about to have a stroke.

ii

By this time Vice-Admiral Fichtner was in no doubt that his movements were known to and were being followed by the enemy. First, the British destroyer and the appearance of the cruisers; then more destroyers, luckily sent to the bottom thus depleting the shadowing force very satisfactorily; then the drone of the aircraft of the RAF and possibly of the British Fleet Air Arm also, distant and invisible in the heavy snowfall but there for a purpose nevertheless, waiting for the *Attila* to show herself. For his part Fichtner had received wireless reports from the German Naval Command, reports based on sightings made by U-boats unable, on account of the heavy weather farther out in the Atlantic, to mount their own attacks, and he now knew

118

the approximate position of the Home Fleet and of the convoy, and he also knew the latter's current course – but that could change and almost certainly would.

At this moment the Home Fleet battleships and cruisers were some two hundred miles south of Cape Farewell and moving north – by Fichtner's estimation to lie off the Denmark Strait and wait for him to steam into their guns. The convoy out of Halifax was another four hundred miles or so to the west of the Home Fleet and had altered course south-easterly. A different approach to Britain was being made, so much was obvious. But again, there could be another alteration. The British, so Grand Admiral Raeder had always said – and so had the Führer – were devious, subject to many changes of mind and plan. The mind of Churchill had permeated to the Admiralty and the British Fleet and nothing could be depended on. The British no longer fought their sea wars on the simple and explicit lines laid down in their own Fighting Instructions, a copy of which every German senior Naval officer had been obliged to study.

Life was being made difficult. Decisions were always difficult, of course; and if you made the wrong one. . . . The Führer was a very difficult man. Vice-Admiral Fichtner conferred with Captain Sefrin and his staff officers. He said, 'The dispositions have changed and are perhaps changing still. I must change with them.'

That, the staff officers considered, was wise.

Fichtner said, pulling the collar of his uniform greatcoat tighter about his ears, which were so cold that they might as well not have been there at all since he couldn't feel them except as a dull ache close to his cropped head, 'Sir Bruce Fraser will hold his battleships off the Denmark Strait. Myself, I shall move round to outflank, leaving him many miles to the north, thus giving myself more time to reach the convoy, destroy it, and return at full speed to Bergen before Fraser can mount any effective pursuit. I shall expect to pick up the convoy about three hundred miles south of the Home Fleet's position, and the same number of miles west of the Irish coast, the southern Irish coast. Well, gentlemen, are there any questions?'

Captain Sefrin said, 'If the convoy alters again to the north,

119

Herr Admiral, we may be too far south to – '

'Yes. We must rely upon receiving further intelligence from time to time, Captain Sefrin, when we shall react accordingly. For now, it shall be as I have said.'

The orders were passed for an alteration of course and from the *Attila*'s signal bridge the lamps became busy, clacking out Fichtner's message to the dark shapes of the *Recklinghausen* and the *Darmstadt*. The snow was falling still, being blown into the faces of the watchkeepers and smothering the gun-turrets and the decks and the boats griped-in to the davits, but it was tending to thin and the visibility wasn't too bad. The ships swung ponderously and as the *Attila* steadied on the new bearing Vice-Admiral Fichtner spoke again.

'The big liners,' he said to Sefrin. 'The *Queen Mary* and the *Queen Elizabeth*.'

'Yes, Herr Admiral?'

'There has been no report of them.'

'Not yet, Herr Admiral. It is a question of time only.'

'Yes. But they must be well outside the expected area, or our reconnaissance aircraft would surely have seen them. When they are picked up and reported to me. . . .'

'Yes, Herr Admiral?'

Fichtner said, 'I have yet to make up my mind about them, Captain Sefrin. I begin to believe that if they are far off from the convoy, then we may not have the time to attack both them and the convoy and still return safely to Bergen. There are two matters to be considered: which is the most important target in the mind of our Führer, and is our safe return of more importance to our Führer than the attacking of *both* targets?'

Sefrin said nothing, choosing to treat the question as rhetorical and in any case not wishing to commit himself to any pre-emption of the Führer's wishes. But he sensed Fichtner's indecision and he was not unaware that the Admiral had a fellow-feeling for all seamen. To attack a battle fleet was one thing and even the victims of the attack would understand that their calling pre-supposed a fatalistic acceptance of death should it come from German shells; but to attack unarmed seamen was another consideration altogether and Captain Sefrin himself was in some sympathy with his Admiral's views. But in his opinion the big British liners were the obvious first target if a choice had to be made. All those thousands of American troops – and the ships themselves! The Führer would never forgive the man who let them go, and much of the opprobrium would rub off upon himself, simply because he was there and in command of the *Attila*. Most unfairly, of course, but . . . no, no. Captain Sefrin checked his thoughts. There must be no disloyalty to the Führer, sent by God to ensure the supremacy throughout the world of the Third Reich; the Gestapo had an uncanny knack of reading minds.

Fichtner said suddenly, 'We must wait and see. It is too early for a final decision.'

'Yes, Herr Admiral. Heil, Hitler!'

iii

IF Petty Officer Clutch had been disbelieving of what Aldridge had done, Aldridge himself was no less so. Nothing in the world could have been a clearer case of beginner's luck: Aldridge hardly knew where the trigger was and he had less idea of how to take aim. He could just as easily have shot up the Captain and the navigating officer . . . he began to sweat at the thought of just what would have happened to him then. It could even have looked a deliberate act after what he'd only just said to Leading Seaman Pittman. He would probably have been charged with treason as well as murder. That would have led to his being put up before a firing squad, most likely. As it was, he'd killed some Germans and, apparently, had saved the ship and the lives of everyone in it. That was quite something; after a while Aldridge calmed down and began to preen. It had showed them all, and it would put Leading Seaman Maloney to shame.

When no further aircraft had come over, Cameron had reduced to second degree of readiness and Aldridge had fallen out from action stations in something of a dream. When the war was over he intended returning to the acting profession just as fast as he could get out of his bell-bottoms and start to live a civilized life again, and he might try to get a part in a war production, even a film perhaps – it was obvious the hoo-ha was going to go on for years, films and stage plays,

121

all would go mad with putting on the heroics of land and sea, and actors who'd been in the armed forces would at least know something about it all and be authentic.

An authentic hero!

A celluloid hero who had actually shot down a Jerry plane and saved his ship. It could establish him in the big time almost overnight. . . .

'Where the sod d'you think you're going?'

Aldridge was brought up all standing. The speaker was Leading Seaman Maloney. Aldridge found himself just about to step overboard where the Jerry aircraft engine had torn away the iron-deck guardrail. He stared in horror and nipped back smartly.

'Blithering little twerp,' Maloney said scathingly, but not so bitterly as he'd always spoken to date. 'Can't bloody lose you now, can we, eh? Well done, lad. Shows you can be wrong about people, I reckon.' He put a rough hand on Aldridge's shoulder and squeezed. Aldridge, not knowing what to say, said nothing; and Maloney grinned and went up the ladder to the fo'c'sle.

On the bridge Cameron stared into the murky weather, where the *Glenshiel* had turned once again to find cover. He spoke to the Officer of the Watch who had taken over from Millard when action stations had been fallen out. 'It's too thick to maintain full speed, Mid. Half ahead both engines.'

The OOW was Midshipman Whyman, RNVR. He said, 'Half ahead both, sir,' and bent to the voice-pipe. 'Both engines half ahead,' he ordered.

Stace was still at the wheel. 'Both engines half ahead, sir.' A pause, then: 'Engines repeated half ahead, sir.' He went through the routine of the order, the repetition, the reporting back. The good old routine of the service, what he'd been used to most of his life, only now it could be taking them all slap bang into the *Attila* if the Jerries were still buggering about under the snow and steaming on all points of the compass. He hoped, when they were back in the thick of it once again, that the skipper would watch out; Stace didn't feel safe with an RNVR middy on the bridge. Whyman was still wet behind the ears, not much more than nineteen and not long left school, or college rather – it had penetrated to the

122

lower deck that the middy had just got into Cambridge and had chucked it up to join the Andrew, which was a mark in his favour right enough but while it spoke for his courage it said bugger all for his ability on the bridge of a destroyer. Baby Face, he was known as, shaved every third day. Poor little bugger . . . Stace wished him all the luck in the world, genuinely, even though he wished he wasn't there. But the skipper was all about, so was the navvy. They would be all right. Stace watched the gyro repeater in front of him, and the clock on the bulkhead at the same time. No relief, and they'd fallen out from first degree ten minutes ago. Leading Seaman Matlock should have been along.

'Lofty,' Stace said.

Ordinary Seaman Nye looked up from a copy of *Men Only*, full of nudes, or as near nude as was permitted to endanger the morals of the public. 'Yes, Chief?'

'Nip along and find out where Leading Seaman Matlock is. Pronto!'

'Yes, Chief.' *Men Only* was put down. Stace glowered at the publication, hissed a little between his teeth. Lads would be lads, natural enough, but himself he didn't get any satisfaction out of looking at pictures of tits and bums and so on. The real thing was a different matter, and such pictures didn't do anyone any good at sea, only distracted the mind. It distracted his now; Mavis didn't look much like the girls in *Men Only*, but it brought her to mind and also brought to mind Bert bloody Cockshutt and what *he* was probably looking at now or would be after nightfall. Bloody reserved occupations! It would do Mr Cockshutt a power of good to be tied to the busy end of a 15-inch gun about to be fired, and . . . Stace grinned as a fragment of a Naval ditty came into his mind: '. . . don't want me privates shot away. . . .'

But war was war and so was all that went with it. Nye came back looking shaken. The casualty reports hadn't penetrated to the wheelhouse till now: Leading Seaman Matlock was the man who'd gone overboard from the midship superstructure. Another relief for the coxswain was on the way.

Chew on that, Stace thought bitterly.

iv

THE British public knew nothing whatever of events out at sea. The families of the men were as yet in blissful ignorance that many of their kin had gone and that the others faced appalling danger; that is, they were unaware in any positive sense. The anxiety was always there, of course, but only in an unspecific way, a constant nag of worry that at certain times of the day made them unresponsive to anything but the BBC News broadcasts, the tones of Alvar Liddell, Stuart Hibberd, Bruce Belfrage, sometimes reassuring, sometimes not. Mrs Aldridge was one of those who never found any of them reassuring, no matter what they said; it was all just propaganda, designed by the Government to stop the public worrying about their boys. She reckoned there was a lot of truth in what Lord Haw-Haw said – and everyone knew it. Sometimes he even mentioned streets that had been blitzed, mentioned them by name with uncanny accuracy. Mrs Aldridge thought he must have a wonderful spy network; even knew the names of the corner shops in various cities – London's East End, Liverpool, Plymouth, Coventry, Portsmouth and others. It all gave his comments wicked point; you felt he knew it all, and in the end Britain couldn't win.

So far, thank heaven, Lord Haw-Haw hadn't made any mention of the *Glenshiel*; Mrs Aldridge always heaved a big sigh of relief when he'd had his say and hadn't referred to her son. Alf must be all right. Mrs Aldridge spent her whole waking hours thinking of Alf and sometimes even talked to him when she walked down St John's Road to Arding and Hobbs, or to the co-op, or Boot's or the greengrocer's, and had a cup of coffee in Lyon's which was where she and Alf went when he was home.

The day the *Glenshiel* turned back into the continuing snow far to the north-east of Rosyth she happened to meet old Mr Sands, whom she suspected of hanging about from time to time so that he could 'happen' to meet her. Although they always called each other Mrs Aldridge and Mr Sands, she knew he had a romantic streak and was lonely since Mrs Sands had been killed getting off a bus in the middle of the

124

road . . . a wretched motor-cyclist in Army uniform. Mrs Aldridge had been ever so sorry about it but reacted to Mr Sands' attentions thereafter even though he was an old-age pensioner.

Gallantly he took off his hat. 'Well, well, fancy. How about a cup of something, eh, Mrs Aldridge?'

They happened to be outside Lyon's.

'Well,' she said doubtfully.

'Come on.' He took her arm.

She could do with some refreshment, filthy though war-time neo-coffee was. 'Thanks,' she said. 'Thanks ever so.'

They went inside and had coffee. Mr Sands enquired after Alf, without much enthusiasm. Mrs Aldridge said she hadn't heard for more than a week and Mr Sands uttered sympathetic murmurs about no news being good news and he was sure the lad would be all right, the British Navy was more than a match for Adolf Hitler and she shouldn't worry.

'The boys in blue,' he said, with a gleam in his watery eyes; Mrs Aldridge was sitting close to him and looked in need of comfort. 'Talk about brave. I salute 'em all, and where would we be without 'em, that's what I'd like to know.' He paused, wiping coffee from his lips with the back of a hand. 'You ever seen *In Which We Serve*? Noël Coward.'

Mrs Aldridge shook her head. 'No. I heard it's good.'

'Me, too.' Mr Sands paused again. 'It's on at a cinema in Balham. All about our heroes . . . you ought to see it, with a lad in the Navy. Thinking of going myself, tonight.'

It was an invitation, that was clear. After some more overt pressure Mrs Aldridge accepted. It would take her out of herself, perhaps, and even though it would remind her of Alf out at sea, or possibly in port for all she knew, Mr Sands was quite right when he said she owed it to him to go and see what life was like for him in the messdeck of a destroyer. So they went to see Noël Coward's sentimental masterpiece, and just as the cinema was emptying the *Luftwaffe* came over and dropped a devastating load of bombs on Balham, the cinema taking two direct hits. Mr Sands and Mrs Aldridge failed to get out in time; the number of casualties was appalling.

V

INSIDE the operational heart of the search for the *Attila* there was something approaching despair. The convoy and the trooping liners were closing towards home waters, but there was little comfort to be drawn from that since they were also closing towards the German guns. The tiny coloured flags on the plot in the Admiralty were being shifted about in accordance with such movements of the Home Fleet as were currently known; but the swastika-ed flag representing the *Attila* was in a sense in limbo: it was there all right, stuck in an area of snow, but its position was nothing more than guesswork despite the earlier reported sightings. It was still believed she would be moving north, still believed that she would turn south down the Denmark Strait and then make at full speed for the target.

'There's no damn pattern,' the Duty Captain said bitterly. 'It's not like the *Bismarck*, sir.'

The Chief of Naval Staff, no sleep for two days beyond catnaps, red in the whites of his eyes as a result of that and too many cigarettes, was inclined to snap. 'Of course it isn't, it's totally different. The *Bismarck* was on the run after sinking the *Hood*. The *Attila*'s after a target. There's no comparison. If it wasn't for the damn weather. . . .'

'Yes, quite. We'd have her by the short hairs, sir. The Nazis must have first-class meteorologists.'

'Yes.' The theory in the Operations Room was that the Germans had been dead lucky insofar as the filthiest and most prolonged bad weather for a decade or more had happened to coincide with the passage of the HX convoy and the Queens; but that didn't mean the German meteorological people hadn't given Grand Admiral Raeder the tip that weatherwise everything would be going for him. 'Got ours beaten! Witchcraft, crystal balls, clairvoyance – or make it up as they go.'

The Duty Captain laughed. The met boys weren't quite as bad as all that, but at best they were right only half the time and any old-style seaman could make rings round them just by sniffing the breeze. CNS was lighting another cigarette when a message was brought in.

'Report from reconnaissance aircraft, sir – '

'The *Attila*?'

'I'm afraid not, sir. *Glenshiel* of the 24th Destroyer Flotilla sighted on a northerly course.' The Paymaster Lieutenant who had brought the signal handed it to CNS. 'The position's given, sir.'

'What's going on?' CNS read the signal, frowning, '*Glenshiel* was under order from CS27 to enter Rosyth. She's bloody useless as a fighting unit! Who's her Captain, do we know?'

'Cameron, sir. Lieutenant-Commander RNVR.'

'RNVR – yes, I remember. Does he fancy himself as Nelson RNVR, or something?'

The Duty Captain said, 'Send a recall, sir, tell him to obey the last order?' Then he too remembered something. 'Can't: W/T's US. On the other hand they may have made a running repair by now.'

CNS prowled, mouth set hard, hands behind his back. 'Leave it. Too much signal traffic at this stage of the game – not a good thing. Necessities only – and the *Glenshiel*'s not a necessity I'm sorry to have to say. Besides, we don't know what's in Cameron's mind – better not to interfere.' He turned, halted and faced the Duty Captain, stabbing a finger towards him in a characteristic gesture. 'But whatever it is, he'd better be right. If he's not. . . .'

There was no need to finish the sentence.

12

CAMERON'S mind was still on the possibility
of picking up survivors, the natural instinct of any seaman.
His imagination flowered: the icy water, the snow that might
be falling on men in open boats or on Carley rafts, the lack of
warm clothing for those who had been below in the engine
spaces . . . hunger and thirst developing and an overall
hopelessness in the fact that they were so far out from land
and were never likely to be picked up. They could row a
certain distance but when they met high seas the strength in
their arms would fade and exhaustion and exposure would
bring the release of death. There would be wounded among
them, burned and broken men for whom nothing could be
done. Cameron paced the bridge, thinking bloody thoughts
of war. The Home Fleet's mission, his mission as part of the
overall force, was to bring the same cruel fate to the ship's
companies of the *Attila* and her consorts, equally acting under
orders. There seemed little sense in it all. No battlefleets on
either side would mean no sinkings, no boatloads of des-
pairing seamen. There was a case for total disarmament, but
only so long as there was rigid international control and
inspection – a World Arms Inspectorate, genuinely sub-
scribed to by all nations. It was a thought for when the war
was over. Command and the need for decisions on his own
initiative, decisions for life and death, had given Cameron a
different perspective as to war, but for now the war was very
much with him and had become a way of life, with peace
something forgotten, something from a very distant past.

Along the upper deck as the *Glenshiel* groped on through the foul weather the talk was also of survivors. Petty Officer Clutch, moving past the torpedo-tubes on his way aft to check the depth charges and well aware of his enhanced importance as acting gunner's mate in addition to his normal duties – for Lieutenant Lyon had overruled Sutcliffe in the event – found the bulky figure of Mr Tarbuck huddled into his duffel-coat and oilskin in the lee of the after screen. Tarbuck, Clutch thought, was showing his age – and in all conscience he was much too old for this lark, one foot in the grave and the other approaching fast. Clutch said, 'I reckon the skipper'll have to give it up.'

Tarbuck looked blank; his mind was elsewhere. 'Give up what, TI?'

'Hunt for survivors, that's what.' Clutch waved a hand around. 'All this muck. Bloody useless! Time to think of 'is own ship, *and* 'is orders.'

Tarbuck said, 'That's no way to talk. Ever been a survivor yourself?'

'No, sir, I have not.' Clutch moved on; Tarbuck, as it happened, had been a survivor and he'd said so more than once. He'd been sunk in a cruiser escorting a convoy through the Gap to Malta, but he had not been long in the drink before he'd been picked up, and anyway the Med was warm enough. Clutch moved out of earshot; he didn't want to hear it all over again. Tarbuck, seeing the way the TI had turned away, knew what he was thinking and felt hurt, but only momentarily. He'd been a long time in the Andrew and his skin had grown thick enough; besides, he knew he'd become garrulous and repetitive, something he ought to watch, but the trouble was, the older you got, the more people you met and in the end you couldn't always remember what you'd said to whom. Anyway, the TI was probably right; this was a wild-goose chase if ever there was one. There couldn't be any hope now, not short of a miracle.

Aldridge, off watch and trying to find sleep in his hammock before the bosun's pipes shrilled again and sent him back to face the appalling cold, was also thinking about survivors and praying that he would never be one himself – or more precisely, that no projy would ever come close enough to put

129

him in danger of death or abandoning ship. He knew he could never cope with the situation if he found himself in a lifeboat or Carley raft; he knew he would die, no two ways about that. It was bad enough just being aboard a destroyer where at least you could get out of the cold and wet from time to time and thaw out. Because of his thoughts, sleep wouldn't come and he lay wide-eyed, staring at the white-painted deckhead close above; and his mind had moved from survivors to Clapham and home when he heard the voice of the BBC announcer reading the news bulletin from London, the suave tones coming from the messdeck radio, bringing a touch of a civilized life still in being somewhere.

Alvar Liddell was reporting news from the Home Front. '. . . raid by German bombers on London last night. It is believed the target was Battersea Power Station, but the aircraft were confused by the heavy anti-aircraft barrage and the target was not hit. A number of bombs fell on Balham and a cinema received direct hits. A number of casualties have been reported.'

Aldridge felt a loosening of his stomach and a sick feeling. Balham wasn't Clapham but it wasn't all that far off and his mother liked going to the pictures. But she wouldn't be daft enough to travel about at night, if she went it would be in the afternoon when you could mostly rely on the buses running – the Jerries didn't come over so much in daylight, or so his mother had written once. The sick feeling died down but left a nagging worry behind it.

ii

SOMETIMES miracles did happen; the hand of God hovered over land and sea. Ordinary Seaman Aldridge was still lying awake with his worries when the bosun's pipes shrilled and the order came: 'Clear lower deck of seamen, all hands off watch lay aft.'

The leading signalman had spotted a whaler, broad on the port bow, drifting. Cameron levelled his binoculars and turned to the First Lieutenant who had just come to the bridge. 'I'll bring her on to the port side aft, Number One.' There was less freeboard aft, easier to embark men. 'Have

130

lines ready, and hands to help the men aboard.'

'Aye, aye, sir.' Hastings went down the ladder, shouting for the buffer. The *Glenshiel* swung to port and steadied; within the minute Cameron had stopped engines in order to drift up to the whaler. On the starting platform Mr Bream eased back his cap and wiped sweat from his forehead, and thanked God in his heart that they'd found something, even one boatload. A few families that wouldn't have to get that Admiralty telegram. On the upper deck the hands stood ready. It wasn't going to be easy to embark any wounded men, they would have to be manhandled aboard, and what medical help could they be offered, with the doctor and the SBA gone? Aldridge had an unworthy thought: If there were enough wounded, the skipper would have to obey his orders and make for Rosyth after all, get them into a base hospital. Aldridge wasn't the only one who was thinking along those lines, that it is an ill wind . . . and once into Rosyth they'd go straight into dockyard hands and there would be leave. Better than chasing the bloody *Attila*. The *Glenshiel* in her current state could well be spared from that chase anyway.

Chief PO Ruckle was first over the side and down into the whaler. There wasn't going to be any leave, not on account of wounded survivors. Ruckle's face told its own story, confirming what was already becoming obvious. There hadn't appeared to be any life in the whaler, no waving arms, no shouts of salvation. Ruckle said in a tense voice, 'They're all dead. Every last one of 'em. All dead.' He clambered back aboard, his face white. He said to Hastings, 'They're *Glenaffrics*, sir. Recognized an old mate.' He asked, 'Bring 'em aboard, sir?'

Hastings nodded. Identity discs had to be examined so that the casualty reports could be made, and there just might be some lingering spark of life, though it didn't look that way at all. The bodies were lying at odd angles, draped over the thwarts like sacks of potatoes. There was another consideration: decent sea-burial, and the words of the committal service, and the White Ensign to honour each body as it went over the side. There had to be dignity in death.

As the bodies were brought aboard and the whaler bumped up and down against the ship's side, Hastings climbed to the

131

bridge to report to the Captain. This time it had been only half a miracle and better in some ways if it had never happened at all. The sight of the whaler's cargo wouldn't be any help to morale in Cameron's view; no one liked to see a projection of what might be about to happen to himself. But in this thought Cameron was proved wrong. It was Tarbuck who said it, his bulbous old face quivering with anger.

'Now we've really got to get the bugger.'

That seemed to be the consensus opinion, on the lower deck as well as in the wardroom. Already turned into a personal matter, it was now much more so. Only a matter of days before, those dead men had enjoyed a run ashore in Greenock, off the Tail of the Bank, drinking in the bars with men from the *Glenshiel*. Now they would never go back, never again catch the drifter from Albert Harbour, out across the busy anchorage towards Helensburgh, never see what could so often be a splendid sunset behind the hills around Glen Massan, never feel the tug of gale-force winds dragging their anchors towards the dangers of Rosneath Patch or see the rapidly changing weather that at one moment brought up the whole great anchorage clear and the next shrouded it in Scotch mist, the teeming rain that blotted out all visibility. The Clyde in wartime had become home to half the Navy, a place to set out from, a place to return to, with memories that would never fade, memories of comradeship and runs ashore. The dead would be missed, but they could still be avenged. Steely determination settled over the *Glenshiel* and the mood was not missed by the First Lieutenant.

He reported to the bridge again, after checking around the upper deck and seeing to the provision of spare hammocks for the shrouds. 'They're raring to go, sir. The spirit's good.'

Cameron nodded, glad enough to have been proved wrong in his estimation of the whaler's effect. 'Rosyth forgotten, Number One?'

Hastings grinned. 'Not forgotten, sir. Just pushed into the background a little longer, that's all. They want to go back with something achieved.'

Cameron nodded again, looked around the close horizons.

He said, 'I'll hold my course a little longer – there could be more boats. Let me know when you're ready for the burial parties, Number One.' He turned to Millard. 'Right, Pilot. Half ahead both engines.'

The *Glenshiel* gathered way and moved on, leaving the now empty whaler to vanish astern into the falling snow. When Hastings reported that the bodies were ready, Cameron once again stopped engines and read the words of the committal service from aft of the starboard torpedo-tubes and one by one the bodies were slid from the plank, under the folds of the White Ensign, lead-weighted at the feet to carry them down into the deeps. Afterwards Cameron went back to the bridge with Hastings, frowning in thought. Hastings asked, 'What now, sir?'

There had been no more boats and the chances of finding living men must now be considered nil. Cameron said, his mind made up, 'I'll alter westwards, Number One, and come out of this weather. Pilot?'

'Sir?'

'Lay off a course once we're clear . . . a course to join up with cs27. We're going into the fight.'

iii

THE Rear-Admiral commanding the 27th Cruiser Squadron had received no further intelligence from the Admiralty and was to some extent out on a limb, a three-ship limb. Still no one knew where the *Attila* was or what her course or intentions might be. There was still the divergence between the hx convoy and the independently-routed Queen liners. It was virtually impossible to assess the mind of Vice-Admiral Fichtner, yet to try to do so was all-important. It was fifty-fifty, a toss of a coin. But there was one aspect that might give a clue. Rear-Admiral Moreton had yarned with Rear-Admiral Horsted, currently in the *Revenge*, at the time that British Intelligence had reported the fact of Fichtner's appointment to the *Attila*; Moreton and Horsted were old friends, and Horsted had told Moreton the same story that he had told the Flag Captain in the *Revenge*: about the old seaman near Southsea Castle at the time of the Coronation Review of the fleet, and Fichtner's comment.

Fichtner was a seaman of the old sort, perhaps a man of chivalry.

It was not a lot to go on, of course, but it was about all Moreton had. He had to make a decision, and make it fast. He was going to assume that Fichtner might shrink from attacking virtually unarmed and unescorted liners when there was a ready alternative for his guns: the convoy and its heavy escort. Fichtner might consider it unworthy of himself and of Germany to avoid action against the British Fleet – just might. Of course, there was the other side of the coin, as there always was: because the *Attila* could expect to suffer damage and casualties when brought to battle, Fichtner might wish to preserve his own men and sink the softer option of the Queens. In any case, the German Admiral would have his orders from Raeder and from the overall boss – Hitler. It was of little use making any attempt to get inside the mind of the schizophrenic Führer, who was to say the least unpredictable and liable to make off-the-cuff decisions out of sheer frenzy. Hitler would presumably have ordered the whole lot to be destroyed but he was possibly unlikely to interfere with the actual handling of the *Attila* or even with the priorities, which would have been left to the Admiral on the spot. Correction: might have been. Raeder, acting as the intermediary, would also have his own ideas.

Moreton gripped the bridge rail aboard the *Monmouth*, gripped until his knuckles showed white. As ever, everything was shrouded in imponderables and uncertainties, and admirals, like captains, were always expected to have crystal balls enabling them to make instant and correct decisions. In another age a warship might well have carried on its Watch and Quarter Bill some such rating as a yeoman of clairvoyance, or a necromancer's mate to advise the Admiral. As it was, one had to do a balancing act and trust largely to sheer luck thereafter.

Fichtner's chivalry had to form Moreton's kingpost of decision. Fichtner would attack the HX convoy first. If the *Attila* could sink a battleship or two, which by all accounts she probably could, and then go in amongst the ammunition ships

134

and tankers and troopships . . . even leaving aside chivalry, it might strike Fichtner as a worse blow to the Allies, or anyway to Britain. The Queens weren't carrying any oil fuel or ammunition or foodstuffs. . . .

Moreton decided to head north to intercept.

iv

'ANOTHER wild-goose chase,' Cameron said bitterly. Once into clear if heavy weather they had made a fair amount of distance north-westerly, closing the area where they expected to find the cruisers; but there had been nothing, nothing at all but heaving, white-capped seas. Never mind all the ships known to be out – the convoy and its big escort, the liners, the Germans and all – they might have been in a deserted ocean. Neither was there any signal traffic: both the Admiralty and the German Naval Command seemed to be in a mutual conspiracy of silence. It was clear enough that the *Attila* had not been sighted again; the luck was all with Hitler currently. All that was known was the fact of the sinking of *Glenaffric*, *Glenorchy* and *Glenfinnan*.

Cameron spoke his thoughts aloud. 'I wonder how many others.'

Lyon was on watch. He said, 'I doubt if there's been any more, sir. They'd have – '

'Broken wireless silence to report – yes, I know. If they'd had the time.' Cameron's eyes were red from constant use of his binoculars and his whole body ached with tiredness; but he had refused to go below. The *Attila* could, for all anyone knew, be close; the Captain must be on the bridge. So there he had remained, drinking cups of cocoa, biting into beef sandwiches, smoking one cigarette after another and crushing out the paper tubes dampened by the spray that was flung over the bridge screen from the fo'c'sle head as the destroyer cut into the heavy seas. If only their radar was working . . . but no use wishing. PO Telegraphist Larkin's misdeeds were with them yet.

So were someone else's. Cameron was back on his scan of the sea when there was a shout from aft, then a high scream, clear above the sound of the wind and water and as Cameron

135

turned towards the quarterdeck he saw Chief Petty Officer Stace going aft at the double, one hand reaching for the lifeline. Stace vanished beyond the splinter screen, then reappeared, cupping his hands.

'It's that Aldridge, sir! Gone berserk, sir!'

13

A lot had been building up in Aldridge's head. He was still desperately seasick and weak from lack of food, which didn't help. His mind roved here and there around his own misfortunes; even the euphoria of his shooting down a German aircraft hadn't lasted. He knew he would never do that again and he knew he had done it only by accident. Cold and miserable and sick, shaking like a leaf inside his duffel-coat, he had kept on thinking about that BBC news broadcast. Balham verged on Clapham, after all, and home was in fact more or less on Balham's brink. The news reader had mentioned only Balham but that wasn't much comfort; he had specified only the cinema and that wasn't much comfort either. You couldn't name every street, every corner shop and so on that might have been hit. A cinema, a place of entertainment, was different. His mother could have been killed or injured for all he knew and there was no way of finding out. Even if she hadn't been directly involved she would be in a state of shock or something, and needing him home.

Aldridge's fists clenched. If it hadn't been for Cameron. . . .

If it hadn't been for Cameron making decisions he had no right to make when he'd had his orders, the *Glenshiel* would have been safe in Rosyth, inwards of the Forth Bridge, and he could have gone ashore and sent a telegram or telephoned Mum's friend Mr Sands for information. Then if necessary he could have got compassionate leave and gone south to the Smoke.

137

But not as things were.

His mind had begun to feel like a sort of fiery furnace, all red and painful inside. Leading Seaman Maloney and the way he was always getting at him, Petty Officer Clutch who was a real bully, the appalling life aboard the *Glenshiel*, the cold and the wet and the stench along the messdeck that worsened the seasickness, the horrible experience of sitting with his trousers down in heads that were largely blocked but still in disgusting use, the coarseness of his companions who were just about the most common people he'd ever come across in his whole life. And everything seemed to boil up to a head when Petty Officer Clutch appeared round the starboard side of the quarterdeck and found him huddled in the shelter of the buckled splinter screen, staring out at nothing.

'Come on, come on, come on!' Clutch said. 'What you at, then, eh?'

'Nothing, PO, I –'

'Nothing. Which is just as I thought. What you *supposed* to be doing, Mister bloody Aldridge?' Clutch's harsh voice beat out at him, the dark, bony face was thrust forward belligerently. 'When you're not on watch in the forenoon, my lad, you work part-of-ship –'

'I know all that,' Aldridge said through set teeth.

Clutch's eyes widened. 'Don't you talk back to me, Ordinary Seaman Aldridge, or I'll run you in so bloody fast your feet won't touch the deck, you bloody little nancy boy, you.'

'Shut up!' Aldridge yelped for the second time in a shortish while. He was approaching frenzy now.

Clutch's head jerked back; he looked almost pleased at the way Aldridge had delivered himself into his hands. 'That does it,' he said. 'Get for'ard – on the bridge. Got you now, I have!'

'I can't take any more. I'll go mad. This ship . . . all the people in it. The bloody sea. Being sick.' Aldridge's voice broke. 'There was a raid on Balham, didn't you hear the broadcast, PO?'

'So what? Bugger Balham.'

'My home's there. My mother. Close, anyway.'

Clutch sneered. 'Mummy's little diddums, then. You're supposed to be a man now, sonny boy. Mummy's in the past.'

138

That did it: she very well might be. Aldridge had learned enough about being a seaman to know that you wore your seaman's knife handy for use, on a lanyard secured outside whatever you happened to be wearing. Aldridge grabbed for it and opened the blade before Clutch, who would never have thought him capable of hitting back, had realized what he was doing. Aldridge lunged with the knife and just in time Clutch saw it and brought up his arm in self-defence. The knife went through his oilskin, into the flesh. The TI yelled blue murder and backed away. Aldridge, aghast now at what he'd done, gave a scream of terror and collapsed on the deck.

ii

'GOD damn and blast!' Cameron said savagely as he saw the procession making its way along the iron-deck for the bridge ladder. As if the war and the current chase weren't enough; but a captain had many extraneous things to endure. This one looked nasty. There was no room aboard a destroyer for a berserk seaman. The procession, led by Chief Petty Officer Stace, looking very official, reached the foot of the ladder. Clutch and Aldridge remained in the lower bridge wing by the port-side close-range weapons. CPO Stace advanced to the forebridge alone, with a clipboard and charge sheet in his left hand. He saluted the Captain.

'Well, Cox'n?'

Stace cleared his throat. 'Beg pardon, sir. I thought I'd cut through the routine and have a word, sir – in the circumstances I thought – '

'Yes, all right, Cox'n. Let's have it straight.'

'Aye, aye, sir.' Another clearing of the throat. 'Petty Officer Clutch, sir, attacked with a knife by Ordinary Seaman Aldridge. That's it in brief.' Stace elaborated a little, telling Cameron about Aldridge's mother. 'TI, he wants a charge of attempted murder, sir.'

'Balls!'

Stace gave a brief grin. 'Yes, sir. Up to a point, sir, that is. If the blade had struck different, it might have been murder.'

'Perhaps. But I doubt if that was the intent.'

'Comes to the same thing, sir.' Stace paused. 'If I might

suggest it, sir, the charge could be bodily harm. Assault on a superior officer.'

'Will that satisfy Clutch?'

Stace said stolidly, 'It could be made to, sir.' The eyes of Captain and coxswain met in understanding. Clutch could be persuaded not to make too much trouble. The TI was largely wind and piss like the barber's cat, but at the same time there was a viciousness in him that couldn't be disregarded; Cameron had to take that into account. He had no wish to see Aldridge charged with attempted murder, which would probably mean referral to the civil power on their return to port and then a long prison sentence, one that a personality like Aldridge's might not survive. On the other hand he had the discipline of his ship to consider; this was no time for the ship's company to write the Captain down as soft and by this time murder would be on the lips of every man aboard. Meanwhile King's Regulations were being torn in shreds. Aldridge and Clutch should have gone before the Officer of the Watch in the first place. Strictly, the Captain had no business to pre-judge the issue or even to hear evidence not given in front of the accuser and accused. But things were not always done in such strict accordance with KR's. War and its exigencies stretched many a point and Stace, in the circumstances as he had said, had done right in Cameron's view.

Cameron proposed to take advantage of that.

He said, 'If Aldridge is brought up as a defaulter on an assault charge now, it's obvious what will have to be done – isn't it?'

Stace nodded. 'Restraint, sir. Cells.'

'Exactly. And I'm not having a man in cells with the *Attila* possibly not far away.'

'Yes, sir.' Stace wasn't going to help any further; necks could be stuck out too far, even with a decent skipper like Lieutenant-Commander Cameron.

'Defer it, Cox'n. He can be brought up when this lot's over. Pacify Clutch and assure him it won't be left where it is.'

'It's unorthodox, sir.' Stace was bound to point that out.

'I know,' Cameron said with a grin. 'Put it down to the fact I'm RNVR if you like. As to Aldridge . . . put him on the sick list. In the absence of the doctor I'll take the medical decision that he's unbalanced. He's to be confined to a cabin . . . Mr Whyman will volunteer to turn his cabin over as a sick-bay annexe. How's that?'

Stace said, 'Not what would be done aboard the *Duke of York*, sir, but we'll make it work out somehow.' He paused, then added, 'I don't think Aldridge'll give any more trouble, sir. Right now he's like a rag doll and crying his eyes out.'

'And Clutch?'

Stace rolled his eyes heavenward. 'An angry PO, sir, very angry.'

'I meant his arm.'

'Sorry, sir. Bleeding, sir. Or was. I put a bandage on it just in case, like, but it's not serious.'

'We'll have to see it's kept clean, Cox'n.' Cameron lowered his voice. 'In your opinion . . . do you think Clutch asked for this?'

'In my opinion, sir,' Stace answered, 'yes. But – '

'Yes, all right, I realize it doesn't alter the charge or give Aldridge an excuse, but it could be a reason, which is a different matter. Thank you, Cox'n.'

'Sir!' Stace saluted again and turned about. Cameron listened to his feet clattering down the ladder from the bridge, then watched the procession making its way aft along the iron-deck. He resumed his binocular vigil of the horizon, looking out for what would be the doubly welcome sight of the heavy cruisers. Not that he would or could off-load his responsibilities vis-à-vis defaulters on to Rear-Admiral Moreton, but the latter's proximity might be more than handy if worse should happen and at least he might, if the exigencies of the chase permitted which in fact they probably wouldn't, be able to ask for a medical officer to be sent across for a proper assessment of Aldridge's mental state. That there was something wrong Cameron had little doubt; he had kept an eye whenever possible on Aldridge and he was not unaware of a certain amount of hazing on the part of Maloney and Clutch. That could get on a weak rating's mind; and Aldridge was far from happy at sea in any case. Then there was the mother: Cameron could sympathize – but it was the same for them all. There might well be other men in the ship with families in Clapham or Balham or parts adjacent, and those

141

from Portsmouth and Plymouth, Liverpool and Glasgow, Bristol and other places faced a constant nag of anxiety also. They didn't stick knives in petty officers. Nevertheless there were extenuating circumstances. Perhaps he was avoiding the issue, shirking it, but Cameron hoped he could delay any formal charge until they were back in port and Aldridge could be landed to a base hospital for a medical check and report. Sometimes procrastination was the better option. In the meantime, although he could have asked Hastings for pusser RN advice, he proposed to do no such thing. There was a rigidity about the RN mind that would see only King's Regulations and Admiralty Instructions and Hastings would think Father had taken leave of his senses. All he did was to send down for the First Lieutenant and put him in the picture, the tone of his voice conveying plainly that he didn't wish to discuss the matter further. Hastings was obviously dubious, but co-operative. A seaman would be placed outside the sick cabin as a sentry.

'What about Whyman?' Cameron asked.

Hastings said, 'I'll fix him up, sir. Hammock in what's left of the wardroom flat.'

'Draughty! But so it is up here. Make my apologies to the mid, please, Number One.'

'Just part of a snotty's lot,' Hastings said. He looked critically at Cameron. 'How about a relieve decks, sir? You look as though you've had enough for a while.'

'I'm all right – but thanks all the same. The *Attila* won't hold off while I take a zizz,' he added.

Hastings said with a grin, 'I'm beginning to think the *Attila* doesn't bloody well exist!'

Something of the same sentiment, however at odds with the known facts, was insinuating itself throughout the lower deck. Surely by now there should have been some sort of contact, even if only by the reconnaissance aircraft? Ships didn't just vanish; and time was closing in – for both sides. The *Attila* couldn't leave her attack until the targets were safe in the shelter of home waters and every turn of the screws was bringing the convoy and the liners nearer home. If anything at all was going to happen, then it had to come soon, as the Buffer remarked in the petty officers' mess.

'Can't afford to crap on the doorstep,' he said. 'I don't like it, I tell you that for free.'

'What don't you like, Buff?' This was PO Clutch.

Ruckle shrugged. 'Just a feeling. Jerries are up to something.'

Clutch jeered. 'We all know that, don't we?'

'I mean something we've not cottoned on to yet.'

'Like what?'

'Dunno. I said, just a feeling.'

'Feeling your age,' the TI said indifferently, 'like Tarbuck.'

'Nothing wrong with Mr Tarbuck.' There was a slight emphasis on the Mr. Any warrant officer had earned the right to that, and the torpedo-gunner was a good old stick in Ruckle's view even if there was a slight aura of the prehistoric. 'How's the arm, TI?'

'Arm's all right.'

'What's going to happen about Aldridge?'

'*Subjudice*,' Clutch said briefly. 'Can't discuss it.'

'Ah. Sorry I spoke, I'm sure.' Ruckle shot a close look at the TI. Clutch was in one of his moods: he wanted to see Aldridge get the full weight of the Articles of War and be shot from the mouth of a 16-inch or something. In the meantime Aldridge, poor little bugger, was being a bloody nuisance, taking up two seamen working watch-and-watch as loony guard when they were already short of hands to work part-of-ship and maintain the sea watches. Better if he'd been shoved in the *Glenshiel*'s single tiny cell, but the 'swain had said the skipper didn't want him to be blown up helpless by the *Attila*, and Ruckle didn't disagree with that – and the cell would have needed a sentry anyway, sure enough. Still, if Aldridge was going to go berserk again then he'd have been a sight safer in a proper cell. Aldridge brought a touch of unease to the ship. He could do anything in Baby Face Whyman's cabin: smash it up, set fire to it if he found the means of ignition, break out past the sentry, anything. And the TI, Ruckle was certain, was the cause of it all.

Which was precisely the thought of Ordinary Seaman Aldridge himself as he lay on the midshipman's vacated bunk and shook as if he had the plague.

None of it was fair. He'd been got at, goaded, and now God

143

knew what he faced. He'd heard that Clutch speak about attempted murder, and of course it hadn't been that at all, not really, it had been just that he'd lost control and couldn't help himself. He was appalled by what he'd done. And in doing it he had delivered himself into the hands of the enemy, not the Germans but the whole might and godhead of the Navy, which could crush out an OD like a beetle and never feel the squirming underfoot. Cameron . . . they said he was a decent bloke, but the fact remained he was an officer, and officers, while unpredictable on some points, were predictable on others. Always they stuck by the chief and petty officers, maintaining discipline; they never believed the junior ratings. Aldridge was convinced he was done for; at best prison loomed and what would be the effect on Mum?

But she might not be alive to know.

Tears streamed down Aldridge's face. All the past came back, making him choke. The earliest memories, the happy memories, were all of his mother rather than his father, who hadn't had much time for him and seemed to resent him. Mum taking him protestingly to school, which he'd hated – all the bullying, about which Mum had protested to the school only to be ignored. After two terms she'd taken him away and sent him to a private prep school, where the other boys had been a load of snobs and he'd had no friends. Mum had dried his tears and soothed him but his father had been mostly in a filthy temper because of the school fees and once the secondary stage had been reached it had been back to the council school. Life had not been easy; if it hadn't been for his mother it would have been impossible. Mum was his sheet anchor, his unwavering support. When his call-up papers had come she'd protested and tried to get him out of it. Fat lot of good that had been . . . all the country thought about was war and collecting everyone's iron railings and whatnot to turn into shell cases.

Outside the cabin, the seaman on guard was relieved by another: Ordinary Seaman Nye.

Aldridge got off the bunk and went to the door. He was able to speak through the slats of the jalousie in the top half and see Nye's outline as he stood there with a rifle and bayonet.

144

'Nye,' he said.

'Yer? Not supposed to talk to you.' Nye sounded dead scared; discipline again.

'For Christ's sake. Look, you heard any more news broadcasts, have you?'

'Yer.'

'Anything about Balham or Clapham? That raid?'

'Didn't hear it if there was, mate. Sorry. I don't reckon there was. Do me a favour and pipe down, will you?'

His hands shaking, Aldridge moved back from the door. No more news. Well, there wouldn't be, of course. They didn't care; it was nothing to Bruce Belfrage and he would have other raids to report. Once a raid had taken place it was out of the news, part of history. The dead were dead; from then on it became private business. Information would be sent to the next of kin, but he wouldn't be told out at sea. He knew his mind was becoming inflamed more and more, it was like a red mist surrounding his brain, nothing he could do about it. Later that day food was brought by a seaman acting as cook of his mess, 'cook' being strictly a misnomer since the cooks of the messes only prepared the food which was then cooked in the galley: bully beef hotted up into a stew, and a mug of cocoa.

The rating was accompanied by Petty Officer West. 'Any complaints, lad?' West asked formally.

Aldridge shook his head; he had plenty but it wouldn't be any use mentioning them, and the sort of complaints he wanted to make were not what West was after.

West hovered, scratching his face uncertainly. Poor little bleeder, he'd never been the sort to go to sea, he'd have been better off in the Army where they'd have found him a soft billet as a clerk or something when they discovered he wasn't fighting material. There was more scope in the Army for that sort, while in a ship everyone was in it together. West said, his voice rough with a kind of embarrassment, 'Chin up, lad. It's never as bad as you think. Look on the bright side, eh? You're a sight warmer and drier down here. That's something.'

Aldridge didn't speak; he just sat with his head in his hands, the picture of misery. West shrugged and left the cabin and the door was shut again, with Ordinary Seaman Dawlish on sentry duty now. Dawlish had the voice of an officer . . .

he wouldn't risk talking through the jalousie. Dawlish was a cw candidate, one of those up for a commission, and he wouldn't put a foot wrong to help his grandmother over a stile. No use asking Dawlish for the latest buzz about the outside world – about the *Attila*, and their own future movements with which Aldridge was much concerned because once they entered port, if ever they did, then the heavens would drop on him.

Fifteen minutes after PO West had left the cabin, the *Glenshiel*, now out into clear weather, swung hard over to starboard, an emergency turn by the feel of it, and from above his head Aldridge heard the thump and crash of the after 4.7 going into action, firing even before the urgent sound of the alarm rattlers blasted into the cabin flat.

14

THE waters north and west of Scotland, if apparently empty in the vicinity of the lone destroyer, had been constantly watched through the binoculars of the Officers of the Watch and the signalmen and lookouts from perhaps more ships than had ever before been at sea together on closing courses. The *Queen Elizabeth* and *Queen Mary*, steaming at more than thirty knots for the Bloody Foreland, the HX convoy plodding along with its heavy escort on the altered track for the Fastnet and up enclosed waters to the Firth of Clyde, the cruisers of CS27 acting as a shadowing force that had not yet found its quarry, and the *Attila, Recklinghausen* and *Darmstadt* now proceeding fast in obedience to the decision of Vice-Admiral Fichtner: the first target was to be the convoy. The *Queen Elizabeth* and *Queen Mary* could be left for the time being. They had sailed from North America after the convoy and as yet were a fair distance off the British Isles. Once he had dealt with the convoy and its escort, Fichtner would detach one of his heavy cruisers to sink the big liners, thus complying with all his Führer's wishes. It was not necessary to be in attendance himself when two unescorted and helpless targets were sent to the bottom. A salvo apiece and that would be that and he would be glad enough not to have to be witness to the discharge of an unpleasant duty. And he had no doubt that the liners would continue to be unescorted although on a handful of past occasions either the *Queen Mary* or the *Queen Elizabeth* had been provided with an escort of light cruisers, fast certainly but of pathetic gun-power – there had been the occasion when the *Queen Mary* had cut into the light cruiser *Curacao*, sinking her as she cut across the liner's bow on the zig-zag. Currently such an escort would be known to be useless and the British had in any case nothing that could match the *Recklinghausen* or the *Darmstadt*, while the Admiral commanding the convoy's own escort would have nothing fast enough to be of the slightest use if detached to join the liners, whose speed would never be reduced so as to fit with the steaming limitations of the slow old battleships.

Fichtner however had to take into account the movements, unknown to him currently, of the British 27th Cruiser Squadron. Its commander might decide, or be ordered by the Admiralty, to place himself across the line of advance of the Queens thus acting as an extended screen into which Ficht-ner's detached cruiser might steam and be engaged, but that was one of the imponderables and would have to be accepted if it happened. In point of fact the 27th Cruiser Squadron might be anywhere. . . .

The point had been raised when Fichtner conferred with his staff officers. Captain Sefrin had made much of the British cruisers. After the convoy had been mauled, he said, both the *Recklinghausen* and the *Darmstadt* should be detached to the next target.

'One alone might not get through, Herr Admiral. Three British cruisers – and the Führer will expect total success, Herr Admiral.'

Always the Führer! Fichtner said irritably, 'Even the Führer will understand that totality is not always possible, Captain Sefrin.'

'But to lose a heavy cruiser, Herr Admiral, even to risk such a loss when two could have been sent to make victory certain . . . the Führer is not always fully understanding of the difficulties facing high command at sea. I would by no means say that the Führer was unreasonable, of course, but. . . .' Sefrin shrugged eloquently and lifted his hands palms uppermost. There was no need to say more and what he had already said was extremely risky, but any defeat would be much more so and it happened that the representative of the

Gestapo was not currently present on the Admiral's bridge, a fact that loosened tongues a little.

Fichtner played safe nevertheless. 'Certainly not unreasonable, Captain Sefrin – '

'By no means, Herr Admiral.'

'There are many strains upon him. Brilliant men are often nervous and highly-strung. Heil, Hitler.'

'Heil, Hitler.' All the staff responded.

'I'm not unaware . . . you have made a point, Captain, and I have noted it. I shall make my final decision on that when I have seen the outcome of the first attack. We cannot assume that we shall have no losses in the course of that attack.' Fichtner moved across his bridge to where charts of the North Atlantic from the Denmark Strait and Cape Farewell to the British Isles had been laid out for him by his fleet navigator. The current estimated positions of the targets had been indicated by pencilled crosses inside small circles: the HX convoy was some eight hundred miles due west of the *Attila*'s position, its course a little south of east. At their combined closing speeds – that of the convoy having of necessity to be estimated – they should meet in not much more than sixteen hours once the *Attila* was able to increase speed in clearer weather. The *Queen Elizabeth*, with the *Queen Mary* a day's steaming astern of her, was as yet thirteen hundred miles out in the ocean wastes, which put her some twenty hours' steaming time currently from the *Attila* assuming she maintained her course. Plenty of time left after dealing with the convoy: Fichtner knew his decision had been a good one. He issued his final orders for the first attack.

'All ships will go to action stations when I am within two hours' steaming time of the estimated position of the convoy, Captain Sefrin. We cannot be certain of the British dispositions, but I expect the *Revenge* to be in the van of the escort – that is, behind the extended destroyer screen. With her I expect to find the aircraft-carrier, the *Furious*. Both are old and useless in modern warfare, and can be destroyed by a salvo apiece. I shall assume the *Resolution* to be in the rear of the convoy. The cruisers, of course, will be disposed along the beam to port and starboard and will attack our flanks as we move in among the ships of the convoy after sinking the old

149

battleships – the *Resolution* will have no more capacity than the *Revenge* to withstand our superior gunfire. I anticipate little difficulty unless Admiral Fraser with the British Home Fleet has joined the convoy. This I consider, as I have said before, to be unlikely. Fraser will be searching for us, to intercept us before we have the convoy at our mercy. That is the British strategy, as we have seen already since the outbreak of the war. And I believe I have fooled Fraser, who will have no idea that already we are so close to the convoy. Also, the British are besotted by the prestige of the *Queen Mary* and the *Queen Elizabeth*, and Fraser will have those ships especially in mind.'

'Then, Herr Admiral, when the attack is made on them – '

'By that time, Captain Sefrin, Fraser will have hastened to the assistance of the convoy.'

Sefrin seemed about to say something further, but changed his mind. The Admiral's tone had been firm and dismissive of any more argument; and he could well be proved right. If he was, then any demur on the part of the Flag Captain could be attributed afterwards to a lack of zeal, even to cowardice. But in his heart Sefrin believed Fichtner to have made a wrong assessment. The battleships of the convoy's escort might be old and slow, leaking like sieves as they were said to be, and held together by tarpaulins and collision mats and pieces of string, but at least some of the battleships of the main British Home Fleet were modern and fast even though their potential couldn't be compared with that of the great *Attila*. If Fichtner's guesses, and they were no more than that, were indeed wrong then the *Attila* could just conceivably be in for a mauling by the heavy units of the Home Fleet and a battered *Attila* could be forced to turn away and run for the shelter of a Norwegian or German port, and if that should happen then there would be no need for guesswork in assessing the Führer's reaction. All at once Captain Sefrin found his confidence evaporating: somebody, either the Führer or Grand Admiral Raeder, and you could take your choice which, had been guilty of overconfidence. Captain Sefrin began to see his decks running red with good Aryan blood. So far there had been a very great deal of luck; had it not been for the concealment offered by the appalling weather, the *Attila* and her cruisers would have been spotted long since and the British Home Fleet would have closed. But perhaps it was not just luck: the meteorologists certainly wouldn't be calling it that, and with their advice the all-knowing Führer had chosen his time well. One must beware of pessimism. The ships' companies were the pick of the German Fleet. There could be no doubt about it that they would fight magnificently; and before dismissing his staff officers Vice-Admiral Fichtner himself made this point. He said also that it was a splendidly useful fact that the British were always so stupidly predictable; that redounded much to the German success: the blindness on the part of the British, who had allowed Lieutenant Prien to penetrate the boom at Scapa Flow with his U-boat and sink the *Royal Oak*; the crass lunacy of the ill-fated British attack on Norway with their ships and troops; the British debacle at Dieppe, and many other instances. Listening, Captain Sefrin had a fanciful notion that the great Führer in the sky must have purposely made the British like that. . . .

Fichtner said, 'I believe my assessment of the British positions to be correct, Captain Sefrin, but there is still that one factor of which I am unsure and of which I have already spoken. The dispositions of the British cruisers, their 27th Squadron. The time has come to fly off a reconnaissance mission by our own aircraft. Please see to it that the pilot is briefed and the plane catapulted at once.'

Sefrin passed the orders. The *Attila* was still steaming through thick weather – surely it couldn't be laid across the whole of the North Atlantic? – and the launch would be tricky, as indeed it always was, even in good visibility. If the weather continued thick, the retrieval of the aircraft could well be impossible from an invisible ship, but the order had been given and that was that. One could scarcely bring the patently obvious to an admiral's attention. But Fichtner, sensing the doubt in his Flag Captain's mind, laid it to rest.

'We shall come into clear weather shortly, Captain Sefrin. The gales to the west of us will be blowing away the fog.'

The aircraft was catapulted away into the murk and the

sound of its engines died away somewhere ahead. The German warships moved on westerly, their engine-rooms ready to inject more oil-fuel into the furnaces the moment the order came down to increase speed and fling the mighty guns into the attack for which they had waited so long. Excitement surged along the messdecks and turrets, the shell-handling rooms, the flag decks and navigating bridges, even in the offices and storerooms and galleys whose personnel would, when action stations was blown by the bugles, desert pens and tins of peas and potato-peeling machines to take their part in what was to be the most devastating and far-reaching action by any battleship, German or British, in the whole of the war to date. While the *Attila* sailed the seas, all-powerful, invincible, unsinkable, no Allied convoy would ever again dare to come across the North Atlantic. The losses from U-boats and aircraft attack had already been cruelly heavy; in the future every convoy would be shattered totally, and the British would starve. The men of the *Attila*, the *Recklinghausen* and the *Darmstadt* would return to Germany as heroes, feted, honoured, marched with their glorious battle ensigns along the Unter den Linden, triumphant, acclaimed by hysterical crowds, by the Führer himself. Their fame, if the Reich should last a thousand years, would never fade.

ii

ABOVE the lonely *Glenshiel*, the spotter plane from the *Attila* flew high, well out of range. The destroyer's gunfire was useless and there was no point in wasting ammunition after the first instinctive reaction.

Cameron ordered the cease fire, stared up at the German.

'We'll be reported,' he said unnecessarily. 'From now on, we stay closed up.'

Hastings said, 'I doubt if they'll bother too much about us, sir. Even from up there, we won't appear to have much potential as a threat. Just one destroyer with pretty obvious damage isn't going to worry the *Attila* a lot.'

There was no response from Cameron. Hastings, frowning, peered closer. Cameron was sitting on the high chair, like a nursery chair that took the weight off the feet and gave the Captain a clear view over the bridge screen. Hastings glanced round, caught Millard's eye. Millard grinned and said, 'He's asleep, Number One. Been doing it on and off . . . I wouldn't wake him. He's got to have a zizz now and again, and he's all about when he has to be.'

'Bloody fool,' Hastings said, but said it tolerantly. 'No one can push themselves for ever and get away with it.'

'I am not,' Cameron said distinctly, 'a bloody fool, Number One.'

'Sorry, sir. I didn't know you'd woken up.'

'And don't put *that* in the log. Captains aren't supposed to go to sleep on watch, are they?' He turned and grinned.

'Extenuating circumstances,' Hastings said. 'A captain's never on watch, strictly speaking. Just always on duty, which is a different kettle of fish.'

'You have a soothing influence, Number One.' As if by some automatic reflex Cameron took up his binoculars again and stared around sea and sky. The aircraft had flown off on an easterly course. Cameron said, 'That wasn't one of the shore-based boys. Embarked spotter aircraft.'

'From the *Attila*?'

'Probably. Unless the Germans have sent out more heavy ships in support. I'm going to assume it's the *Attila* or one of the heavy cruisers. If I'm right, we have a fair guide as to where she's lurking. Agree?'

'Don't know, sir.' Hastings frowned into the now-empty sky. 'The pilot could be laying a red herring as it were.'

Cameron nodded. 'Could be, I suppose. But he'll have to be watching his fuel, I'd have thought. I've a hunch the *Attila*'s not so far off.'

'And that she's to the east of us.'

'Yes.'

'Enough of a hunch to break wireless silence, sir?' Hastings asked.

'No. Not yet, Number One. I don't want to confuse the issue by jumping the gun on a hunch, even if that means I'm not backing my own judgment. I want a sight of her first, and we could get that any moment.' He waved a hand towards the bank of dirty weather, now some ten miles to the eastward. 'If

153

the Germans are moving in to attack as we expect, then it can't be long before they show.'

Millard, from behind the binnacle, said, 'If they're there, I reckon that's right, sir.' Like Vice-Admiral Fichtner, Millard had done his sums. He, too, placed the convoy around two hundred miles to the west of his current position and his estimate of its speed had told him that within forty-eight hours the merchant ships and their escorts would come under the umbrella of Coastal Command and additional escorts – if they were available – from the UK ports. The *Attila* could not afford more delay; but the Captain could be wrong and the Germans might be far to the north or south for all anyone could say for sure. It was to be presumed that C-in-C Home Fleet and even the shore-bound brass of the Admiralty were equally in the dark; the signal traffic picked up on the repaired W/T had continued to consist entirely of routines, no operational signals at all being made. This wasn't surprising if the *Attila* had lurked throughout in the fog and then the snow. The Germans were being accorded a monstrous advantage, the ability to lurk like a tiger in cover, and then pounce at speed across a narrow gap before the defence had time to re-dispose its forces to the succour of the convoy. Everything would then be up to the escort, those elderly, worn-out capital ships and a handful of cruisers and destroyers.

Cameron's mind seemed to have been working along lines similar to Millard's, and the navigator understood what he meant when he said suddenly, 'Just us now – if the *Attila*'s close. Unless CS27's handy, it's just us between the Jerries and the rest.'

'We'll cope,' Millard said. 'God knows how – but we'll cope!' You had at least to sound confident; anything less, and the whole ship's company could become affected. The forebridge was the nerve centre of the ship, and the lower deck, however disrespectful the *sotto voce* comment could often be in regard to officers, still tended to believe that God lived there, especially at times like this. But Millard felt his stomach turn to water at the thought of what might happen so soon now, and inside himself he didn't believe for one moment that any of them were going to come through. This feeling was confirmed inside the next two minutes when the leading signalman made a report.

'Green six-oh, sir . . . masthead moving into view. Looks like the bloody Jerries, sir!'

15

'PORT twenty,' Cameron ordered. 'Emergency full ahead both engines.' He bent to the voice-pipe to the wireless office. 'Leading Telegraphist to take down a sighting report.'

The helm and engine orders went down to Chief Petty Officer Stace, at his action station on the wheel. His face was set: this was it now. The skipper was turning away in order to make his sighting report – if he was given time before the guns of the *Attila* opened. Below in the engine-room Mr Bream felt the shake and judder of his engines as the shafts came up to full spin and sent the destroyer surging through the restless water. The confused sea that he'd noted when last on deck was with them still and might help to throw off the radar and the aim of the German gunnery control officers in their high fighting-tops – the old *Glenshiel* was a small enough target.

As so often before Mr Bream thought of his wife. This time, she did look like being a widow; never before had Mr Bream had the feeling so strongly. It was as though fate had made a signal in advance, a preliminary shortly to be followed by the executive. A lot of the past went through his mind at great speed, quite automatic as he watched his dials and gauges and kept an eye on the telegraph from the bridge while the destroyer reeled from side to side as Cameron made frequent alterations of course to make it harder for the enemy to lay and train. In Bream's past lay sins of omission and commission vis-à-vis his missus: often he hadn't been loving enough, had displayed temper and a lack of understanding

156

and sometimes he'd been mean. Worse: when younger and doing a spell with the China Squadron in the old *Sussex* there had been a Chinese girl in Hong Kong, slant-eyed and attentive, who'd thought chief engine-room artificers, which he'd then been, were wonderful and mysterious and romantic. Or so she'd said. It hadn't lasted long because he was none of those things and she'd moved on to a commissioned signal bosun, whose little bit of gold lace worked miracles for an ageing mariner. Now Mr Bream, who had forgotten her rather involved name and thought of her facetiously as Who Flung Dung, was mindful, in what he believed would prove his last few moments on earth, of his infidelity. It was late to ask forgiveness, but he did so all the same, in the midst of the thump and shudder of his engines and the mouthed blasphemies of CERA Downs as the latter slid about the greasy deck plating each time the *Glenshiel* swung hard to port or starboard.

Any minute now. . . .

ii

'MAKE to Admiralty, repeated C-in-C Home Fleet, CS27, Commodore HX68 and Senior Officer of the escort in *Revenge*: *Have enemy in sight in position 56 degrees 38 minutes north, 38 degrees 10 minutes west*. That's all, Hunter. Make it in plain language.'

'Aye, aye, sir.'

'Don't lose any time. She'll open any moment.'

Cameron lifted his binoculars towards the German squadron. For some reason or other they hadn't opened yet and the range was increasing all the time. Maybe they would get away with it. But even as he thought that, one of the German cruisers, he wasn't sure whether it was the *Recklinghausen* or the *Darmstadt*, opened fire. There were puffs of smoke from her turrets and soon after there came the express-train sound overhead. Spouts leaped up from the water on either beam. Cameron twisted and turned, keeping up a solitary zig-zag, moving at his high speed between the shells as they took the water, increasing the distance. Within the next three minutes the bridge was called by the wireless office.

157

'Message passed, sir!'

'Well done, Hunter.' Now it didn't matter so much – not to the chase anyway. The *Attila* had been flushed out and reported. In the meantime the Germans were not mounting a chase of their own: they were maintaining their course, not closing. They would have picked up the transmission, of course, and would know the score. Now they would be concentrating on reaching their target as fast as possible before the defending forces could close in. It was a case of first things first, and *Glenshiel* was redundant to the German tactics now. Inside another four minutes the response to his signal came from the Admiralty: someone there was awake and taking notice, a miracle in itself. It was a one-word signal addressed only to the Glenshiel: *Shadow*.

'Which is what I'm doing,' Cameron said with a grin. 'Or will be doing as long as possible.' That might not be for very long, in fact: to shadow he would have to remain within sighting distance of the enemy and it must be only a question of time before he was sunk if he did that. But there were other ways of remaining in contact, ways that carried a lesser risk though they would be a lot less effective than if he'd still had his radar. Cameron spoke to the navigator. 'Pilot, I'm maintaining my course away out of range. I'll nip back in at intervals for a look-see. It's the best we can do.'

Millard nodded. Talk about overwhelming odds . . . heroism was all right, but useless foolhardiness was another thing and one destroyer remaining inside the gunnery range of a battleship and two heavy cruisers simply was not on. You couldn't shadow once you'd been sunk. 'Sheepdog effect, sir?'

'Not exactly. More like a keeper, watching the poachers from cover. It could have the effect of rattling the Germans into thinking there's more of us around.'

Millard said, 'Yes, it might. For what it's worth, sir.'

'Keep 'em guessing,' Cameron said. Back to the binoculars as the German ships dropped astern. There was distant smoke and a ripple of flashes as one of the cruisers fired a last salvo, but Cameron's zig-zag tactics were working well and the *Glenshiel* remained unhit. The day was darkening now, the short northern day, and that helped. They were going to live to fight on. Cameron tried to assess the broader movements of the British defence. Where would Sir Bruce Fraser be now, with the main weight of the Home Fleet, where was cs27? Much depended on the current positions of those two formations, the Home Fleet capital ships especially. Even *Nelson* was far from fast: twenty-three knots flat out, very little more than the *Revenge* and *Resolution* with the convoy. But her 16-inch guns could be effective enough once she was within range. Would Fraser slow his fleet in order to carry the slow coaches with him, or would he steam at his maximum and rely on the guns of the *Duke of York*? His overall tactics must surely be to place his ships across the convoy's line of advance, between them and the German squadron. Fichtner would know this, and was presumably confident that he could blast his way through the screen. On the other hand he might alter course in an attempt to outmanoeuvre the Home Fleet and come up in rear. If so, then he might move north for the purpose, or he might move south.

The *Glenshiel*'s shadowing was vital, at least until the RAF reconnaissance aircraft had picked up the *Attila*'s reported position. But no RAF showed. Too dark already? And they were being pursued by the dirty weather still. All the luck was with the German ships. Hastings, coming to the bridge after a tour of inspection below, was scathing about the lack of air support that had been a feature of the chase all along.

'Another cock-up,' he said. 'You'd think they'd be able to pull their fingers out for a special occasion!'

Cameron agreed wholeheartedly, but said, 'We shouldn't be too critical, Number One. We don't know all the facts. Goering may have laid on his own support – saturation raids on the airfields to stop take-off, something like that.'

'Or their compasses are all pointing the wrong way.'

Cameron grinned into the encroaching darkness. It was a diverting thought, to visualize the Brylcreem Boys all haring flat out in the wrong direction, heading down for Freetown and not realizing it, but this was no time for humour. The enemy was out and not far off his target by this time.

Time. That was now the nub of the whole show.

Cameron looked at the luminous dial of his wrist-watch:

1550 hours, and now almost full dark. The British ships would have a good seventeen hours of that cloaking darkness . . . so would the *Attila*, who would carry out her attack during the night, making it all a more hideous encounter. Night always confused an action, and the advantage would lie with the attacker as it always did. So many targets, so many warships that could end up firing at their own side once the *Attila* was through the screen and in amongst the merchant ships. Of course, the convoy would scatter, but scattering was not a panacea for every ship.

Cameron looked fore and aft along his decks, the long, dark shadow of the ship cutting through the water. She still had her engines, still had her speed – but that was about all. One 4.7-inch gun was laughable . . . no radar, and a jagged hole in the after screen, a shattered wardroom, a depleted ship's company, and her torpedo-tubes. That summed it up. But one thing in particular nagged at Cameron's mind as once again he turned his ship towards the *Attila* in order to maintain his contact, though by now she would be getting much harder to pick up: flat out, he had a knot or two over and above the speed of the Germans. Something might be made of that.

iii

WHEN *Glenshiel*'s sighting report reached Admiral Fraser to the south of the Denmark Strait the main body of the Home Fleet, allowing for the poor speed of the oldies, was some seven hours' steaming from the estimated position of the convoy. Immediately upon receipt of the intelligence, Fraser turned the fleet one hundred and eighty degrees to the south to cut across the convoy's course. Once again, the time factor was crucial: speed had to be of more importance than gun-power. If they didn't get there in time, the presence of every modern battleship in the British Navy wouldn't help.

'All other heavy ships to detach and follow,' Fraser ordered as he increased speed to full. 'It'll be ship to ship when we get there. *Duke of York* against *Attila*. Whoever gets the first hit in will have the initial advantage and that's going to count.'

160

He passed orders that the gunnery control officers were to open without orders from the bridge the moment the radar raised the *Attila* and her consorts. It could be taken for granted that nothing else as heavy as the Germans would be coming through on the expected bearing.

As the Home Fleet swung on to its new course the engines thrust onwards at full power, each Commander(E) on the starting platforms and giving the shafts all possible in the way of power. *Nelson*, with the other slow ships, was soon left behind, wallowing along in the hope of adding her immense gun-potential late but not not too late.

Aboard the *Revenge* south of the Home Fleet's position Rear-Admiral Horsted passed the word by blue-shaded signal lamp to the Commodore of the convoy: the scatter order would come within the next three hours. In the meantime the ships would remain on course and in convoy. Horsted didn't want them too widespread over the ocean, to become the easy prey of U-boats lurking and waiting their chance in better weather. Farther south still and as yet some way to the west of the convoy, *Glenshiel*'s report had been passed to the Masters of the *Queen Mary* and *Queen Elizabeth*. The great liners continued ahead at full speed; there was nothing else that could be done. Broadcasts were made to the packed US soldiers along the troop-decks; they were being kept fully informed. Hands felt for the assurance of the US Navy-issue lifejackets lying flat around their waists ready to be inflated by a half-turn of a fitting that would cause the small bottles of CO_2 to be pierced and blow them up like encircling balloons, or so many soda-siphons waiting for a fill. The mood was sombre: not long now, the party was over. Mostly the thoughts were of home – back in New York and Texas, West Virginia, Montana, Oregon . . . all over the United States. After a while a GI aboard the *Queen Mary* began singing in a low, melancholy voice a song that was taken up by a number of the men:

'Carry me back to old Virginny,
That's where the cotton and the corn and taters grow . . .
That's where I worked so hard for ole Massa
Day after day in the fields of yellow corn. . . .'

161

'Old Virginny' was a far better prospect than the cold, the bitter cold of the winter North Atlantic if the cookie should crumble that way, crumble them overboard from a sinking, shattered ship. There were plenty of men aboard the liners who trusted the British to see them through, but there were also plenty who hoped to the Almighty that the limeys knew what they were about.

iv

ALDRIDGE had been released on Cameron's order the moment the *Attila* had come into sight and he remained at liberty. He would remain thus until all danger was past, the risk being taken that he might cause trouble. But he was being watched closely and Cameron believed it unlikely he would do anything stupid again. The lesson had sunk in. Aldridge was like a jellyfish, no fight in him. He would be worse than useless as an effective member of the ship's company but that also had to be accepted even if in fact he proved to be a liability, which he probably would. Currently, at action stations, he was being employed on the searchlight platform: he couldn't do too much damage there, always provided he didn't illuminate the ship at the wrong moment, and up there he could be contained easily enough by Able Seaman Backhouse in charge of the searchlight. Backhouse was a beefy man in his middle thirties, unambitious, but dependable when it came to his seamanship duties, which was more than could be said of his general behaviour. Backhouse would have been a stripey had he been able to earn and keep his good-conduct badges, but he was too fond of the bottle and more often than not returned aboard from shore leave drunk as a fiddler's bitch. So he was in the curious position of being a badgeless stripey. But he was immensely tough and could be relied upon to sit, literally, on Aldridge if there was any panic or further signs of aggression towards Petty Officer Clutch.

Stace had already had a word with Clutch.

'Keep away from Aldridge,' he'd said.

'I didn't come down with the last shower, 'Swain.'

'Just a word of warning, that's all. Pass orders through a leading hand whenever that's possible.'

'Oh, yes!' The TI was sarcastic. 'I should think so! What comes first, safety of the ship, or bloody Aldridge's feelings, eh?'

Stace said patiently, 'I'm not going to argue the point, Reg.'

Clutch stumped away angrily. Some people! All the same, he'd taken the point, which was a valid one. If there was direct contact his own temper might get the better of him and if he clocked Aldridge one then the boot would be, as it were, on both feet at once, since it was just as much a crime for a PO to take a swipe at a junior rating as the other way round. He went aft to the depth charges and torpedo-tubes. All nice and handy – the only remaining 4.7 wasn't far from the charges or the tubes and he could keep an eye on everything at once. Aldridge included, as it happened; and if Aldridge put a foot wrong, coxswain or no coxswain, temper or no temper, then the lad was for it as a clincher. Clutch had a feeling the skipper was leaning over backwards to avoid the charge of assault; but if there was another charge he wouldn't be able to avoid it and then the ship would be rid of a useless article that let them all down by not pulling his weight.

Clutch shot his cuffs beneath his duffel-coat sleeves as he saw the dark outline of Mr Tarbuck coming aft from the bridge ladder, shambling along like a tenth-rate bear in a zoo and cannoning off the bulkhead as he swayed to the destroyer's heavy roll. The sea was up still, and breaking over the fo'c'sle head. The Gunner(T) was being pursued by dollops of North Atlantic.

Coming up, breathing heavily, he said, 'That you, TI?'

'It is, sir, yes.' Clutch's voice was brisk; maybe the old donkey was going blind now. But he seemed to be excited about something, and happy at the same time. He was almost rubbing his hands. Clutch asked, 'Anything on, is there?'

'You could say that. By gum you could! Three guesses, eh?'

The TI's lip curled; Tarbuck was like a kid at a party. 'There's a war on, sir,' he said.

Tarbuck stared. 'What?'

'Oh, never mind. But let's have it, eh? We haven't got all night. The *Attila* – '

'We've got the time all right, that is if everything's on the top line, which it is. I told the skipper so. There's no call to be sharp, Reg, you're in this as much as I am and it's going to be a big thing. Something I used to dream about . . . till I thought, well, me old lad, it's a blooming pity, but you're past it now. But I was wrong, see.'

Clutch looked at the elderly warrant officer closely; Clutch was beginning to have an inkling . . . and if the *Glenshiel* was to go into independent action largely under the aegis of old Tarbuck here, then God help them all. His mind was back in about 1916, probably thought he was still sailing under Jellicoe or Beatty.

'Well?' Clutch asked.

Tarbuck took a deep breath. The inkling had been spot on: Cameron intended to carry out an attack with torpedoes, using his slightly superior speed to close the great side of the *Attila* and then trust to luck thereafter, hoping to get the tin fish away and thus slow the *Attila* into the guns of the Home Fleet before the *Glenshiel* was ripped apart by the German armament.

His voice high with excitement as he saw a lifetime's dream coming into sharp focus, Tarbuck asked, 'What d'you think?'

Clutch exploded, loudly. 'Think? Christ above, I'm past bloody thinking, Mr Tarbuck! That bloke's gorn right round the bloody bend! This is bloody suicide!'

16

PERHAPS it was crazy: Cameron was prepared to concede the point if anyone had put it to him. But the purpose in life of a destroyer was to destroy, and the *Attila* was out there waiting to be destroyed. Cameron's mind had gone back a few years, as far back as Tarbuck's, to the days when destroyers had been known by their full classificaton of torpedo-boat destroyers. Well, the *Attila* was no torpedo-boat but the *Glenshiel* still had her full complement of tin fish, and battleships were notoriously susceptible to being struck by torpedoes. Even the anti-torpedo bulges along the sides of the British R-class and *Warspite*-class battleships were not a lot of use, their chief effect being to slow the vessels down.

It could be done, and Cameron was convinced of the absolute necessity of giving the Home Fleet time. And Tarbuck had backed him to the hilt. Tarbuck had said it could be done.

There were the warning voices, the cautious voices of Lieutenant Lyon and the First Lieutenant. They'd have to be lucky, Hastings said. True it could be done, but only if they could get under the Germans guns. They would be picked up instantly by the radar as they closed to the maximum torpedo range of some seven thousand yards and from that moment on everything would be flung at them. They would steam into the jaws of hell. The Germans must be at least half expectant of such an attack.

'Not necessarily,' Cameron said. 'They'll know our job's to shadow and report.'

'Not to be sunk?' Hastings asked, tongue-in-cheek.

165

Cameron shrugged. 'We all know the risks, Number One. But you've made a point as it happens. Maybe Fichtner won't be expecting us to be suicidal, bearing in mind the known importance of shadowing to the Admiralty . . . and if that's the case, then he'll see our approach as being no more than a recce probe.'

'Could be, sir. But the shadowing – you've just said that's important, which it is. So – '

'All right, Number One, I know what you're going to say. I've weighed all that. The end result of shadowing is sinking. To go in is more direct, that's all. And I believe it's much more important to slow her down than to keep tabs on her. We can take it the Admiralty will be moving to block her escape routes, so she'll be picked up whatever happens.'

Hastings was doubtful. 'Not enough heavy ships available, sir, not unless they bring some back from the Med – and there's obviously no time for that. I doubt if the Jerries are worried, anyway.' He blew out a long breath. 'Well, sir, it's worth a try, I suppose. Tarbuck's all in favour anyway!'

The Gunner(T) had left the bridge by this time, hurrying aft to pass the word to his torpedo party. Cameron said, 'It's mainly up to Mr Tarbuck. All I can do is to put the ship into position. Think he'll cope?' He had addressed the remark to Lyon, the gunnery officer. 'He's no chicken in body. I'm not too sure about the mind! He's going to have to react in a split second.'

'He'll do, sir. He lives torpedoes. Nothing he doesn't know. He'll aim and fire by instinct! It's going to be his big day.'

'Correction,' Cameron said. 'Big night. I'm going in now.'

ii

THE word was passed throughout the ship. The consensus of lower deck opinion was that the skipper was right even though he was once again about to disobey his specific orders. In a sense he had the *Attila* in his sights and there could be no doubt about the fact that to slow her down would put her at the mercy of the big ships when battle was joined. They all felt they were now about to steam into history

166

as the ship that saved a big HX convoy and the great Cunarders – that was, if they brought it off. In the first flush of excitement not many of the *Glenshiel's* company thought too much about what was likely to be their own fate. It would have been pointless to dwell on that since they were now committed for good or ill. Yet, as the orders went down to the engine-room and the wheelhouse and the ship swung in for the attack and the minutes passed towards what might well be eternity for some or all of them, there came a change, a period – one that wouldn't last beyond the point of action – almost of detachment from the reality of what was happening. Their training and experience held and there was no relaxation of alertness or efficiency but there was a part of each man's mind that had gone home across the sea's dark desolation to what had been left behind. Stace thought of his wife and wished her well; if she had to be a widow within the next hour or so, probably less, then let her go to Bert Cockshutt with his blessing. No point in being dog in the manger and if she could be happy as Mrs Cockshutt then so be it. There wouldn't even be any need for her to worry about the divorce he hadn't let her have. What in a funny way bothered Stace more than his domestic upsets was the fact that if the worst did happen advancement in the service would not now come and he wouldn't be getting that eventual commission he'd set his sights on.

Ruckle, Chief Bosun's Mate, thought about a happy family whom he might not see again. He knew just what his loss would mean to them, could see the shadow spreading over his home. There had been so much to look forward to, though you didn't ever look too far forward in wartime. You were always on the brink. Linda, his younger daughter, just sixteen, working in Woolworth's, her hopes set ahead to when she could join the WRNS and wear the uniform of the Senior Service; Janet, three years older and with a steady boy-friend, seeing herself married before much longer. His son Freddie, at seventeen set on the RAF though God knew why. . . . All happy, all with hopes. There would be a blight. Ruckle had to come through this lot somehow.

Midshipman Whyman had only his parents to think about, being unmarried at his tender age and not having any specific attachments elsewhere. He was one of four brothers and there

167

were three sisters as well. Naturally, he would be missed; but he could be spared, no shortage. Simply because of that, he had a strong feeling he was going to come through, and he was able to give a thought to Ordinary Seaman Aldridge, whom he knew to be an only child – he'd had a natter with Aldridge more than once, being a friendly person. He knew that Aldridge's mother was a widow and since Aldridge had never mentioned Mr Sands he assumed she would be very much alone if the *Glenshiel* went. It was always rotten for the parents of only children; their world came to an end with vicious suddenness.

Lieutenants Hastings and Lyon, Dartmouth trained, had no home thoughts at all unless it was a brief nostalgia for the playing-fields and parade-ground of RNC. Dartmouth had been their father and mother, their nurse and their home since the age of thirteen-and-a-half, when they had started to become seamen and to think and react as Naval officers whose calling was war and the axiomatic acceptance of being killed in action. That had been bred into them, or if not precisely bred then forced in by the petty officer instructors, by their term lieutenants, and by the Commander of the College – even by the padre, who had preached sermons about it after Sunday Divisions. So their thoughts were purely practical ones directed wholly towards the ship and their duty. Each had had a succession of girl-friends but nothing serious, and even had any of those girl-friends been turned into wives then they too would have understood that the ship and the service came first along with King and country. Wives, to the wardroom, were not important. They belonged to the shore.

That, however, was not the case with Mr Bream, deep in the oily heart of the speeding destroyer. As RN as any Dartmouth officer, the training had been different – harder because it had been lower deck, and with a different emphasis – more technical and not so much of what he would have called bullshit. There hadn't been the same grinding in of leadership – some would have said arrogance – and the need to put everything else aside in the greater interest. Mr Bream regarded his missus as being the most valuable thing he had; and now, as he started on the last hell-bent leg to close the

Attila, he saw her plain. Every handwheel in his engine-room seemed to hold her face, and every face was crumpled with weeping, just as if she knew already.

He regarded that as a bad omen.

He was called up by the bridge. Answering, he said, 'Engine-room, Warrant Engineer.'

'Ten minutes, Chief. All right below?'

'All right, sir.'

'Good luck,' Cameron said.

'Thank you, sir.' Mr Bream wiped his hands automatically on his ball of cotton-waste and glanced down at his white overalls – white for an officer, blue for the ratings. They were oily; he gave a bleak grin. Should have put on a clean pair to bloody die in, he thought. His missus always liked him to be clean and tidy, it was quite a fetish with her. Now he felt he was letting her down in a funny sort of way, disregarding her wishes, but it was too late now. He wished he didn't keep seeing her face. . . .

Aft, Mr Tarbuck was standing by with Petty Officer Clutch. They were at the starboard tubes, which would be the first to be fired. To port was the LTO, Leading Seaman Pittman. Clutch was watching out for old Tarbuck, certain he was going to make a lash-up of it. Clutch himself was bang up to date, having taken his courses after the outbreak of war at the *Vernon* in Pompey. Tarbuck had done his, probably, when Whitehead was inventing the first torpedo and would have been too senile to benefit from his refresher on being recalled to service.

Tarbuck was now busily making sure that all hands knew the orders backwards. 'Listen, lads. Captain's going to make his approach to around two miles, inside maximum range, all right? Then he'll put the helm over to port and expose our starboard side to the *Attila*. We fire just as soon as the sights come on. Soon as the fish are away, the skipper makes another turn to present the port tubes, and we loose off again. All right? Any questions? Right!' Tarbuck turned to the TI. 'Going over to port, Reg –'

'Say it all over again, are you?'

'That's the idea, no harm in making dead sure.'

Clutch made an indistinct sound as Tarbuck shambled

169

across aft of the splinter screen. In the Gunner(T)'s temporary absence he checked everything, so far as possible at this stage, once again. No snags that he could bowl out, though you never knew what might happen when the tit was pressed. Queer things, torpedoes, you never quite knew, and the sea wasn't helping – too disturbed, more than enough to throw the fish off their courses even though they had a deep setting on them to take the *Attila* nicely below the armoured belt. . . . With luck, and it would be luck rather than skill, they might blow the magazines and that would really be a sight for sore eyes, the pride of the Jerry fleet going up in one big bang. Like the *Hood*, poetic justice really, though the *Hood* hadn't been hit by tin fish but by the big guns. Which reminded Clutch of his recently acquired extra duty as GI.

He shouted up to Number Three gun.

'All right, up there?'

The captain of the gun answered. 'All right, TI.'

'Don't suppose your perishing pea-shooter'll be used, but let's have you on top line just in case, right?'

'We'll be there, TI.'

'Good.' Clutch heaved himself half-way up the ladder from the iron-deck to give himself a sight of the searchlight platform and the searchlight's crew. He could see only one man, Able Seaman Backhouse, standing against the rail.

'Where's that article Aldridge, eh?'

Aldridge had been sitting with his back against a stanchion. He got to his feet and called down, 'Here, PO.'

'Been resting on your bum, have you?'

'Sitting down for a – '

'Which is what I said, so don't be bloody impertinent, my lad. Keep on your feet from now on, understand, do you?'

'Yes, PO.'

Clutch thought he detected a sulkiness in the tone and was about to say so when suddenly he thought, why bother? Why bloody bother? None of them might have much longer to go. Somewhat thoughtfully he got down from the ladder and moved back to the tubes, running a hand along the sea-wet metal. Clutch was not a religious man, far from it; on the other hand he was not a disbeliever. Some instinct told him there was something on the other side, that you didn't just

170

snuff out like a light. That was logical: it would be a waste. The years spent on earth must have some sort of point, and the point could be found only by continuation. One of the things Clutch had occasionally reflected upon was the undoubted fact, a fact that could be gainsaid by nobody at all, that the world had gone on for ever – or rather, the space in which it floated had gone on for ever – and would continue to go on for ever. Even if it was replaced by something else, then that something else would go on for ever, and so on *ad infinitum*. You could never get away from that space, empty or otherwise. Likewise in a physical sense, if you got shot up into the air, in any direction you cared to name, you would zoom on for ever and never come to an end. Even if you did, say for example there was a brick wall, well, what was on the other side of that? How could you possibly come to the end of space? And the human mind couldn't begin to hoist in the fact of 'for ever', literally world without end. Only the superhuman could take that in. For superhuman, read God.

The TI began to feel it wouldn't be long before he found it all out for himself, first hand. It was a little late in the day, but he'd better watch it. As in the service, past records would count. He knew he'd always been a bit of a bully; and Aldridge had brought out the worst in him, a temptation he ought for his own soul's good to have resisted. . . .

iii

MILLARD said warningly, 'It's not going to be easy to pick 'em up, sir. And they'll have the advantage with their radar.'

'I know that, Pilot, but we'll still have a good chance under cover of the dark.'

'Yes . . . our only defence really.'

Too true, Cameron thought, head sunk on his duffel-coated arms as he stared down at the fo'c'sle and ahead into the night's blackness. One hundred and twenty-odd men hurtled through that darkness . . . had he the right to make the decision that would very likely kill them all? Doubts came in lurid legions, as they came inevitably to all but the most case-hardened commanding officers at sea or on land or in the air. But to him as to the others, the answer had always to be yes so long as it was in the greater interest, the interest of saving more lives in the long run. If his life and those of all his ship's company had to stand between the *Attila* and the many thousands of men now approaching British shores, then so be it. It had to be.

Cameron spoke again. 'The gun-flashes, Pilot. When they open – that's when Tarbuck'll get his point of aim.' He didn't add, if it's not too late by then. Millard could work that one out for himself. The whole thing was a risk, a sheer gamble, but that was so often the way battles were won. Cutting through those doubts, thrusting them aside as impediments to his concentration, Cameron kept a close vigil ahead, eyes more red-rimmed than ever behind the binoculars as he searched for darker shapes in the night, the vaguely seen blur that would tell him he had a ship ahead, then perhaps the confirmation of a tumbling wake that might stand out, with luck bringing a little luminosity from the sea's phosphorescence, though such really belonged to the waters of the Mediterranean and the more southern seas.

The ten minutes signified to the engine-room had half gone by now, but the time had been no more than an estimation based on the German squadron's last known position, course and speed. Any of those might have altered in the meantime. The minutes passed, rasping at the nerves. Cameron's hand shook on the guardrail before him; the wind made by the destroyer's onrush tore at the hood of his duffel-coat, and spray was flung back over the fo'c'sle head as it dipped and lifted again. On the fo'c'sle a figure moved, and Cameron called down.

'Who's that, down there?'

'Chief Buffer, sir. Just checking the slips and stoppers, sir.'

'Bugger the anchors, Chief. You're more important. Leave it.'

'Aye, aye, sir.' Ruckle sliding a little on the wet deck, moved back aft. If the skipper said leave it, you left it; but Ruckle read into Cameron's words more than had been expressed. The skipper didn't think they'd ever need the anchors again. He was very likely dead right, of course, but Ruckle's lips were pursed in silent disapproval. Call him

172

pernicketty if you liked, but it went against the grain to go into action with anything adrift on deck. He'd be willing to bet any money the Nazis wouldn't. They might be the worst set of villainous murdering buggers the world had ever seen, but they were smart and shipshape.

Somehow Chief Petty Officer Ruckle had managed to convey all this in the way he'd said those three words: 'Aye, aye, sir.' All the older generation of chief and petty officers was adept at that, past masters of the art. Cameron, well able to interpret, grinned briefly to himself. Those old-timers were the very salt of the earth, of the seas themselves, no one like them. . . . As Ruckle moved out of sight Cameron felt a prickling sensation running up and down his spine like a premonition, a warning. By this time, assuming Millard's estimation of the Germans' whereabouts to be more or less correct, the *Glenshiel* might be being picked up on the radar and reported. In this he was correct.

iv
'THE one ship only, Herr Admiral.'

'The destroyer.' Fichtner's tone was flat.

Captain Sefrin said, 'Yes, Herr Admiral, the destroyer. That is the assumption.'

'The obvious one, I think. The bearing again?'

'Port sixty degrees, Herr Admiral, at eleven miles distant.'

'And the HX convoy at this moment, Captain Sefrin?'

'Estimated fifty miles to the west, Herr Admiral. We should be in action in a little more than an hour – less, if the British extended screen is far ahead of the convoy. And we have no updated information as to Fraser's battleships, Herr Admiral. For all we know they may be close.' Sefrin gave a cough. 'I think perhaps the destroyer is not very important now, Herr Admiral. She is almost at the end of her shadowing. On the other hand, the sound of gunfire. . . .'

'Yes, Captain Sefrin?'

'Such might be heard over a long distance, and bring the British battleships, Herr Admiral.'

Fichtner nodded. 'I have considered this. I have rejected it, since we are already so close to action.' ˙

'But with great respect – '

'Yes, yes, Captain Sefrin.' Fichtner was shivering; it was most damnably cold, and with age the blood thinned. He knew his hands were blue beneath his woollen mittens and thick leather gloves. 'I think you have forgotten something: the destroyer is closing, and she carries torpedoes.'

Sefrin gave a gasp. 'But that would be impossible – '

'No. If the British have one thing above all it is courage. Also determination. Nevertheless, we must make it impossible. The destroyer is to be sunk.'

Already the *Attila*'s great triple turrets had been laid and trained on the radar bearing and within seconds of Vice-Admiral Fichtner's order being passed from the bridge, the gun-ready lamps were glowing in the gunnery control positions fore and aft in the flagship.

17

BY this stage the tension in the Admiralty's Operations Room was high. The Prime Minister was not present; for some hours he had been engaged in a highly important conference with some Russian generals in his concrete dug-out. It was in a nail-biting atmosphere that a report was made to the Chief of Naval Staff.

'From *Glenshiel*, sir. A – '

'A sighting?'

The Duty Captain said, 'A battle. *Glenshiel*'s engaging – '

'Engaging, by God! Cameron must have taken leave of his senses! Go on.'

The Duty Captain did so, wishing CNS had the gift of listening in silence. 'Engaging with torpedoes. She's come under fire from the *Attila* – '

'Position?'

The Duty Captain gave it. CNS said, 'Inform the Home Fleet and the convoy escort immediately, in plain language.' The Admiral paced the Ops Room for a few moments, frowning, then asked, 'Where's Fraser at this moment?'

'The map's been brought up to date, sir.' The Duty Captain gestured across the room, to where two WRNS ratings were moving the flags indicating the whereabouts, as just notified, of the *Glenshiel* and the Germans. The Home Fleet was currently closing the HX convoy's van and with luck should be across its track within a matter of hours – three or four depending on the weather, which was said by the met experts to be improving south of the Denmark Strait and towards sea area Hebrides.

CNS said, 'We still don't know if Fraser can hold the *Attila* off, but one thing's certain enough: the *Glenshiel* can't possibly last.'

'But if she gets her fish into the *Attila* before she goes – '

'Ah, that'll alter the whole situation, the whole balance.'

'It will indeed, sir. And at least we're beginning to reckon up the score now. It's all going to be up to the Home Fleet capital ships.'

'Yes.' Those ships were still problematical. Some lucky salvoes . . . but the luck might go to the Germans. It was touch and go and the moment of truth was coming fast. CNS went to a red-coloured telephone and reported urgently to the Prime Minister.

ii

AHEAD, the ripples of flame had been seen as the *Attila* opened on the *Glenshiel*, now closing fast to within torpedo range. So far it seemed as though the *Recklinghausen* and the *Darmstadt* were holding off, though Cameron had a nagging idea they would be ordered to detach and either put themselves between his torpedoes and the *Attila* or steam towards him and finish him off at closer quarters while the *Attila* moved away towards the convoy. But so far it was the *Attila* only.

Tarbuck was on the sound-powered telephone, agitating. Cameron said, 'Hold it a moment. I'm starting the run to port now.' He had the ship himself by this time and had just passed the helm orders direct to the wheelhouse. 'Once I'm ready . . . then we have to be bloody quick, before the *Attila* turns away – or turns towards us, which is likely enough.'

'Aye, aye, sir.' Tarbuck didn't need to be told that: the normal tactics when under torpedo attack were to present the smallest possible target, either the bow or the stern, and Tarbuck reckoned Cameron was right that the Jerries would turn towards rather than away, thus giving themselves a better control of the situation. There was a risk in it for them, of course; the idea was to steam in between the torpedo trails, but at night they'd find it impossible to detect the trails until they were almost on top of them. It wasn't going to be all

176

German luck and old Tarbuck spat on his hands in the anticipation that tonight Adolf Hitler was going to have his balls wrenched off.

Now *Glenshiel* was coming round on to a westerly course parallel to that of the *Attila*, who was still firing. The heavy shells were coming across, whistling eerily in the wind, falling over and astern, so far. At any moment the German gunners would get the range and deflection. . . . Cameron's nails dug hard into his palms as the destroyer came to her new course. Watching his bearings on the azimuth circle on the binnacle in front of him, he passed the final orders.

'Starboard ten.'

'Starboard ten, sir. Ten of starboard wheel on, sir.' Stace lit a fag as he moved the wheel to meet the port swing and check it. Not long now: lucky Bert Cockshutt, the bastard.

'Midships . . . steady!'

'Steady, sir. Course, 270, sir.'

'Steer that.' Cameron nodded at Millard, now standing by the telephone to the torpedo tubes.

Millard, with the handset already in his hand, ordered, '*Fire starboard*!'

In the same instant Tarbuck repeated the order to Leading Seaman Pittman. 'Fire *one* . . . fire *two* . . . fire *three*!'

Off they went, hissing defiance towards the enemy. Tarbuck's lips moved. It could have been wicked and God might be excused for taking no notice, but the Gunner(T) was praying that they might all hit true and blow up the bloody *Attila* and be done with it. Tarbuck had enough imagination and enough past experience as well to know in detail what dreadful inferno would result aboard the *Attila* as her innards shattered and melted, but never mind. *Them or us*, he thought, *and it's got to be us that comes out, it's just got to be*.

Now the German shells were coming closer; Cameron was once again flinging his ship about the sea, zig-zagging crazily, knowing that if he was unlucky he might succeed only in putting his ship slap beneath the fall of one of those massive projectiles, but he had to do what he could to throw off the German radar that acted as the eyes of the gunnery officers in the control positions. While he zig-zagged he was counting down to the torpedoes' arrival at their target. They were taking their time and hopelessness began to set in: they'd missed, all of them. Down by the tubes Petty Officer Clutch was thinking the same thing, and thinking it savagely. If they had to go down, he wanted to take the *Attila* with him. He vented his frustration on Tarbuck, insubordinately, not that it would matter now.

'Balls-up,' he said briefly, furiously. 'Bloody poor aim or you got the depth settings wrong.' He'd queried the settings earlier but had been overruled. Now the chickens had come home. 'Told you an' all, didn't I?'

'Just wait, Reg, just *wait*. We've got three more fish ready, don't forget that.'

'And *I'll* bloody fire 'em off! You've forgot it all, you're bloody past it – '

'That's not fair, Reg, not fair at all. I – '

'We're not going to win this war on what's fair!' Clutch was shouting now, loud and clear. He could be heard all over the after end of the destroyer. Tarbuck shouted back, telling Clutch to shut his trap. Up by the searchlight Ordinary Seaman Aldridge heard it going on and all his hatred of the TI came to the surface. He hadn't had much to do with Mr Tarbuck, but the old warrant officer had seemed kindly when they had spoken, like a father, what they called in the Andrew a sea-daddy, and everyone aboard liked him, except for his own TI. There was something rather sad about him, sad and humble. Aldridge clenched his fists, forgetting the appalling danger he was in as the *Attila*'s gunfire came close and the *Glenshiel* became drenched by falling spray and shuddered through all her plates at the impact of the 16-inch shells as they took the water. When they did that, the angry voices fell away, only to come through again. Aldridge remembered what Petty Officer Clutch had said about his mother. Then he saw Clutch shaking a fist in Mr Tarbuck's face and he saw Tarbuck fall back against the port torpedo-tubes, now ready for firing once the ship had turned to present her port side to the enemy. He saw Tarbuck stagger and collapse on the deck as if he'd had a heart attack. The TI's hand fell to his side, and Aldridge, his hate for the petty officer rushing to the surface and over the brink, started for the ladder down to the iron-deck.

'Oh no, you don't!' Able Seaman Backhouse shouted and made a grab, but missed. Aldridge reached the ladder and went down, cack-handed and unseamanlike as ever, just as the *Glenshiel* began the sharp turn under maximum helm and at full speed to bring her into the next firing position. As the destroyer lurched heavily, Aldridge lost his grip, gave a piercing cry, fell to the solid metal of the tubes, and bounced over the side into the disturbed water as the stern and the whirling blades of the screws swept round to meet him. In almost the same instant there was a sudden flash of bright light, broad on the port beam, and an explosion that was carried back on the wind to the *Glenshiel*. Flame shot into the sky and one of the German cruisers was seen to be on fire.

'Must have got a magazine,' Millard said. Fire didn't normally follow a torpedo hit: the fact of the explosion and penetration brought water in with it. A moment later there was another explosion, another bright flash. Two of Tarbuck's fish had taken the *Recklinghausen* on her port side as she had steamed to place her protective bulk between the flagship and the British attack. In the glare of light from the blaze the *Darmstadt* was seen clearly, astern of the *Attila*, which was also standing out starkly to the east and steaming fast to the westward, her turrets in action as she ran towards the convoy's position.

Cameron was ready now to make one more attack, the last chance he would get before the battleship drew too far to the west. He passed the firing order down to the torpedo-tubes and Petty Officer Clutch, now in undisputed charge, took it from there with a feeling of satisfaction.

'Fire *one* . . . fire *two* . . . fire *three*!'

That was the last Clutch knew: the third fish was on its way when the *Attila*'s gunnery control got the *Glenshiel*'s range and bearing spot on, and a shell took the quarterdeck just below the waterline. There was a sheet of white-hot flame that shrivelled Clutch and the torpedo crews into cinders while water surged into what was left of the engine-room and boiler room and started to take the destroyer down fast by the stern.

iii

CAMERON had been knocked out by the blast; Hastings had been killed, along with Lyon. Millard took charge and managed to get a Carley float away with all that were left: the Captain, Chief PO Stace and his telegraphsman, Ruckle, the leading signalman and Ordinary Seaman Nye. It had been a holocaust. Cameron came to after about an hour, shivering violently as the icy sea slopped over into the Carley float.

'All right, sir?' Millard asked.

Cameron tried to focus; he had a blinding headache and felt sick. There was noise all around, and a good deal of light, but both seemed distant. No doubt they had drifted. . . .

Millard said, 'It's all right, or soon will be. We're all that's left – but we got the *Attila* . . . just two fish. Enough to slow her, which was the object.'

'The battleships,' Cameron said. 'Fraser – '

'Just come up, sir. That's what you can hear.'

'Just come up,' Cameron repeated in a flat voice.

'Yes.'

'It wasn't worth it, was it, Pilot? I mean . . . Fraser wasn't far away after all. . . .'

Millard said, 'I reckon it was worth it, all right. Not just because we slowed her . . . but because she's lost her manoeuvrability. She's something of a sitting duck now, even for the *Nelson*.'

iv

IN fact the *Nelson* had not caught up; but Fraser had the *Duke of York* and with his cruisers was making rings around the damaged *Attila*. One torpedo from the *Glenshiel* had taken her amidships; the other had taken her stern and two of her four screws had been blown from the shafts. Her steering was non-existent, her rudder gone, and as soon as the guns of the *Duke of York* opened Vice-Admiral Fichtner had known that the Führer's gamble had failed and that his flagship was doomed. The British gunnery was uncannily good; after two ranging salvoes, the *Attila* was taken by a broadside as the British flagship turned to bring all her main armament to bear. The 14-inch projectiles ripped into the German's sides, some taking her below the armoured belt, some smashing into the superstructure, shattering the fore turrets and bringing fire to sweep upwards towards the navigating bridge, the flag deck and the admiral's bridge itself. Within a comparatively short time the *Attila* was an inferno as the internal explosions ripped her plates apart and spread the fires below, an inferno in which desperate men were cremated in seconds and the steel ladders melted or twisted into white-hot spiders' webs. Her after guns courageously returned the British fire until more heavy shells came across and the cruisers closed in to add their own impact to the deluge. But Fichtner, standing with Captain Sefrin on his bridge as the flames mounted, refused to strike his flag. Helpless, he watched in awe as his command disintegrated before his eyes. Tears ran down his cheeks: his men, his loyal and brave men, had been sacrificed by a fool's whim, by a megalomaniac ex-corporal of the Austrian Army, an upstart who had fancied that if he decreed anything it must be successful. Vice-Admiral Fichtner, with what remained of his staff, stayed at his post and continued to fire his guns until they fell silent because no more ammunition could be sent up from the shell-handling rooms on hoists that lacked all power. Fichtner was there at the end, with the German battle ensigns still blowing out from the fore and main mastheads until the licking flames burned them away. The end came when another explosion deep down in the ship split her virtually in half and blew the bottom out of her. She settled and went down fast, bows first, stern rearing up into the air in the terrible light of the fires that burned on until great spouts of steam rose in their place.

Cameron saw it all from the Carley float, saw it in as much awe as Fichtner had seen it. The death of a great ship: not a sight anyone really wished to see, nothing to gloat over. In a moment like this, seamen had no nationality. As they watched, the guns fell silent over the whole area; and soon after that, in the glare of searchlights, they saw the boats moving in from the Home Fleet to pick up survivors. Away to

181

the east the *Recklinghausen* had already gone down and her men were in the water: there would be few survivors. The *Darmstadt* had come under concentrated attack from the British cruisers: cs27 had been alerted by the Admiralty and had swung down to join the Home Fleet in the closing stages. With his command ablaze from stem to stern *Darmstadt*'s Captain had hauled down his flag in surrender only a matter of minutes before she went down. But the Germans had exacted their own toll as well: the *Monmouth* and the *Leicester* had gone down, the former taking the Rear-Admiral down with her; and there had been considerable damage to two modern cruisers of the Home Fleet.

Millard was ferreting about inside his duffel-coat. He brought out a Verey pistol, and fired it into the night. The flare shot up into the sky, described an arc, and came down in the sea some distance off. 'I've got some more, sir,' Millard said. 'It won't be long before we're picked up. And the sooner the better. It's been a long day!'

Cameron nodded; he was too tired to think straight. The full impact would hit him later. All he could register now was the horrible sight of the sinking battleship, the raging fires that had ended in that uprush of steam. That, and something that had weighed so heavily on his mind: he would not now have to adjudicate between Clutch and Aldridge. Both dead, they would go deservedly on the war memorials that would one day be set up, their names shown as killed in action. The slate was clean now.